101 WAYS TO DIE
A Magical Romantic Comedy (with a body count)
Book 21

R.J. BLAIN

101 Ways to Die
A Magical Romantic Comedy (with a body count) (Book 21)
by R.J. Blain

Officer McMarin of the NYPD is in for the ride of her life when the Chief Quinns storm into her station, promote her to the rank of detective, and relocate her to Manhattan. Saddled with the dubious honor of being Chief Bailey Quinn's primary rider is only the beginning of her woes.

Her first case delves into the dark waters of the many ways in which a person can die.

At the heart of the mystery is one Alec Mortan, a forensic accountant with a knack for being at the wrong place at the wrong time. Witnessing so much death is hard on a soul, and she can't help but admire his tenacity and desire to help her uncover the truth.

When the forces of the heavens and the many hells involve themselves in the case, McMarin's beliefs and skills are put to the test. If she's not careful, she'll lose her witness to fate right along with her chance for a happily ever after.

Copyright © 2023 by Pen & Page Publishing/R.J. Blain

All rights reserved.

No part of this book may be reproduced in any form or by any electronic or mechanical means, including information storage and retrieval systems, without written permission from the author, except for the use of brief quotations in a book review.

Cover design by Rebecca Frank of Bewitching Book Covers.

ONE

The hell and the high water had already come calling in the form of the Chief Quinns.

CAPTAIN HUGH FRANKSON of the NYPD stormed to my desk and slapped a file down on the ever-growing stack of misdemeanors I needed to register in our database before I could leave. Any other day, I would have indulged in an anxiety attack over the man's unexpected appearance.

Whenever the captain showed up at my desk, hell came chasing on the heels of high water, as he went out of his way in his idiotic attempt to prove women had no business being on the force.

Today, however, the hell and the high water had already come calling in the form of the Chief Quinns, who haunted the station somewhere, doing whatever it was chiefs did when checking in on precincts they were responsible for. In addition to dodging jabs over my gender, I'd likely escape from being ribbed over my mixed heritage thanks to their presence. Aware the captain would lose his shit if he believed I wasn't taking him seriously, I set aside the case I'd been working on and picked up the folder.

Before I had a chance to flip it open and behold the terrors within, the captain announced, "You're being transferred." His declaration carried through the open room, loud enough everyone could hear—even the cops busy on the phone. A still quiet fell over the cubicle farm, except for the cops forced to continue their conversations. "I'll take your cruiser keys now. You'll have a ride to your new place of employment."

Well, screw me sideways with a baton while lighting me on fire. With a little luck, the poor bastard saddled with my cruiser would survive the experience; it had needed to retire years ago, but I kept the damned thing running through investing a few hours every week at home convincing the engine to keep trucking along. I opened my drawer, grabbed my keys, unclipped the dying vehicle's keys, and handed them over. "Effective immediately, sir?"

Captain Frankson snatched the keys out of my hand. "Yes."

Before I could say another word, he blew through the cubicle farm in the direction of his office and turned the corner. A moment later, a door slammed.

"Damn, McMarin. What did you *do*?" my now ex-partner, Kit, demanded in an amused tone. "I haven't seen the captain that pissed since the day you were assigned to our station."

If Kit ended up with my cruiser, I hoped he survived the experience.

"I did something?" I heaved a sigh, well aware I had an audience. Bracing for the worst, I flipped open the folder and checked the file. A single sheet of paper informed me I'd been promoted to the rank of detective third grade and instructed me to report to my new place of employment under the direct guidance of Mr. and Mrs. Chief Quinn.

My mouth dropped open, and I blinked several times before rereading the sheet, which remained the same. I passed the sheet to Kit, who read it over and joined me in attempting to catch flies in his mouth before he leaned over to hand the news off to the next cop in line.

Typically, those up for promotion endured tests, trials, and tribulation along with a warning of the impending changes. I viewed my daily life as some ridiculous challenge where I needed to prove I could be just as good—or better—than the boys. While the captain loathed me, the boys in blue liked me around, or so Kit often told me. The fact we got requested to serve as backup often implied there was something to Kit's claim.

The news of my promotion ushered in stunned silence.

"I'd ask you who you slept with, but the incubus at the bar bust this morning made it clear you're a pure and pristine maiden," Kit teased.

I regretted the morning half of my shift, which had required me to decline the incubus's offer. Taking him home would've beaten the damned jokes. However, my status as single and unlaid didn't bother me in the slightest. I was married to my job, so I grinned at my partner and replied, "I reduced him to begging, too. I'm quality, Kit. I put some serious thought into taking a half-day, writing my number and address on a napkin, and taking him up on his offer."

My ex-partner cackled. "I can't say I blame you. I would have covered you, too. You know how awful those unexpected stomach bugs can be."

"Should've said I'd contracted the flu," I stated, gesturing in the general direction of the window. In the morning, we'd gotten snow, which had been reduced to slush, the normal state of January in Brooklyn.

Everyone laughed, and my promotion announcement made its way back to me along with two empty filing boxes. I doubted I'd fill one; Captain Frankson preferred when his cops were white and male rather than mixed and female, so I'd done my best to keep my desk clutter at a minimum just in case I needed to bail out in a hurry. Being half-Irish somewhat appeased the asshole, and my sparkling record had spared me from termination.

The half-Mexican part of my heritage tripped his trigger, reminded everyone in our precinct we worked for a racist bastard, and resulted in a careful dance of the sensible people doing their best to mitigate the damage his idiotic prejudices did to the community we served.

In his book, Mexican was one step up from anyone else who wasn't white or European; he claimed most Mexicans were at least *part* Spanish. If my parents found out about his idiocy, they'd give him a talking to, as I was a solid fifty percent Mexica, and my mother was damned proud of her heritage, which hadn't been conquered by the Conquistadors.

In good news for everyone involved, Captain Frankson generally knew better than to test his luck against the labor board, opting to keep his discrimination somewhat to himself.

My pens and journals went into the box first with my prized dry-erase markers following in their wake. As I had zero scruples about reminding the men that a woman worked among them, I placed my stash of feminine hygiene products on top. I chuckled at the mix of blatantly pink to plain white to camouflage, making certain there was a little something for everyone who crossed my path and might need to make use of them.

My personal stash stayed in my locker, which I would raid as soon as I had half a moment. The rest would eventually find their way into the hands of the needy. I put the lid on and gave the box a pat. "I'm ready. Give the poor bastard inheriting my desk my condolences. He'll need it. If he needs some love, don't warn him about the chair."

It took skill to sit without the devil-spawned chair establishing dominance and declaring itself the winner over its latest victim, usually me. On a good day, it dumped me on the floor. On a bad one, it attempted a cruel violation before dumping me on the floor.

A door slammed down the hall, and Captain Frankson yelled, "Move it, McMarin!"

Damn. Who had pissed in the captain's coffee? Picking up my box, I hauled it to his office to discover the Chief Quinns lounging together on his couch.

I stepped into the doorway, forced my expression to be calm and neutral, and held my box as though I meant to go to the filing room rather than my locker to empty out my gear. "Sir?"

"Chief Quinn will be taking you to your new station. They have need of a detective, and you were up for promotion. Empty your locker on the way out. Dismissed."

For a woman rumored to be pregnant yet again, Chief Bailey Quinn hopped to her feet with admirable grace, although her husband beat her to the door and snagged my box, claiming it.

"Sorry for the lack of notice, Detective McMarin," he said, and he herded me out of the captain's office, snagging the door with his foot and easing it closed. "The commissioner dumped a huge stack of files on our desk yesterday. I was permitted to bring in one new body to help deal with it. A new hire wouldn't work, so I inquired with Captain Frankson who would fit well in the position, can handle excessive amounts of paperwork, and has a high tolerance for bullshit, as he's got the most robust numbers in the area. Upon reviewing your file, Bailey decided we were taking you, and as she's willing to fight me over it, I thought it wise to cooperate. Don't mind Captain Frankson's temper. He's annoyed we took his best paper pusher, and the commissioner has also decided he isn't accepting no for an answer. First things first; unless reporters are nearby, I'm Sam or Quinn. She's Bailey."

Chief Bailey Quinn glared at her husband and the box he held. "If you want to put him in his place, call me Gardener. It drives him crazy." Placing her hands on her hips, she continued to glare at her husband. "I could have carried that."

"You could have, but you won't." Chief Samuel Quinn grinned. "As I'm busy carrying this box, I won't be able to defend your saddle, which I happened to bring with me today."

The woman bolted down the hall, hit the stairwell door at full throttle, and bounced off it before yanking it open and plunging down the steps.

My mouth dropped open, and I struggled to come up with a single thing to say.

"The kids are at their grandparents' place today, and she is enjoying her freedom. As she's no longer nursing, she had her first cup of coffee today since month five of her first pregnancy. This time, she gets to have coffee until month eight. This will delight her until she realizes that she's already working on her timer before she's cut off again. She has not had coffee in months. She's once again forgotten cindercorns don't appreciate the cold, which should have been her first clue she'll be losing her coffee rights again by the end of the year. Have you ridden a horse before?"

I grimaced at the memory of being stuck with one of the force's worst assholes of a horse during my training period. "I have basic mounted patrol training, but I was passed over for duty," I reported.

"That'll do. You'll ride Bailey to the station. Maybe that'll calm her down. I've a pair of goggles for you to wear, and I had a vest made for her so she's not cop bait. She is excitable today, and cindercorns have a habit of disregarding speed limits when excited. Hell, who am I kidding? Cindercorns hate speed limits."

I considered running away and searching for the incubus I'd rejected earlier in my shift. Testing my luck with the incubus seemed a great deal safer than riding a unicorn with a habit of breathing fire and destroying entire city blocks at her whim. "Understood, sir."

"You're going to be one of the ones who struggles with first names, I see. We have a rule for the newbies at the station: those who don't use our first names get extra paperwork."

"Are you serious?" I blurted.

"Not really, but it's fun making the more formal cops squirm. You'll get used to it."

No one had warned me Mr. Chief Quinn was as crazy as his cindercorn wife. Doing my best to mask my skepticism, I replied, "If you say so, Samuel, sir."

"I'll take it. Let's hurry up before Bailey creates extra trouble or breaks something in her general excitement. Had

I been a little wiser this morning, I wouldn't have reminded her she can now have coffee. It's your first day with us, and I'm already going to have to issue you a hazard bonus for coping with my wife's insanity. I'd say I'm sorry, but I'm really not."

All I could do was hope heaven might help me, as I doubted there was any other force in the universe capable of stopping a pregnant fire-breathing unicorn with a reputation of creating havoc wherever she went.

CHIEF SAMUEL QUINN observed while I emptied my locker into the duffle bag I kept in the bottom, aware I ran a high risk of being let go at any time. My firearm would be returned to Captain Frankson with the promise I'd get my choice of new weapon as soon as we made it to the station. I'd also be receiving a new badge, I would have an office of my own, and I would have my choice of partner from a pool of thirty men and women being shuffled as part of their reorganization.

The reorganization, according to Mr. Chief Quinn, might be the thing that shattered his flagging sanity, although he loved the perks of working with his wife, even when she was a demoness high on her first cup of coffee in months.

Ten minutes after I started emptying my locker, returning everything belonging to the station and otherwise regretting I hadn't taken a half day to enjoy a dalliance with an incubus, Chief Bailey Quinn pranced into the locker room, her dark head held high. Her hooves clicked on the floor, and she lashed her tail.

Up close, the cindercorn seemed a great deal less dangerous than expected, although I respected that her horn could inflict a great deal of damage. The red mottling her black coat resembled smoldering embers, and I wondered why she didn't smoke or steam.

Snorting, she went to her husband and nuzzled his chest. He smiled and dug his fingers into her thick fur. "We'll tack you up in the garage, and we'll see how Detective McMarin takes to riding you. You may do one and only one teleportation test with her, so pick your test wisely."

"Only one?" the cindercorn whined.

"Only one. The goal is to see if she's able to handle teleportation, not break speed records getting back to work. You also need to remember that most people get sick from your teleportation, and I'd rather if you didn't end up in the bathroom holding her hair for a few hours because you got rambunctious again."

Heaving a sigh, the unicorn with a reputation of destroying anything that got in her way regarded me with a dark eye. "Most cops throw up when I teleport. Hope you don't. You seem nice. Tolerant. I need nice and tolerant. Mostly tolerant. Please don't throw up."

Chief Samuel Quinn snickered, gave his wife a final pat, and grabbed my bag, tossing it over his shoulder before taking my box. "Bailey, why don't you return the detective's vest and gun? Make sure he gives you the return receipt so he can't be a pain in my ass later. You know how annoyed I get when the captains try to claim we didn't return the vests and firearms after stealing one of their cops."

"Much annoyance, much whining." The cindercorn

grabbed the vest and holster in her teeth, lifted her head, and stepped with care to keep from tripping over the straps. Her husband opened the door for her.

Once she left, he said, "All right. Let's get downstairs and start sorting through her tack while she inevitably starts an argument with Captain Frankson. And if anyone asks why I allowed my wife to cause trouble, I'm just going to ask how they expect me to stop the fire-breathing unicorn. That usually stops most of the complaints. He annoyed her. We can talk down in the garage."

Without anything to carry except my purse, I led the way, holding the door for the chief while he wrestled with my possessions. "Thank you, sir."

"Don't thank me yet. I know what's going to be put on your desk as soon as you arrive at the station. While you're getting that promotion you're overdue for, you'll be earning it."

"Wait, overdue for?"

Chief Samuel Quinn snorted. "That's part of why Bailey is going to pick a fight with him. His prejudice has cost the NYPD a detective for at *least* three years now. Part of my job as a chief is to monitor the staff in all stations and precincts we're responsible for. Since the restructure, I've been going over the Long Island precincts. Your record is as good as it gets, you're active on the streets, there have been virtually no complaints from your partners, and it's no accident you're the only woman in that station. Captain Frankson has just enough seniority to cherry pick the new recruits, and the only reason he ended up taking you was because one of the other chiefs told him if he didn't improve his diversity numbers, stat, the commissioner would be coming in to take a look at the situation."

Ah. As I checked off several diversity quota boxes, I could understand why my ex-captain would tolerate me. He'd be able to claim he had a woman, a second-generation immigrant, and someone of mixed heritage. At the next family dinner, I'd have to thank my parents for coming to the United States as children and getting their citizenship young, not that they'd been given a choice in the matter.

My parents would have a field day when they found out about my transfer.

The chief waited until we were in the garage to say, "Captain Frankson is going to be particularly displeased when I come around next week, as I will be clearing out half his station and requiring him to do a full diversity hire. I'll be spreading people around, giving him a pool of cops he must pick from, and none of those cops will be white and male. It's time he joined modern times—and ran his precinct more in line with our values. Don't get me wrong; he has a lot of good cops, but he also has one of the highest incident rates for non-violent racial disputes in his precinct. I'm hoping having a more diversified pool, better matching the residents of the public he serves, will resolve some of those problems. He was smart in how he used you, but he could do better, and honestly, this should have been addressed years ago."

"Well, someone started to address it. I was hired," I replied.

"While true, this should have been taken care of already. The chiefs allowed themselves to think his precinct was predominantly Caucasian. It's not. It's surprisingly diverse, but there's little of the racial violence we have in other precincts with this sort of mingling. I was hoping you could shine some light on that, actually."

I considered my ex-precinct, which included parts of Crown Heights, Weeksville, and Prospect Heights. In some ways, I felt bordering the Brooklyn Botanical Garden helped.

The people who lived in the precinct viewed themselves as belonging to the middle and upper classes, laid back enough compared to other neighborhoods, and more concerned with accumulating wealth and raising families than causing trouble. While the precinct had its fair share of crime, it also had a diligent patrol, one I'd participated in from the day I'd been issued my badge. "I'd say it's less about the staff diversity and more about Captain Frankson making it clear he'd be rather angry if he had any reports of brutality or anything that smeared his reputation. He's very concerned about his reputation." He cared more about his reputation than he cared about the public we served, but neither Chief Quinn would hear that from me. "Our demographic helps. People are concerned for their own safety, they're typically diligent, and there are several active security companies patrolling the communities here. That keeps the crime figures low. It doesn't hurt there are folks with stronger magic who have made it clear they like their neighborhood quiet and peaceful."

"That definitely helps. A self-policing populace makes our job easier—if the self-policing populace also follows the rules. Still, there are enough racial problems in this precinct it has drawn the commissioner's attention." The chief set my box on the hood of his cruiser, unlocked it, and put it in the back seat along with my bag. He then went to the trunk and began the process of unloading a saddle, bridle, and various pieces of protective gear, some of which I recognized. "All right. Bailey is fast, she's got a ridiculous amount of endurance, and she has zero respect for lights. It's impossible to run a siren on a cindercorn; it annoys her and she eats the damned thing. Flashing lights? Those also annoy her into eating them. I have not convinced her that sirens and running lights aren't edible, so I stopped trying to get her to wear them. Instead, she gets this nice blanket that protects her body and chest. It is bulletproof, and while she complains it's heavy, it doesn't slow her down. Unbeknownst to her, it's heavier than it needs to be because she needs more exercise, so it's weighted so she builds healthy muscle. Once she's back to a good weight, I'll exchange it for a lighter one."

I admired the man's sneakiness. "That's really clever."

"I'm a dead man when she finds out," he admitted in a cheerful tone. "Have you ever jumped a horse before?"

"No, I can't say I have," I admitted.

"Do your best. Bailey does slow down when she's about to jump usually, but be on your guard, keep your heels down, and do your best to stay astride. Hold on tight with your legs and don't worry about pulling on her mane. Her rider's cursing amuses her, so go to town if you want. If you handle teleportation well, you'll end up in rotation on our team. We hadn't anticipated it being so difficult to find people who could ride her without throwing up afterwards."

The clop of hooves warned me the cindercorn had returned, and she trotted over, trails of smoke streaming from her nostrils. "Why can't I bite him?"

"You can't bite the captains who annoy you, sorry. He put up a fight about the receipts?"

Bailey bobbed her head. "I stood over his shoulder until he sent it, faxed it, *and* texted it to Perky. Perky texted back a con-fir-may-shun of receipt to the captain's phone, but I will confirm with Perky when we return." Bobbing her head, she turned her nose away from us and snorted flame. "Why no bite?"

"He'd give you indigestion if you ate him. That's why."

"True. Probably taste bad, too."

"How about I order you a burger and some of those greasy fries you love as compensation for not being able to bite the captain?"

The cindercorn's ears pricked forward. "Extra mayo? Coffee?"

"May everyone in the station forgive me, but yes, you can have some more coffee to go with your lunch, and I'll make sure they slather your burger with mayo."

The cindercorn pranced in place, and the idea that food motivated the woman that much would amuse me for at least several hours. "Okay. No bite idiot captain."

"Detective McMarin has not ridden a jumper before, so you need to be extra careful so you don't lose her. If she does handle your teleportation well, we'll enroll her in riding lessons so you'll have a proper rider while on duty. I'll have whomever she picks as her partner trained as well. Unlike you, I don't view sunshine as a mode of transportation, so I'm compatible with anyone who can ride a horse."

"Not my fault I fast, beautiful, and magically inclined to ride sunshine. Blame my daddy, I dare you."

"No. I value my life and don't want to find out what your daddy would do if I complained that your decision to use sunshine as transportation causes me trouble. Don't you love me anymore? Why do you want your daddy to deal with me?"

"Extra fries or I'm telling my daddy you're complaining

about my perfection. And if you protest, we hunt sea bugs this weekend."

Chief Samuel Quinn laughed, went about putting the bulletproof blanket on his wife's back, and replied, "I'll make sure you get extra fries, and we can go look for some sea bugs this weekend if you want."

"Extra fries mean I feed you fries, and you eat less than bird." The cindercorn stilled while waiting for her husband to finish strapping her saddle and bridle into place. "Okay. Show her gear check. Not like other horses. I far superior."

"Yes, you are the most marvelous of cindercorns, although our cindercorn children are also marvelous cindercorns."

"All our children are best children," she replied in a solemn tone.

"All right, Detective McMarin. You should be familiar with most of this gear, but if there's a problem with her tack, you may struggle with it, so listen up." The chief ran me through the differences between a regular horse's tack and his wife's tack, which boiled down to extra straps, a slightly different placement on her back, and allowing only one finger's worth of space instead of two. "Her bridle has no bit, so all it's there for is to help you balance and give her cues if you want her to look a certain direction. If you see something dangerous, if you pull really hard, you'll astonish her into stopping, as I'm always gentle with her reins. If in doubt, pull as hard as you can and dig your heels in. Generally, she's good at spotting trouble, but sometimes she wears blinders, especially if she's thinking about lunch."

"Should have eaten lunch before coming, you right," the cindercorn complained.

The man laughed and rubbed his wife's neck. "You'll

survive until you get to the station, and I'll call in your order so you don't have to wait long. Try not to create too much mayhem on the way, okay?"

"Will do best, but very hard. Snow and slush and ice make drivers stupid, not all idiots have broken their cars yet this year. Where I go, mayhem follow. Where snow go, more mayhem follow."

I took that as my cue to get onto the cindercorn's back, and I mounted as I'd been taught, hurrying to get into the saddle to mitigate how long she dealt with all my weight on one stirrup. Chief Samuel took my purse. "I'll make sure you get this back. If you get pulled over, just tell them to give me a call, and I'll explain there's no such thing as licenses to ride crazy pyromaniac unicorns here. They'll cope."

"They better," the cindercorn replied.

TWO

"Bailey Ember Quinn, what have you done?"

UNDER NORMAL CIRCUMSTANCES, it should have taken at least an hour to reach Manhattan's lead precinct from Brooklyn, but Chief Bailey Quinn did the run in less than ten minutes. The first time she teleported, it reminded me a little of being punched in the gut. The second time triggered a headache. After the third time, I decided to register the cindercorn as cruel and unusual punishment.

Upon arrival, I did not throw up, but I oozed off her back, failed to stay on my feet, and leaned against her steaming legs, debating if I wanted to cry over my lot in life or crawl into a hole to die. Several cops came out of the station, and they stared while the cindercorn nuzzled me. "You do good. You survive! You not only survive once, you survive *twenty-two* times! You are the best detective to ever detective. You deserve medal. Gold stars. Lunch. You deserve lunch."

"Bailey Ember Quinn, what have you done?" one of the cops demanded, and he stood with his hands on his hips.

"You are not supposed to be here for another twenty minutes at the earliest."

The chief flattened her ears and snapped her teeth at the cop. "Perky mean!"

"I'm not mean. I'm concerned for your victim."

"She a little oozy but good. No vomit. Not even turn green. Yelped only twice. She good. Twenty-two times she jump. No throw up, not even once! Even learn to ride actual jump. Car in way, no want to stop, so jump. Smart, adaptable. Mine."

The cop lifted his hand and pinched the bridge of his nose. "You didn't actually teleport her twenty-two times, did you?"

"Twenty-two times," the cindercorn reported before nuzzling my cheek. "You ooze because not ride horse in long time. You fine."

While fine was a stretch, I would manage. I used her leg to help stagger back to my feet and brush myself off. "Thank you for the ride, Chief Quinn."

The cops stared at me as though I were the unicorn rather than the actual unicorn, who pranced in placed. "See? See? She *perfect*. Ride me, no problem. Twenty-two times! I picked the best detective, Perky."

Perky sighed. "Please forgive Bailey, Detective McMarin. She's excitable today. She was supposed to teleport you once to test if you could handle it. While Sam can deal with her teleportation magic, most of us cannot. By cannot, we tend to spend the rest of the day ill. I am one of the ones who can't handle it at all. Come with me, and I will show you to your new office. I also have several firearms you can choose from along with the rest of your gear. Someone else can deal with the gas guzzler."

"No gas today but promised more coffee and lunch."

"Yes, we're aware you were promised lunch. Sam called me and asked me to take care of it. At the same time, he told me what the original plan was, which you opted to completely ignore."

"Lunch and coffee here, not there. Brooklyn give hives." The cindercorn lifted a hoof and revealed a claw. "Not allowed to slice or bite idiot in Brooklyn, so come here for lunch and coffee. No mean, tell Perkette."

"I'm not being mean. I'm informing you that as soon as I take Detective McMarin to her office, I'm telling your husband what you've been up to, and you'll have to deal with him. And no worming around on the steps. You might break your saddle again, and we don't have another spare."

"No break saddle, but you cruel and mean!"

"Come with me, Detective McMarin, and ignore the gas guzzler's whining. She'll resume being a professional sometime after the coffee wears off or she gets used to having coffee again." Perky gestured to the doors leading into the station, and I followed him. "I'd apologize, but if I apologized for every time the chief got excitable, I'd never get any work done. The first time you see her in public, you won't believe it's the same woman. She has two modes of operation, and she's in her interior mode. In good news, her interior mode keeps morale up, as she's insane and hilarious to watch."

"So mean!" the cindercorn complained, trailing along behind us. "Stale chips?"

Perky laughed. "I'm sure I can scrounge up some stale chips for you, and if you stand quietly while someone strips off your gear, I'll take care of the detective's orientation so you can get some work done before the responsible chief arrives."

"Children?" she demanded.

"I checked in on the entire herd of them, and everyone is fine, although you're going to have to talk with the whelps about reading during playtime again. Apparently, the point of playtime is to be social, not to read books."

"Don't want to," the cindercorn complained.

Perky chuckled, led us to an elevator, and pressed the up button. "Your foals are napping, and your father is making sure they're a good temperature. The experimentation with solid food is going well, and I've been informed to tell you that you are clear from pregnancy and breastfeeding restrictions until your next batch of parental woes arrives."

"No woes, only lack of sleep and much joy." The cindercorn did her best to cross her eyes. "Much joy." Heaving a dramatic sigh, she regarded her saddle and snorted fire at it. "Would roll and kick hooves, but break gear."

"What happened now?"

"Vomit. Much vomit everywhere. Of the bile variety. Beauty in-tol-er-ant now to pineapple of all things. She eats pineapple, she throw up pineapple. Beauty see gorgon doctor tomorrow. Perkette check and tell if we need specialist or if pineapple no longer a Quinn household food item? All in house sad."

Perky reached over and patted Bailey's shoulder. "I'll have the wife swing over tonight if Beauty is throwing up that badly. Won't take her more than an hour to do an evaluation if you're all right with more bile to clean up during the tests, although she'll do some blood tests, I'm sure. She's between projects."

"Oh, yes, that very good. Please."

The elevator pinged, and we stepped inside, and the cindercorn eyed the weight capacity sign, which declared cindercorns should take the steps while it declared two cindercorns and two people could safely occupy the elevator at one time. I pointed at it. "What's that in pounds?"

"We had the elevator redone because of the frequent presence of cindercorns, so it's rated for ten thousand pounds now, but Sam loves toying with Bailey, so the signs constantly get changed." Perky pointed across the elevator, where a small but proper placard announced the elevator's actual capacity. "The elevator cost the city a fortune; it actually ended up on the last ballot because renovating the building for cindercorns cost taxpayers a million dollars. The vote for a temporary tax increase to pay for the city's cindercorns passed with a rather wide margin. The people love when Bailey comes out in her fur coat, and Sam's earning a following, too. He's shier than she is about shapeshifting."

Both chiefs could shapeshift into cindercorns? I questioned if the city would survive, although I remembered the vote, which had hit the entirety of New York City. I'd been among those to vote yes to the measure, as I appreciated not having been turned to stone during the 120 Wall Street incident.

"I am best cindercorn. Children also best cindercorns. All cindercorns are best cindercorns."

"Yes, you are the best cindercorn." Perky hit the button for the eighth floor. "We are all residents of the eighth floor, as Bailey decided her new detective needed to be close by. Your office locks, and you do not need to let her in if she's annoying you. Honestly, when you see the pile of paperwork in your office, I'm sure you won't be speaking to the Chief

Quinns for a few days. To compensate you for the nightmare ahead of you, I have secured a digital murder board *and* a digital whiteboard for your exclusive use. You'll have earned it within a week."

I recognized when trouble headed my way. "What kind of case is it?"

"We suspect a serial killer, but we don't have sufficient evidence to bump it over to the specialists yet. Honestly, I stopped counting after fifty of these cases crossed my desk, so you'll have to get a headcount, identify the common links, and do what you can. Some of the cases are fairly fresh—as in from this morning. We have several teams out gathering evidence for you now. With the number coming in, there's no way one pair can handle it, but you'll be the central point for our investigation. Bailey thought a pair of fresh eyes with a new detective's badge might be able to give us additional insight, and Sam liked the idea enough he started digging through personnel records for the perfect person, which is you."

For the case count to be well over fifty, I struggled to believe a single serial killer held responsibility, especially if there were several new cases in one day. "Time between killings?"

"This morning, the murders were within a three-block radius and happened within a thirty-minute window. They all shared a similar murder method."

All right. I could understand why someone might believe a mass murderer might be responsible, but a serial killer? "Why is this being classified as a serial killer and not a mass murderer?"

Perky smiled, although it was grim. "The fact you understand there is a difference between a serial killer and a mass murderer puts you ahead of the game. We have been dealing with a week-long argument about the differences because of these cases."

"Well, it depends on which definition of serial killer you go with. Some specify there needs to be a cool-down period between incidents, and psychologically, many like to believe there is a sexual component to the crimes."

"Ewww," the cindercorn said, and she shook her head. "No want to think about sexual conduct between killer and goo of steamrolled people."

Torn between dismay and laughter at the woman's reaction, I replied, "It's not the sexual relationship between the murderer and the corpse, typically. We call those necrophiliacs rather than serial killers."

"Still ewww," she replied.

"Someone went on a joyride in a steamroller and killed several people this morning?" I asked.

"That's the problem. We don't know how the steamroller got to the various murder sites. It's like the steamroller manifested, ran the victim over, and teleported to the next victim before disappearing. We have eyewitness accounts there was a steamroller, the physical evidence claims there was a steamroller involved, but there's no steamroller."

The elevator pinged before opening, and I followed Perky out, staring at him with wide eyes. "The steamroller disappeared?"

"Honestly, that's the most normal part of the whole case," he muttered. "Okay, gas guzzler. Go to your office and leave us alone. Your lunch will be here in twenty minutes, so get your gear off and make yourself pretty. If you're pretty when Sam gets here, he might even forgive you for tormenting the new recruit."

"She fine. Not even green. Order her whatever she want for lunch, she earn it. I pay because twenty-two teleports. It twenty-two teleport penalty, issued in food." The cindercorn lashed her tail and trotted down the center of the massive gauntlet of cop cubicles. She stopped at every desk on the way to investigate, where the officers gave her some form of junk food in exchange for an opportunity to pet her.

"I'm very confused," I confessed. "I'm concerned I damaged my brain this morning when I rejected the advances of an incubus."

"Ah, you're the incubus case? We heard about that. The incubus 'reported' an incident to Sam, claiming that it is criminal for the NYPD to have a gorgeous virgin cop and refusing to give her paid time off to resolve the issue. I'm letting you know so you're prepared for the flurry of speculation. Unless you're looking for a date, play stupid. If you *are* looking for a date, just tell Bailey you're lonely. She'll go on a mission to end your single days. Honestly, she's pretty good at it, so that's something."

Oh, right. I'd rejected the incubus by stating I had no more PTO left, and however much he'd be a great start to my day, I would have to decline his invitation. Had I remained at my old precinct, the jokes about my virginity would have become relentless, with an equal mix of good-natured ribbing and maliciousness. "Doctor's appointments," I complained. "My next appointment is unpaid."

"Right. Okay, so, your healthcare works a lot differently here than in the other precincts." Perky gestured along the wall where a bunch of glass-fronted offices observed the cubicle farm. "These offices are for those who are supervising the rowdy cops in the cubicle farms. We rotate them, so every month someone gets to escape the farm to enjoy an office before the shuffle resumes."

Interesting. At my old precinct, offices went to the captain's favorites without exception. "Why am I getting an office?"

Perky led me through the cubicle farm to a hallway, and I discovered the chiefs had a pair of offices next to each other with a removable wall, which was opened so they shared their space. "Bailey said so, and Sam agreed after looking over your file—and we have a bunch of offices for detectives on this floor. Since you're coming in with the shit cases, you get an office as your transfer reward. Anyway, if you have any problems with your sexual health, you need to go see Sam. He's part incubus, and if he can't resolve the issue, one of his family will come in and resolve the problem. It turns out a quarter of the women in our precinct had various issues of one sort or another, which were corrected. About a quarter of the men had issues, too, which were likewise resolved. As a result, everyone is happier. When the ladies aren't grouchy because they're in pain, us men are more likely to survive to the end of our shifts. As for us men, heightened testosterone levels are addressed along with any sexual health issues, as these can cause problems for everyone. We also have a zero tolerance policy for domestic violence or excessive force while on duty, and a condition of employment is that the spouses or significant others of everyone working here have direct access to the Quinns in case of emergency. Let's just say it's worked well and leave it at that."

Huh. I'd have to battle a mass murderer or serial killer to get to stay at what appeared to be the ultimate workplace for a female cop. The challenge enthused me almost as much as the change of pace and improved environment. "What's the catch?"

"If you have something wrong with you, you will get unexpectedly called in the chief's office—and which chief you get depends on which one notices first. If Bailey notices first, she will start nagging angels until one shows up to fix the problem. If Sam notices first, you get a consultation in his office, whatever therapy you need he can handle, and the rest of the day off work because your emotional health will have undergone severe trauma and you deserve to go home with hot chocolate, coffee, or some other treat along with strict orders to enjoy your freedom from work."

"What is traumatizing about a consultation and therapy?" I blurted. "If it works, bring it on."

"Hold that thought," Perky said, and he turned, lifted his hand to his mouth, and whistled. "Hey, gas guzzler! Moment, please?"

The cindercorn trotted over, and in her hurry to come when called, she still had her nose in a bag of chips.

Perky sighed, supported the bottom of the bag so the cindercorn could munch at her treat, and said, "Call Sam and ask him to give your new detective a check over. It looks like we've got another one."

The chief pulled her head free of the bag and eyed me. "Erratic periods, excess bleeding, or the wrath of god in your uterus?"

Well, that was one way to handle the situation, especially as the rest of the cops went back to work and made it clear they had zero interest in our discussion. Had I been asked in my first days in the force, I might've fallen over dead from embarrassment, but dealing with the problem directly suited me. "Wrath of god," I admitted.

"Will call asshole. Take her to office, asshole fix. Asshole owe favor, balance scales, make Sam happy." Chief Bailey Quinn went to the nearest desk, lifted a hoof, and pointed at the phone. "Move that, press out button," she ordered.

The cop chuckled and obeyed.

With care, the cindercorn dialed a number and pressed the speakerphone button.

"How is my sweet little granddaughter today?" a masculine voice answered.

"You come station, fix new detective? She has wrath of some cruel mean god in her uterus. You clear debt, Sam made happy, I be rewarded for good behavior tonight. All go sleep happy, with new detective happiest of all."

The man chuckled, and his laughter reminded me of the chiming of bells. I altered my thought on who she spoke to, as I'd run into enough angels to understand they weren't quite men or women. "How sensible of you. Are you enjoying your coffee?"

"Oh, yes," Chief Bailey Quinn breathed. "So much coffee, much happy."

"I can do as you wish but on one condition."

"What condition?" the cindercorn demanded, and she turned her ears back while lowering her hoof back to the floor, clicking her claw against the tile. "No condition, owe favor."

"I would like your detective to investigate someone. It would be most prudent of her to do so. That is all I ask."

The cindercorn grunted. "Fine, but if I do not get my reward for good behavior tonight, I will be very sad. Especially if Beauty is intolerant to pineapple. Very, very sad. She see Doctor Perkette tonight about the pineapples. Then other doctor tomorrow, too."

"I see you are as vigilant as always regarding your children," the angel praised. "I shall be over promptly, although I will delay long enough for your detective to see the marvels of her new office before I assist in this matter. Do prepare your couch, as she will surely become a temporary resident of your office once I finish with her."

"Can do. Foals are with my father if you would like to visit with them. They eat solid food as of today. They have graduated! I am free, free to have all of the coffee!"

"May *He* safeguard us all from your wicked ways," the angel teased.

"You the one most wicked. See you soon. No halos, and no smiting!" Lifting her hoof, the chief disconnected the call before turning to the cop at his desk. "You make couch ready. You late shift tonight?"

"I'm on late shift tonight. I'll make sure Detective McMarin makes it home. Do you have her cruiser keys?"

"Sam has keys. You steal from him, be in charge of my detective. If she wish to get started on case once she is up from her nap, keep eye on her. Order her soup and good food, give me receipt. She have hard day. Twenty-two teleports."

The cop whistled. "Well done, Detective McMarin. Welcome to the eighth floor. If things get a little crazier than you're used to, just come over for a chat."

"A *little* crazier?" I asked, wondering what sort of hell an angel would put me through for me to end up on a couch in the chiefs' shared office.

"She's from a Brooklyn precinct, Nilman," Perky informed the other cop with a grin. "You know how they can get there, not often graced with the presence of cindercorns and what-else we got kickin' around here."

A sympathetic sound came from every cop in the cubicle farm along with several condolences for my suffering.

"Don't worry, Detective McMarin," Nilman said, winking at me. "We'll take good care of you here. Our precinct is the best, and I'm not saying that because Chief Bailey is willing to make us coffee when we do a good job. Good luck with your cases, though. If you need any help, just ask. Having helped them move the filing boxes into your office, you're going to need all the help you can get."

THREE

"Angels are assholes."

I GOT SUCKER PUNCHED by an archangel and woke up on a couch in the shared office of the Chief Quinns, who engaged in a lively argument over the schedule. Chief Bailey Quinn had returned to her human form, and she sat on her husband's desk with her arms crossed over her chest.

Sitting up, I yawned and tried to piece together the circumstances leading up to the archangel giving me a whack to the gut I'd never forget. "Is it normal for angels to punch people?"

My question halted the dispute, and Chief Bailey Quinn grinned at me. "That's my fault, I'm afraid. I specified no halos and no smitings, but I neglected to tell him no assault or ambushes. Apparently, he claims he was doing you a favor by making sure you were knocked out for his work. Honestly, he probably was doing you a favor, so I'm ignoring it. Holy fire hurts like hell, and angels lack regard for human pain tolerance."

"I didn't even get a diagnosis. I got a punch to the gut. I mean, that is not a complaint, but it's unexpected."

"Angels are assholes. You'll get used to it. He had other things to do, but he wanted to clear an owed debt, so he did so. A little warning would have been nice, but I guess he noticed Sam behind you so you wouldn't hit the floor hard."

Samuel waved from his position behind his desk. "Polycystic ovary syndrome due to faulty hormonal production. That's something I could have handled, but Sariel informed me he has addressed any and all other health issues to make certain the debt was paid in full. We've been looking over your work performance records, and I suspect you'll be happy enough without having to go to the doctors as frequently."

No kidding. I discovered my purse on the floor near the couch, and I checked my phone to discover I'd lost four hours of my day. "Did I even get to see my office? I can't remember."

"You did," Bailey informed me. "Sariel warned me you'd have some memory issues, and he told me to tell you not to worry about it. Holy fire tends to short circuit humans for a while. I'll show you to your office so you can get settled."

Samuel cleared his throat.

"What now?" the woman complained.

"Why don't you make her one of your magical cups of coffee while I show her to her office? At the same time, you can make yourself a cup, as you're about five minutes from crashing out from your first cup."

"I am not going to crash out from a single cup of coffee. I can survive a while without my next cup of coffee. But I will go make McMarin a cup." Bailey slid off the desk and left, whistling a merry tune as she went.

"Don't mind her. Do you want to be called McMarin or something else?"

"I have a first name?" I asked, tilting my head to the side.

"According to your badge, it's Josefina," the chief informed me. "I have trained my wife to use my first name sometimes, but if you hear her wailing Quinn, she's talking about me." He rose to his feet and headed to the door. "Expect Bailey to pass out on your couch. She's stubborn, she's tired, and she refuses to admit she's tired. I'll remove her when we head home, as my grandfather has informed me she will be down and out for the rest of the night. The freedom got to her."

I chuckled at the thought of the cindercorn being defeated by something as simple as a single cup of coffee after not having any for months. Getting to my feet, I slung my purse strap over my shoulder and followed the chief into the hallway. "I'm sorry for the trouble, Samuel, sir."

"You're no trouble. It's not the first time a new officer in our precinct has ended up on the couch after getting smote by an angel. We take care of our own here, and I have a list of angels who owe me favors a mile long, as they come to the chiefs to handle touchier situations with humans. I have the angels patch up my cops to clear out the debts, so if they can come to me, they do. They enjoy doing good for humanity despite the rules generally barring them from participating in random acts of kindness. You'll get used to it."

I would? "How will time off and salary work here?" In

an effort to maintain the casual atmosphere, I forced myself to drop the sir.

To my astonishment, I didn't spontaneously combust or descend directly to some hell.

"I'm having your paid time off reset, as those days should be for rest and relaxation, not trying to get a medical diagnosis. I already discussed it with the commissioner. Your starting salary will be average level for third grade detectives with an unplanned transfer bonus. You'll get to negotiate your salary at the end of the year when we're doing the budget. Normally, we'd do the negotiation immediately upon promotion, but I needed you yesterday, and the commissioner gave me some leeway with your bonus. Part of your bonus is a relocation package if you live more than an hour from our precinct. Oh, and that's with traffic at rush hour."

I stared at the man, wondering when he had lost his mind. "Who *doesn't* live more than an hour from here during rush hour?"

"Everyone except myself, my wife, and Perkins; we're terrorizing Queens right now, although we're going to need to get a bigger place, yet again, due to the number of children and others underfoot."

My current apartment gave me a two hour commute on a bad day to get to Brooklyn, and I expected closer to three hours to get to Manhattan.

Would my new salary allow me to live somewhere closer? I supposed I could have moved closer to Brooklyn on my pre-promotion salary, but I hadn't had the time needed to search for a new place to live. I decided I would deal with my living arrangements sometime after I came to terms with having a new job at a new precinct.

"Others?" I asked.

"My wife adopted an entire species of... honestly, I have no idea what they are. They look like mice, but they're sentient, and they've outgrown the basement of our place. My wife wants more kids, and we agreed we'd adopt as many as we have, so we're going to end up with at least two more kids. Add in our rescue wolves, and our current property in Queens isn't going to cut it for much longer. This is driving me crazy because we just moved. I underestimated my wife's interest in an entire herd of children. I need to stop underestimating my wife."

"At *least* two more?" I blurted.

The chief led me to an office, opened the door, and ushered me into a work paradise with the promised digital whiteboard and a digital murder board, both of which I would form close relationships with. There was a couch and two guest chairs along with enough space I'd be able to spread files out without needing to resort to using the hallway. The presence of twenty filing boxes stacked in a corner concerned me, but I would tackle it the same way as always: at the beginning and with a purpose.

I wouldn't miss my squeaky dry erase markers, and I would donate them to someone still stuck with a traditional board. I spotted my filing boxes on my desk, and I dumped my purse on the polished surface before exploring, checking out the cabinets to discover a precinct-branded travel mug inside with my name on it. "We have named cups?"

"You have four more where that one came from. The mug wars got ridiculous, so we just keep a stash of these and engrave owner's names on them. Bailey has one of yours in the break room making your coffee. According to your file, you live on the mainland?"

"I do. It was what I could afford at the time I joined the force, and I haven't had time to find a closer place to live."

"With your permission, we'll call in a real estate agent to help you find a new place, and part of your hiring bonus will be getting you moved closer to the area. Cops who have to drive several hours to get to work are crabby cops, and we don't stock enough pixie dust to keep everyone from being crabby due to the commute."

My mouth dropped open. "Pixie dust?"

"Oh. Frankson is one of those, is he?" The chief snorted. "I'll make sure to have a talk with the Brooklyn captains and make sure they review their operations. We basically throw low grade dust around our precinct like it's sugar. It keeps everyone in a slightly better mood, improves general work performance, and lowers incidents on the streets. Happy cops work better with the public, and the low grade dusts don't impair. Sure, we have to budget for it, but pixie dust is definitely cheaper than some of the court cases we've had to deal with due to overly cranky cops at the end of a long shift."

I returned the mug to the cabinet and explored the drawers to find a stockpile of new general supplies. A post-it gave me a temporary username and password for the computer along with instructions on how to make my username. "Anything else I should know before I get started on this?"

"If my wife starts talking in her sleep when she passes out on your couch, ignore it or record it. If you record it, send me a copy, because once she starts talking in her sleep, things get weird."

I raised a brow. "You mean they aren't already weird? I got sucker punched by an archangel today."

"Weirder," he replied with a grin.

Armed with a mug with my name on it, Chief Bailey Quinn invaded my office and set my prize on my desk. "I have decided that because I subjected you to twenty-two teleportations today, I will make your first twenty-two coffees. That almost makes up for torturing you on the way here."

I accepted the cup, chuckled, and asked, "How long do you think it would take you to run to Stony Point?"

Bailey checked her phone, tapping on the screen. "What's out in Stony Point?"

"My apartment."

She dropped her phone, which clattered on the floor, and she cursed before scrambling to retrieve it. "Oh, good. I didn't break this one. Okay. That's too far, Sam."

"I know it's too far. We'll look into arrangements."

"It's really too far."

Samuel sighed. "You want to run her to and from work, don't you?"

"Twenty minutes flat with how good she is at handling teleports during daylight hours, and maybe an hour after dark if people and the roads are stupid."

"Or I can book her into the extended stay hotel ten minutes from here until we can move her properly. That way, I keep my wife as sane as possible. I'm challenged enough without you running how many miles each day?"

Bailey sat on my couch and regarded me with a frown. "Do you like hotels?"

I shrugged. "If I have a ten minute commute? I'll love everything to do with that hotel. Will I be allowed to take my cruiser home?"

"Absolutely. The choice is yours if you take it home or bring your own vehicle to work."

I had a vehicle? Rather than tell him that, I replied, "I can handle a long commute for a while until I find a place to move closer. It doesn't bother me."

"While it may not bother you, it bothers us." Samuel glanced at his wife and laughed. "And she's out."

Sure enough, Chief Bailey Quinn had fallen asleep on my new couch, still seated upright. When her husband stretched her out to be more comfortable, she didn't stir. I wondered how I'd get anything done if I needed to keep an eye on a woman with a reputation of destroying entire city blocks. "Is she all right?"

"She's fine. We've just been busy because of the cases you just inherited. If you're too tired to drive home, a hotel will be arranged."

I turned in my chair to regard the stacks of boxes. "A hotel might be a good idea, because leaving that to breed will give me hives."

The chief grinned. "I'll come back with where you'll be staying tonight, and I'll make sure you have clean clothes for tomorrow. We have a system. One of the ladies will stop by to get your sizes and make sure you have everything you need to be comfortable on your first real day."

"Thank you, Samuel, sir."

"Glad to help. Nilman will be around most of the night, so if you have any issues, go see him. You'll see Nilman a lot, as he's usually partnered with Officer Perkins. Right now, we're on split shifts because of this mass murderer or serial killer case, and Nilman's wife is out of town, so he can afford to lose some sleep. If he finds anything new on those cases, he'll come find you."

"Excellent. I'll get started on this, then."

"One last thing. What do you want for dinner? Some soup will be served because Bailey believes soup can cure anything."

"Something good and hot with a side of something I can claim is healthy. I'm not picky, and I don't have any allergies. I also have no idea what's good around here."

"I'll order from the Chinese place down the street. Are you vegan or vegetarian?"

"I'm not."

"I will return with your reservation and your supper, and when it's time for me to take Bailey home, you can take some pictures when I toss her over my shoulder because she gets embarrassed if I carry her like a princess."

"How is being tossed over your shoulder not embarrassing?"

"Apparently, I'm so manly when I do it she breaks something in her head and forgets she gets embarrassed. I've learned to just not ask."

"What about the situation with the pineapples and your daughter?"

"Ah, Beauty will be fine. I asked my grandfather, and if gorgons don't get enough of a certain vitamin, pineapple and some fruits can become problematic. Bailey is being assertive, so I'm pretending I don't know what's going on while happening to mystically acquire the appropriate vitamin, which will be slipped to our daughter along with a lecture she needs to eat more and stare less at her food."

"And what about the person I'm supposed to investigate?"

"Oh, him. He's our main witness for the murders, and

honestly, I'm concerned he's one of the targets. So far, he's witnessed at least twenty of them, and the poor guy is going to need some serious therapy to get over it. He was at the steamroller incident this morning on his way to work, and the steamroller kept popping up and killing pedestrians. After we put up the bulletin, he called the non-emergency line and told us he'd witnessed it. His name is Alec Mortan, and he's with a therapist right now. We haven't questioned him yet, mainly because when my grandfather suggests to get the witness into therapy before having you investigate him, I listen. I'm considering witness protection for him, but we might settle with a hotel—perhaps a room next to yours. That would make you accessible to keep an eye on him."

"Connecting?" I asked.

"I will ask the hotel if they have one. That should keep me busy until it's time to take the firestarter home so she can sleep off her most exciting day. I am sorry she teleported you that many times. I didn't think the coffee would be *that* bad."

"It didn't bother me."

"Right. Speaking of which, that just got you a free ride to a magic evaluation, courtesy of the CDC, because I'm the only other person who can tolerate a lot of her jumps, and I'm up there on the charts. Your academy records say you passed the basic aptitude tests for being up to a detective, but there was no mention of your official test results."

"I couldn't afford the official tests," I admitted. "And since I was already grateful enough to make the cut, I figured I could get tested later."

"Well, as the CDC wants to know how Bailey ticks and why so few can tolerate riding her when she teleports, you'll get an all-expenses paid test, and it'll be official so you can use it for work. We'll take care of it after you've had time to settle here. I'll leave you to your work. If you need anything, find Nilman. If Bailey does something I'll regret, come find me. Otherwise, try not to stress too much on your first day. Tomorrow, the rodeo truly begins."

FOUR

I imagined the apocalypse unfolding in our precinct.

I SPENT several hours registering the cases in my new murder board and recording case numbers on my digital whiteboard before calling it quits and heading to the hotel a few minutes away. As Nilman didn't want either chief to freak out over the idea of me driving after a long day, he dropped me off at the hotel with a promise to have somebody pick me up in the morning.

In retrospect, I should have realized I would end up riding a cindercorn to work again, although judging from the larger size, I'd gotten Chief Samuel Quinn instead of his wife. "Is Bailey all right?"

"Bailey is in a state I can only describe as partially comatose," Samuel replied shaking his head. "I carried her into our office, put her on the couch, and upon hearing you needed a ride to work, decided to give you a more traditional trip, as I'd already sent the patrols out for today and didn't have any spares. It's busy today."

Uh oh. When the chief claimed it was busy, I imagined

the apocalypse unfolding in our precinct. "What happened?"

"Two more murders, and our traumatized witness is in your office with one of the other cops because he's rattled. I can't say I blame him for being rattled. I thought the steamroller yesterday was bad."

"What happened today?"

"Defenestrations onto fences. One was a wrought-iron fence, a second was onto a glass-topped stone wall, and the third was onto a concrete median with a steel decorative fencing. That one was impressive, as the median was over twenty feet from the edge of the building. The defenestrations occurred in Lower East Side, but we have jurisdiction despite it not happening in our precinct. In a way, I'm glad we overhauled jurisdiction for the chiefs; it lets me pluck cases from various precincts and move them to ours. This case would have become a true nightmare if all the involved precincts had to handle the cases individually."

As the chief had run down the street to pick me up, I wasted no time stuffing my foot into the stirrup and mounting. "How long does it take you to make the run?"

"Ten minutes. While I can run almost as fast as my wife can, I do not teleport. As I'm trying to teach my wife to be sensible when she has four hooves and is making use of public roads, we'll obey traffic laws."

"What, you don't have lights or a siren?"

"I'm guilty of trying to eat them, too. The sound and flashes are just intolerable in this shape," he complained. Once confident I wouldn't fall off, he moved into a canter, sticking to the roads, although he wasted no time weaving between vehicles at his whim.

He did, as promised, generally obey traffic laws. Technically, cindercorns couldn't signal, and I couldn't blame him for blowing some flame and smoke at an idiot dumb enough to honk at a chief of police. As two could play the game, I flashed the driver my new badge and raised a brow.

The honking stopped.

Unlike my last ride to the precinct's primary station, Samuel trotted up the ramp alongside the steps, bumped the handicap access button with his knee, and strode on in, angling for the elevator. I took care to dodge banging my head into anything.

If he wanted to handle the walking, I would sit in the saddle without complaint.

Perky met us at the elevator, and I took advantage of the wait to dismount. "Good morning, Perkins."

"You may as well just call me Perky. Everyone else does unless we're being official or I'm in trouble nowadays. How was your commute?"

"I had to show an idiot driver my badge because he thought it was a good idea to honk at a cindercorn. I figured I should stop that nonsense before the cindercorn torched his car and made a mess of rush hour traffic."

The chief whinnied and bobbed his head. "I gave a warning snort. The drivers need a reminder now and then that some of the mounted police have fiery tempers."

"And he doesn't mean the cop," Perky muttered. When the elevator opened, he waited for the chief to step inside before going in. "Your office is a warzone, and I'll make you your coffee this morning until Bailey can teach you to handle the machine she's having a relationship with."

"Relationship?" I asked, joining them in the elevator and pressing the button for the eighth floor.

"Since she hasn't been able to drink any of its blessed

ambrosia, she's been cuddling and cooing to it," Samuel admitted. "She does the same with the one at home. I'm expecting tears when she realizes she can have as much coffee as she wants today, assuming she decides to join us."

"She's on the move, and she's whining because she's misplaced her gorgon-incubus doohickey. Before I came down to wait for you, she was roaming the hallway rubbing her eyes and questioning how she got to work in the first place."

The chief whinnied again. "Hasn't figured out she can have coffee yet?"

"Nope." Perky checked his phone. "She is now sitting on Amanda's desk trying to figure out which day of the week it is, how she got to work, what happened to her actual uniform, as it appears you dressed her in jeans, a t-shirt, and why she's wearing your favorite of her leather bulletproof jackets."

"I'm a man with simple needs, and if she wasn't going to dress herself, I was going to dress her as I like. And I really like her in that jacket. I brought her actual uniform. I was going to call the commissioner and report a downed chief, but it seems I've been foiled."

"That worked the first time you tried it, but he's onto you now and just asks why she's that exhausted."

"While true, it still amuses me."

The elevator pinged open, and because I needed coffee, I gathered the chief's reins. "I'll return him to the chief so they can get to work, Perky."

"Ask for a coffee and suggest Bailey should make herself one. Then she can take her cindercorn somewhere to change into his proper attire while you deal with the disaster in your office. If you need therapy after your interview with him, come to my desk, and I'll get you in touch with somebody."

Uh oh. "Do you need therapy from this case?"

"It's a possibility. I had nightmares about steamrollers chasing me all night. It was not fun."

"I dreamed about dismemberment, and I'm not sure if I want to trade you or not," the chief admitted.

Rather than bite my hands off or incinerate me, the cindercorn followed when I led him through the cubicle farm in search of his wife, finding her in the heart of the maze, yawning and listening to a pale-haired woman, who had rolled in to work ready to model while enforcing the law.

Damn. I needed to ask for advice on her makeup game, as she rocked a subtle shadowy look that drew attention to her eyes. I bet the trick worked wonders when she patrolled, and I meant to master the look, assuming I could get home long enough to retrieve my makeup kit.

"Bailey, I apprehended this cindercorn blowing smoke and flame at a honking driver," I announced, showing off where I held his reins.

Samuel bobbed his head, whinnied, and reached out to nuzzle his wife. "I fully understand your hatred of people honking at you now."

"It's so bad," the woman complained. "But, as we have been unable to come to the bottom of this mystery, why am I wearing this?"

"You didn't want to go to work and refused to put on your uniform, so I dressed you how I selfishly wanted while packing your uniform in a bag. I'm really not sure why you willingly got into our cruiser after protesting going to work in your sleep, but here we are. To be fair to you, you were pretty much asleep when it happened."

"We both need some coffee," I informed Bailey, and I handed her the reins. "I have a critical disaster to attend to in my office. If you can find something for the poor man to drink while you're at it, that might be a good start."

"Try one of the calming teas," Samuel suggested. "Dust it with B or A, but make sure he's in retention of his faculties. We need to get a coherent interview out of him without traumatizing him. Detective McMarin, your office is wired to be recorded and observed, so notify him he is being recorded and make sure he understands he can request an attorney if he would like for the questioning session. He's been pretty cooperative, but don't take any shortcuts."

"Understood, sir."

"Good luck. You'll need it."

I nodded and headed for my office, to discover a small party in the hallway, in the doorway, and on the couch. According to the chatter, which involved a heated dispute over what sort of hell weather we'd face in the next week, my new co-workers had opted to distract the man seated in one of my guest chairs with small talk.

I took a moment to look him over. From average brown hair to average brown eyes with an equally average appearance with no truly distinctive features, he was the type of man detectives complained about when attempting to pull together a sketch from witness accounts.

He could be anybody, with his skin, eye, and hair color being his most distinguishing features, meaning he could be one of millions of men in the New York City area.

If he turned to a life of crime, I pitied the detective who

needed to work on the case. His appearance would complicate the situation more than I cared to think about.

To put an end to the party, I checked the forecast on my phone, listened in until somebody made the correct guess for the afternoon's proclaimed weather, and said, "According to the meteorologists, we will be wise to bring umbrellas with us in the afternoon, but I wouldn't hold your breath. We are in New York, after all. Mr. Mortan, I'm Detective McMarin, and it's a pleasure to meet you." Wiggling through the crowd, I offered him my hand and shook with him before circling my desk and taking a seat. "I asked someone to make us drinks, but I think I'm going to get away with that exactly once."

Alec Mortan grinned at me. "We'd been talking about how you'd just been promoted and transferred to this precinct. I'm just going to apologize now for the trouble."

"You're no trouble, Mr. Mortan," I replied, unlocking my computer so I could pull up the starting notes for the case. Once I had it open, I grabbed the new digital pen for my whiteboard, herded the other cops out, and left the door open so coffee and tea could be delivered. "Be advised that this conversation will be recorded, and if you would like legal advice from an attorney, you may request it at any time."

"I'm used to the routine. I don't need any legal advice. I'm just the world's most unfortunate witness. Honestly, this office is a lot nicer than the interrogation rooms."

My office was; I'd been in interrogation rooms enough times to understand how uncomfortable they could be, something done on purpose to encourage criminals to start talking. It sometimes backfired on innocent witnesses, but the method tended to work, which resulted in nobody being happy during an interrogation.

As everything I'd heard about the man indicated he wasn't lying to me, I nodded. Anyone who'd witnessed at least five deaths over two mornings was either cursed or truly unfortunate. "I was brought in to provide a fresh perspective, so I'd like you to introduce yourself and tell me when the trouble started."

I turned on my digital whiteboard, opened a new file, and prepared to take notes.

"My name is Alec Mortan, I'm thirty-four years old, and I work as a forensic accountant. I'm currently employed by a corporation on Wall Street to expose any internal fraud, embezzlement, and so on. My job is to investigate questionable accounts at the company, identify any suspicious money movement, and learn who might be behind the transactions."

Well, I already had a pile of potential motivations for someone to target Alec Mortan. Even in Brooklyn, we'd encounter cases of somebody trying to knock off a nosy accountant who'd exposed some form of fraud or another. "When did you start working as a forensic accountant?"

Most witnesses tended to give basic answers, but Alec backtracked to the moment he decided he wanted to transfer from marketing to accounting at the age of twenty-six, guided me through his education, explaining how he'd taken night courses while paying the bills working in marketing, eventually graduating at the top of his class for his first degree in accounting. At thirty-one, he'd accomplished his goal of qualifying to work as an accountant, and it had taken him two more years and more schooling to land his first job as a forensic accountant.

"And that's when the trouble started," Alec announced, and he sighed. "It was during lunch on my first day, and my new boss took me to a restaurant down the street. It was a nice day, so we ate out on the patio. A driver decided to use the sidewalk as the road and killed ten people and injured a bunch more. I still don't know why he did it. The guy didn't seem drunk, especially not after he got out and made a run for it. Nobody told me what happened to that guy, but he took off down the street at a sprint."

On the digital whiteboard, I made a notation of the murder method. "Hit and run, with the culprit running away on foot." Alec gave me the date, time, and location, which I added to my notes. "Did you know any of the victims?"

"Know? No. Would have known given time? Yes. Two of the women killed were going to be working in the same department with me. My boss was really shaken up. They'd both been working for him for a long time. I hadn't met them yet; they were doing an audit in a nearby building that morning."

I made the appropriate notation, drew a box around the note, and marked it as the first case, leaving room to pull out the various case numbers for my digital murder board. "Were you questioned about it prior?"

"Yes." Alec got onto his phone, and to my astonishment, he told me the case number. "I was told to keep the case number handy in case they had any other questions for me. They said something about me being able to request therapy about it if I referenced the case number."

I nodded, as the NYPD did what it could to help those who'd witnessed a violent crime. Having a front row seat to the murders of ten people counted. I went to my computer, plugged in the case number, and pulled up the file. "The culprit was charged with first-degree murder, as one of the victims was an ex-girlfriend known to walk in that specific location at the time of day of the crime. He was imprisoned, and he's still serving his sentence."

"Good."

I nodded, returning to the digital whiteboard and making notations with the verdict, case number, and a note to check over the trial's transcription. "Before that incident, were there any strange accidents around you?"

"What sort of accidents?"

His question worried me, and I wondered how I could get the best information I could out of him. "Let's start with moderate to severe injuries that could have easily led to death, especially if the accident involved someone else."

Alec took his time thinking about it, and then he shook his head. "Nothing is coming to mind. There were plenty of rubberneck incidents, but I never saw any of those happen."

As rubbernecking was a way of life in the area, helping to create traffic calamities every time there was an incident, I accepted his comment at face value. Unless something in the case indicated the standard city car accidents were relevant, I'd eliminate them. I made a note on the whiteboard I hadn't pursued rubbernecker incidents to remind myself of another angle to pursue if the cases went cold on me. "What happened next?"

"Someone ran a red light in Times Square and hit a bunch of pedestrians. I heard later their brake lines had been cut. One of my co-workers, Rachelle, was crossing the street to meet me for a show. She died a few hours later. I went to the hospital, but I didn't get to see her, not while she was still alive. She died while they were operating on her."

Alec sighed. "I didn't get a case number for that one. Too many witnesses, too little time, I guess."

Times Square had been out of my league and on the wrong island before my transfer, but I could imagine the nightmare of trying to get statements from everyone who'd witnessed it. Some would have stayed, some would have tried to help the victims, and some would have bailed without a second look back, concerned more about their schedules than becoming involved with a police investigation. I gave credit where credit was due; most New Yorkers would check to make sure there were enough helpers on hand before bailing.

Alec gave me the date of the incident, which I recorded to look up later. "After that?"

"Someone with a grudge started shooting at drivers on Broadway during rush hour. There were several car accidents and quite a few deaths. I didn't know anyone, but my car got totaled. I sprained my ankle." Alec checked his phone, and he gave me the insurance information from the incident along with the date and time. "After that, something broke off a building not far from my work and flattened a car. I got hit with some rock debris from the accident. Not sure what the deal with that was, but since I got cut, I got a case number."

With startling efficiency, Alec referenced his phone and continued going through the list of ways he'd witnessed people die.

One driver had managed to flip his car off a bridge during a crash. Another had been slammed into the median. One pedestrian, who'd decided to jog along with traffic on the George Washington, had gotten hit and tossed into the water. In what I could only think of as a freak accident, someone had gotten killed through being strangled by his jumper cables. Alec had no idea how somebody could get one part plugged in, get spun around, and have the other end wrap around his throat, but he'd fallen and gotten hanged as a result.

Alec had, upon coming across the scene, tried to rescue the man, but CPR couldn't save a corpse.

That case had led to his first therapy session.

To my horror, his brush with the steamroller yesterday hadn't been his first; a supposed mechanical malfunction in the braking system had resulted in someone being crushed against the side of a building. After the steamroller had punched through the wall, it had killed three more people inside.

A co-worker's cousin had been one of the victims.

A freak crane accident dropping a slab of concrete had crushed someone near him, close enough he'd been covered with rock dust and blood.

The mental images from that incident would haunt me for a while.

While I'd been told he'd witnessed twenty killings, I uncovered that the number was well over fifty when he exposed the incidents he hadn't gotten case numbers for. He took all the deaths seriously, recording everything he could about each event in case someone asked him what he'd witnessed. Not only had he recorded everything, he'd detailed the scenes, dutifully took pictures, and made comments about each one, who he'd known that was no longer around, and his relationship with the victims.

My heart hurt for him, and I asked for a copy of the file, which he sent to my email without question.

As it would take me several hours to work through it, I

asked him to wait, visited the chiefs' office, and requested he be put up in the same hotel with me just in case, mentioning he'd witnessed more murders than anticipated. Both sighed and promised it would be taken care of.

By the time I returned to my office, I dreaded the next few weeks of my life, which would be rather complicated.

Add in I'd been asked by an archangel to investigate the poor man, I worried about what the future would hold.

FIVE

"I have a 10-10 N partnered with a rain of frogs."

My future held chaos, but not in the form of witnessed murders. Instead, I got a rain of frogs. The frogs, conjured by an idiot of a practitioner, would make the rest of my night interesting, as the incident took place in the hallway outside of my hotel room. An hour earlier, I had enjoyed the upgrade to a nice suite on the top floor so I could be next door to one Alec Mortan.

Now, I regretted everything, beginning with having told the Chiefs Quinn I'd be fine without constant monitoring and supervision. I also regretted having opted for late-evening room service.

Conjured frog slime did a great job of killing my appetite.

Alec regarded the frogs with a puzzled expression, nudging one of the amphibians with the toe of his shoe.

The frog attempted to bite him, but it failed to get a hold of him.

The practitioner, drugged or high as far as I could tell,

sat in a sea of slime and giggled, his bloodshot eyes focusing on something new every other moment.

Great. Just what I needed: a drunk druggie hallucinating to go along with his conjuring act. Once I added in the swaying and some other symptoms, I suspected he had taken a potent mix of narcotics, alcohol, and who-knew-what before playing with magic.

I inhaled, counted until ten, and exhaled. "Alec, if you don't mind, please go into my room."

Careful not to step on any of the hopping frogs, the man obeyed. "Any other time, I'd be flattered, Detective McMarin." He sighed, nudging a frog out of the way before easing by me. "I'm sorry to have caused you all this trouble."

Poor guy. "You're no trouble," I assured him. "I'd just rather be between you and that practitioner right now. He appears to be rather unstable."

"Does it make me less of a man to admit I'd rather have you between me and him right now?"

"Considering I'm armed and you aren't, it makes you quite sensible, really." I dug my phone out of my pocket, wished I hadn't investigated the odd noise outside of my door, and thumbed through the contacts until I found Officer Nilman's number.

One day, the man might be able to head home, hopefully before his wife came back to town. I connected the call.

"Detective McMarin," my new co-worker greeted. "How can I help you this fine evening?"

"As the Chief Quinns would surely panic if I contacted dispatch, I have a 10-10 N partnered with a rain of frogs, and I'm fairly sure the perp has mixed and matched his substances." I eyed the frogs, some of which were brightly colored and screamed poisonous. "I'm not up-to-date on my amphibian identification, but some of these look like they dabbled with a box of crayons."

"And Mr. Mortan?"

"He is currently in my room, where the potentially poisonous amphibians or their drugged and probably inebriated conjurer won't get him. Send medical assistance for the practitioner along with any antidotes, or whatever it is people use to prevent poisonous frogs from killing someone. I'd rather not add a tally to Mr. Mortan's checklist. I have not engaged the probably hallucinating gentleman, who has settled into rocking and muttering to himself."

Sometimes, my job as a cop was to stand and do nothing until someone qualified to handle the situation showed up, and outside of a rain of potentially poisonous frogs, he hadn't harmed anyone. Yet.

Thanks to the late hour, no one else had come to investigate the amphibians, who protested their new environment in ribbits.

"What checklist?"

"Of witnessing 101 ways to die, of course. I suspect he's up to his fifties by now, and I'd rather not he be able to add drug overdose or encounter with lethal frog to the tally."

Behind me, Alec Mortan snorted a laugh. "That's true isn't it? That's definitely one way to look at it. It's been a unique experience. I shouldn't be laughing about this, but my therapist would probably praise me because it beats generalized depression."

Yes, a little laughter even in the face of something terrible generally beat generalized depression. "It's unfortunately true. The first time I witnessed someone die while in the line of duty, I got a week with a therapist, and he suggested I add morbid humor as a stage of grief. I haven't counted the ways yet, but it might make for one hell of an interesting autobiography. While slightly horrifying in a way, laughing at what I couldn't change actually helped." One of the bright colored frogs hopped in my direction, and I redirected it with my shoe, grateful I'd had the sense to put them back on before investigating the chaos outside of my door. "Nilman, just so you're aware, there are literally hundreds or thousands of these frogs, and I don't know if they were conjured or teleported in from somewhere else, and there are more species than I can shake a stick at."

"I'll make sure dispatch understands there might be endangered species in the lot," he replied. "Please don't lick any frogs."

I blinked, took the phone away from my ear to confirm I'd dialed the right number, and once I had it back in its proper position, I asked, "Why would I lick a frog?"

"I just ask myself 'What would Bailey do?' and react accordingly. She would absolutely try to give a frog a kiss, especially when a cindercorn."

Behind me, Alec snickered. "You don't seem like the type to lick a frog, Detective."

"Please just get someone here who can handle this mess, and I'll hopefully keep the practitioner from falling over dead or adding to the chaos."

"On it. Expect the cavalry within the next five to ten minutes with the CDC hot on their heels. Let's just hope there aren't any fatalities. If there aren't any fatalities, we won't have to notify the Quinns until later. Much later."

"10-4. Call me back if there are any issues." I hung up and settled in to defend my hotel room from frogs while I kept an eye on the perp, who needed more help than I could provide and a stint in an emergency room to detox him of whatever crap he'd taken before deciding to experiment with magic.

THE PRACTITIONER FELL over dead on me, and as I'd sworn an oath to serve and protect, I did my best to resuscitate him while waiting for emergency services to arrive.

Luck wasn't with me—or with him.

Thanks to the frogs, numerous of which were deemed rather toxic to people in general, I got to enjoy a trip to the emergency room to make certain I wouldn't join the practitioner in reaching a premature expiration. Alec insisted on accompanying me, even though my co-workers attempted to talk him out of it.

After the first thirty minutes, I appreciated his company.

"What do you think killed him?" Alec asked, and he eyed the monitoring equipment I was attached to with a frown.

"It'll take a while for the toxicity reports to come back in, but judging from his behavior, a drug overdose in conjunction with poisoning from the frogs he'd summoned. Bad things happen when you mix various narcotics, and if he had alcohol on top of it, overdose and chemical reactions can happen in a hurry."

Drug overdoses had taken the top spot for non-natural fatalities at my old precinct, with gun-based violence coming in a close second. Domestic violence tended to be the reason someone hit up the drugs or squeezed the trigger, but the underlying causes rarely made it into the reports that reached the public.

Heart disease and asthma reigned as the crowned champions of 911 calls resulting in death.

Too often, the asthma calls involved children.

"Is that why they stole a bunch of your blood?"

"Yep. They're going to run every blood test known to man before letting me out of here. If I'm lucky, nobody will notify my boss."

Someone knocked at the door, but before I had a chance to say a word, Mrs. Chief Quinn poked her head in.

"Speak of the Devil," Alec stated in a wry tone.

"Don't," Bailey ordered. "If you do, he might show up."

"Yes, I might," an amused masculine voice stated from behind the woman.

Bailey squealed, spun around, and judging from the thumps in the hospital hallway, commenced with beating her target.

Mr. Chief Quinn came into the room, and he heaved a sigh. "Nilman called, because he knew if he didn't, he'd have literal hell to pay in the morning. I'll just apologize in advance."

Alec's brows furrowed. "Is… is that the actual Devil?"

"Yep. He's also my uncle, and he almost always listens in whenever his name is invoked anywhere near Bailey. I'm sorry about them." Samuel closed the door, eyed one of the chairs as though considering barricading it so the troublemakers would remain outside, and sighed again. "I've been updated on the rain of frogs, in case you are curious."

"Actually, yes. I am. The toxicity reports won't be back for a while, right?"

"I pulled in a favor from the CDC for access to one of

their scanners, which was able to churn through most of the common narcotics. I wanted to make sure there wasn't going to be anything you might need to be treated for due to secondary contact. Beyond the dart frog toxins, which is why you're here under observation instead of enjoying your hotel room." My boss eyed Alec with interest. "Thank you for keeping an eye on my cop, by the way."

"I'm pretty sure I'm the cause of the whole problem," he replied with a grimace.

Samuel went to the door, opened it, and said, "Hey, Lucy. Come here a second, please."

Lucy? I frowned, but before I could ask, a tall, dark-skinned man with flaming hair, curved horns, and wearing a designer suit ducked into the room. At eight feet tall, he fit what I expected from the Devil, although nobody had warned me he rocked in the sex appeal department.

"My wife likes this look on me, and I'm trying to earn some spots," the Devil informed me. "But thank you for the compliment."

Well, that would leave me pondering the mysteries of the universe for at least a few nights. "You're welcome."

"You got a sturdy one this time, Sam. You should keep her."

"That's the idea. I stole her from a precinct in Long Island after she got passed over for promotion for several years despite her obvious qualifications. I have to start her as third grade, but I expect she'll move up at the minimum allowed promotion rates." My chief grabbed a seat, sat, and propped his feet up on my bed. "Word on the wire is your wife really wants to babysit cindercorn foals again, and she wants the really young ones, so you're just going to have to bargain with me to get what she wants."

The Devil laughed. "All right. What do you want now?"

"No deals!" Bailey complained, coming into the room and placing her hands on her hips before stomping her foot.

"You're getting a babysitter for the next batch of Quinns out of the deal," he replied.

She spent a few minutes thinking about it before she relented with a nod. "But do I get his wife? I only want the premium babysitters, and that means him or his wife. The rest are pushovers."

The Devil laughed. "She'd take over my many hells if I gave her a chance and a reason."

"She really would. Here's the problem. This is Alec Mortan, and there's no way one human could have the infernally bad luck as to witness so many murders, accidents leading to death, and otherwise unexpected deaths as he has without some form of magic being involved. While I understand you may not be able to solve the mystery for us, a clue or two would be appreciated."

The Devil looked me over. "You should watch where you put your mouth, young lady."

"I'll start keeping the appropriate mouth guards in my purse or pocket," I promised, rather dismayed over the number of times I'd been forced to perform CPR during the course of my career. "Usually I have one, but I was not expecting an incident outside of my hotel room."

"I recommend you move them into the same hotel room, as this will limit the amount of anxiety your cop will experience rather significantly. It won't change the number of incidents, but she'll appreciate her ability to be able to act when they happen."

"How much is this advice going to cost me?" Sam asked.

"I get the foals tomorrow."

"Take them, and take the other kids with you. You can even take the doohickeys out for a jaunt if you want for all I care. If you're going to charge me in a day off from being hover dad, I'm not going to complain about this. Just try not to teach them too many bad habits."

Bailey bobbed her head. "What he said. I'm too tired to hover mom, and I'm still trying to figure out why Beauty keeps puking pineapple."

Sam shot the Devil a glare.

It amused me that the Lord of Lies held his hands up in surrender. "Beauty will be fine, and I will make certain there are no dietary issues while I'm watching the kids. My darling is brooding, and if I throw enough young things at her, it tames the beast."

"So, can we have that clue or two?"

"As a matter of fact, yes. I can give you a clue or two regarding your witness's particularly foul luck." The Devil stepped closer to Alec and held out his hand. "I'm Lucifer. It's a pleasure to meet you."

To my amusement, Alec shook hands with the Devil without any evidence of discomfort. "It feels strange to say it's a pleasure to meet you, and I'm not even lying about it."

"You've been tempered, so my presence doesn't bother you."

"Tempered?" the Chief Quinns demanded.

"Yes. Once a mortal soul has witnessed hell on Earth sufficient times, it creates a tolerance. I could likely unshroud without him being at any risk, although his genetics play a part in that. I won't, as your detective does not have that tolerance. We could bargain for that to change, as it might be useful for you to have a detective running around with the capability of withstanding the realities of my nature."

I considered the past few days, which had included being sucker punched by an archangel. "The lack of an angel's head is a shroud, then?"

"Precisely. To see the face of an angel is to see *His* face, which has an unfortunate tendency to destroy mortal souls, resulting in death. Mortals can be tempered to withstand such a sight, but it takes a great deal of work and some genetic alterations. Your companion has seen so much death in his life that he has flipped his gene marker, which is a gift from a very distant relative—one of the first instances of a divine having a child with a mortal. But that's only part of the problem."

"Okay." I considered Alec, as it hadn't occurred to me to do a genetic test on him, something we *could* do if there was a solid enough reason a judge would sign off on the appropriate warrant. "And you're not a problem, by the way."

The Devil chuckled. "Don't mind her, Mr. Mortan. She's one of those goody-goody cops who wants to make sure everyone is as happy as possible. It'll only drive you a little crazy after a while."

The Chief Quinns didn't seem impressed with the Devil's statement, and Bailey leveled a glare at him. "She's *my* goody-goody cop. I teleported her twenty-two times, and she didn't vomit."

"I'm more impressed she didn't die," the Devil admitted. "But now I have a better understanding about why my favorite little cindercorn was making absurd chants in her head trying her best to get me to come over. You finally found a cop who can handle you at your worst and your best, and you were going to worry yourself sick over it."

Bailey turned her back to the Devil and lifted her chin. "I don't have any idea what you're talking about."

"Just let her win, else she'll try to hold visitation rights over your head until she gets you to do what she wants again. I don't know why you taught her that trick. It bites you every time," Samuel muttered, shaking his head. "I swear you like when she steps all over you."

"I do. It took some careful cultivation to enjoy the fruits of my labor. Now she's learning to be properly assertive without being embarrassed about it. You should be thanking me."

Bailey turned and glared at the Devil. Her husband smirked.

"Should I be worried about having accidentally poisoned myself or been exposed to drugs through attempted CPR?" I asked.

"You were not poisoned or exposed to drugs. He took his cocktails via syringe, which will be discovered later, and he'd consumed the alcohol well in advance of his frog summoning incident. You had some minor exposure to dart frog toxin, but at most, you'll develop a rash in the next few hours, and it won't be uncomfortable for you. It'll just be a skin discoloration. Mr. Mortan, on the other hand, would have suffered through an allergic reaction to their toxin, which would have ruined your evening severely, so you were wise to herd him into your hotel room away from the frogs." The Devil engaged Bailey in a staring contest. "They're natural frogs, transported from their native environment, so you can amuse yourself trying to identify where they came from and return them rather than continue your amusing attempts to concoct ways to make me suffer should I fail to do what you want."

"Damn it. I did not want to have to relocate those damned frogs!" Grabbing her phone, Bailey went into the hallway, presumably to make a call regarding the amphibian infestation plaguing the hotel.

"Now that she'll be occupied for at least twenty minutes, that leaves us with the problem of your current mystery."

"I'd settle with the knowledge it's not a serial killer," Samuel admitted.

"It's not a serial killer," the Devil announced.

"I don't suppose you'll tell us what it is, will you?"

The Devil's sly smile worried me. "It's a curse, and it's not one of my little cupcake's makings, fortunately for you. The who, where, when, and why are your problem, Detective McMarin."

Ah. The archangel's demand I investigate Alec Mortan made a great deal more sense when framed by the existence of a curse targeting the poor man. "Will this curse try to kill him?"

"No. He's at no risk from the curse beyond the understandable trauma from facing death so many times. It's quite unhealthy, really. But, for your safety, I recommend you use these." Stealing Samuel's handcuffs, he held them up. "The curse will not bother you if you're connected to him directly, but I recommend against taking him to the station for any lengthy period of time. It wouldn't end well for your new toys."

"Knowing how much those toys cost, I'm officially banning you from the station until further notice," Samuel Quinn announced. "But you can have a laptop in the meantime. I'll have one brought over for you. Laptops are cheaper than those toys Bailey made me get you."

With a snicker, the Devil handed me the handcuffs.

"Oh, and once on, they'll only come off when you're changing or removing your clothes, and during that time, you'll get a more magical ball and chain making sure you two stay sufficiently close enough to mitigate the curse—for the most part."

The Devil's smile worried me even more than the realization I'd be handcuffed to Alec Mortan for an unknown period of time. "For the most part?"

"You'll see," the Devil promised before he teleported away.

Samuel sighed. "Well, it could be worse."

"How?" Alec blurted.

"He's letting you change your clothes. Trust me when I say you're going to be grateful for that after a day or two. I've learned one thing about my uncle since he came storming into my life to stay: when he gives a warning or recommendation to a mortal, it's a damned good idea to listen to him. He might be called the Lord of Lies, but he uses the truth as his ultimate weapon. I'll see about getting you out of here, McMarin. In the meantime, decide which hand you want cuffed—and I'll find something to wrap those in so you're at least somewhat comfortable."

Alec turned to me and said, "He's serious, isn't he?"

I stared down at the cuffs in my hand. "This is some form of revenge for rejecting an incubus, isn't it?"

"The only difference between revenge and a reward is if you like it, Detective McMarin," my boss announced before leaving the room. "I'll go see about your discharge while you decide your fate. Choose wisely."

SIX

Life rarely worked out that way.

IT WAS one thing to give a drunk druggie CPR to save his life, but to handcuff myself to a witness so I wouldn't be the next one hit with his curse took the cake. As I had a healthy dislike of death, I went along with the idea.

The idea would have been a great deal easier to tolerate if the witness lacked appeal, failed to mind his manners, and otherwise served as a brutal reminder not all of the good men of the world were married. The incubus defined what it meant to be attractive, but Alec Mortan would test me in more ways than I liked.

After some serious reflection, I decided to blame the archangel. His sucker punch to the gut had removed some of my common sense and replaced it with a rather strong itch and a desire to leave the pool of single virgins.

The last thing I needed was to be handcuffed to someone kind, sensitive, and attractive. I gave my peace of mind a lifespan of no longer than an hour.

"I'm so sorry about this," Alec muttered.

"Did you ask to be cursed?"

"Not as far as I know. I mean, who would ask to be cursed?"

I thought about that for a moment. "A masochist?"

"I am not a masochist, but you make a good point." Alec wrinkled his nose and eyed the handcuffs, which had been wrapped in black velvet to keep the metal from biting into our wrists. My bosses, after adjusting the handcuffs, had gone off to secure my freedom from the hospital, leaving us to our fate.

"Are you right handed?" I asked.

"Unfortunately, since you're also right handed, and as I can't use a gun and you can, you should have access to your right hand."

Damn. "I guess we'll just stick close together until we're out of here, then we'll put on the cuffs and deal with the situation until I get to the bottom of this curse. That means I'm going to have to do a full interview about your life, by the way."

"That's fine. I do feel guilty, though. If I'm actually cursed, then I'm responsible for all of those deaths."

"No, I wouldn't say so. Look at the case of the vengeful ex who committed that hit and run. You didn't influence him to make that decision. You just happened to be at the wrong place at the wrong time. It's entirely possible that the curse is putting you in the place where a death or crime is about to be committed, forcing you to witness it. I will look into the average death rates in the places you've lived and worked to see if there was a jump in the numbers, but we *do* look for that sort of thing yearly. We try to address the problems as much as we can."

I often felt I failed that part of my job, but I did the

best I could with the resources I'd been given. In my former precinct, we rarely had the number of cops needed to take care of everything, but whenever I was on shift, I'd always tried my best. In some ways, trying my best all the time put my normal at a higher level and made it harder to shine.

I recognized that didn't apply to everyone else in the force.

I could tell when other cops tried their best, because it showed. In some ways, I wondered if constantly trying to make my best my normal had bitten me in the ass. Then again, my best couldn't beat prejudices.

Life rarely worked out that way.

"I hadn't thought about it like that. I might not be the cause of their deaths?"

"And even if the curse is responsible for the deaths, the source of the curse is to blame, not you. You're a victim of a curse, not a murderer."

"That doesn't explain the steamrollers, defenestrations, or the other deaths lately," he countered.

In good news for my patience, Alec already attended therapy. I worried I would need to attend therapy, too, if I needed to stay handcuffed to him for longer than a few days. Judging from the water cooler talk at my previous precinct, cases could take months to resolve.

Months handcuffed to Alec would test me in more ways than I cared to think about. Months handcuffed to anyone would test me, but everything I'd seen about him indicated he was nice and single to go with his good albeit average but attractive appearances.

When partnered with nice and single, average had a tendency of becoming ridiculously handsome in a hurry.

I needed to not think about Alec classifying as handsome when there were handcuffs involved.

"You're right. It doesn't. But if we can find out the details on this curse and why you were targeted by this curse and free you from it, everyone is better off. Especially you, though."

"I really can't think of anything I've done to justify being cursed," he said, frowning and staring in the general direction of the handcuffs. "I'm also not sure what I'm supposed to think about these handcuffs."

"To say the least, I fully understand your hesitancies. I'm supposed to be doing the cuffing, not being cuffed." As I realized how that sounded, I shrugged and added, "And since we're going to be involved in a rather unique relationship moving forward, my name is apparently Josefina. That's what my license and badge state, but I've been called McMarin for so long I forget I have a first name."

"I noticed the cops tended to address each other by their last names. Why is that?"

"I honestly don't have a clue. The day I became a cadet, I underwent a mystical transformation, switching from Josefina to McMarin."

A snorted laugh indicated the Chief Quinns had managed to sneak into the hospital room without anyone noticing. "It's easier to read the name tags, which go by our last names. Without those name tags, we would be lost, confused, and surrounded by nameless co-workers," Samuel informed me. "It's also efficient, as we don't get many cases of matching last names in the precinct, whereas there are at least ten Michaels working in our precinct, and two of them are on our floor."

"I can see how that would become complicated," I acknowledged. "Do I get to escape this joint tonight, sir?"

"That's more paperwork for my new detective," Bailey said, and she snickered.

"We don't get to give her any extra paperwork, as she is being handcuffed to our witness. That's punishment enough." Then, he shrugged. "It might be a reward. Who knows? Are you feeling rewarded or punished, Mr. Mortan?"

"Having met many cops, I feel I have been slated to be handcuffed to one of the highest quality members of law enforcement," he replied. "I can't state I am being punished at this point in time."

All-in-all, I gave him full points for his dignified tone and bearing, as he made his announcement with a straight face and no sign of cracking under pressure.

"Oh, that's a good one," Bailey said, and she stared at her husband with wide eyes. "It was the perfect rebuttal."

"You got side zinged, and you can't help how much you enjoy a good zinger," her husband replied.

"It's true. I can't even feel bad for losing. I'm taken and get to go home with my good catch. But I don't get the handcuffs."

With a raised brow, Samuel stole her handcuffs. "Are you sure about that?"

"I will go make sure the doctors hurry up with that paperwork," Bailey announced, and she fled the room.

"You're not going to actually handcuff her, are you?" Alec asked.

"I probably will, otherwise she'll try to follow you back to your hotel room and hover because she doesn't know any other way to approach the situation. You do not need an audience to go along with your case of cuffed for the foreseeable future." With a grin, he went to the door and peeked into the hallway. "She is picking a fight with the nurse in charge of your discharge. The nurse is amused, so I can't tell which one of them is winning yet. As she'll have a meltdown if I don't take you to your hotel and see you safely inside, you get to deal with us hovering for at least thirty more minutes. Unfortunately, I am going to ask for you to figure out how you're handling the cuffs, as the last thing I need is either one of you getting in trouble on the way back to the hotel. I'll leave you two to that discussion."

Well, so much for having limited freedom until the hotel. "Understood, Samuel, sir."

He chuckled. "You'll be fine, McMarin. If either one of you becomes uncomfortable, just give me a call. I'll arrange for a sleepover party."

As I could see the sleepover party resulting in someone's premature demise, I would make certain neither one of us had a reason to make that call. "I'll keep that in mind."

After he left the room, I sighed. "He forgot about the IV. We'll deal with the cuffs after I've been freed from the IV and get changed. We'll pretend that you standing outside of the bathroom is the appropriate distance before we get this show on the road."

"I am so sorry about this."

"Don't be. I'd rather deal with being handcuffed for a few days than the alternative. I'll just keep this in mind when it comes time to ask for my next raise."

EXHAUSTION MADE COPING with the reality of being handcuffed to a witness easier than I anticipated. Upon making it back to my hotel room, which had become our hotel room, we acknowledged our exhaustion would win within a few minutes. After a brief dance to use the bathroom involving averted eyes and a determination to handle the basics like adults, we flopped onto the bed and passed out. Alec started snoring within moments, and I joined him within five minutes, after waging a brief battle with the handcuffs and the blanket.

My alarm went off, resulting in a tangle of arms, legs, and blankets. Curses from my new roommate and unconventional partner reminded me of my life's odd left turn into the absurd. After a brief struggle to free my right hand, I silenced my phone. "Sorry about that, Alec."

Stifling a yawn, Alec snagged his phone with his free hand and blinked at the display. "That's okay. Mine goes off in ten minutes, and when I call in that I'm attached to a cop for an undetermined period of time, I'm going to end up losing my job."

Crap. I could understand that; finance auditors often worked under NDAs, and my status as a police officer wouldn't override his contractual obligations. "I'll call the chiefs and ask about that situation once I'm a little more awake."

"That's not necessary. I have a bit of a reputation as the grim reaper in my office anyway, so they'll probably be relieved I'm gone. I'll have to figure something out, though."

It bothered me I would get paid for being handcuffed to him, but he would face all sorts of consequences for his situation. However, it said a lot about the man that he would rather pay personal prices to protect those near him, in this case, me. "I'll discuss the situation with my bosses. Hopefully, we will resolve this sooner than later."

"I have some vacation time. I can probably get off for personal reasons if I can get one of those waivers from the CDC."

"Waivers from the CDC?"

"Yeah. They give me these waiver things I give to my boss, which allows me to take time off to deal with the investigations. I don't really get how it worked, but the CDC sends someone to cover for me. They keep staff in most fields for this, apparently."

While I longed for a cup of coffee, I tapped my phone's screen, located Mr. Chief Quinn's number, and connected the call.

"Good morning, McMarin," he answered. "How was your first night handcuffed to your handsome witness?"

Handsome witness? His question beat what my former captain would have asked, so I accepted it with a soft chuckle at more evidence of the absurdity infecting my life. "We were both so tired we had a consciousness span of approximately five minutes upon arrival. There have been no incidents to report, but I had a question."

"Ask."

"Mr. Mortan says he has been getting CDC waivers and coverage to help with his time off. While I will be paid for being handcuffed to his person, I suspect his work is sensitive enough he can't take a cop to work without there being issues, however willing I am to accompany him and do my work with my free hand."

"Ah, yes. I've already taken care of it. More accurately, my uncle has taken care of the matter, as he is the one who insisted on the handcuffs. He'll be covered and paid as normal. Now, that said, my uncle's general interest in your witness is concerning. When he takes an interest, he's usually causing trouble or matchmaking."

"Did you just say matchmaking?"

"Yep. At heart, he's still an angel. He's just openly naughty rather than covertly naughty. Angels love matchmaking. He wouldn't lie about the curse element, but it wouldn't surprise me if he lied about the absolute necessity of you being handcuffed. If you're handcuffed, his matchmaking ploys have a higher chance of success."

"Yes, I would say that archangel was covertly naughty right up until he sucker punched me in the gut." I remembered I lacked a free hand and didn't give my stomach a rub to discover if I was still sore from the unexpected angelic assault. "This is because I rejected an incubus, isn't it?"

"I would count on it. You're handling things better than I thought you would."

"I considered taking half a day to take the incubus home with me," I admitted, and I sighed. "But there's no reason for me to be embarrassed; if this sort of talk bothered me, there would be no way I could handle my job. I was the only woman in my entire precinct."

"That is being addressed, but I understand. How is your witness handling the conversation?"

Apparently, my witness had passed out again, as he'd resumed snoring. "I believe he is suffering from fatigue and would like to go back to bed. I didn't even notice him go back to bed. He's asleep." I wondered at which stage Alec had passed out.

Hopefully before the mention of matchmaking. What was left of my pride would appreciate if the man remembered nothing about the call with my boss.

"Good. He has had a rough few days, and sleep is good for him. How are you feeling?"

"I'm fine beyond having lost access to my left hand."

"Honestly, you're probably fine to go to the bathroom without an audience, unless you feel there's a potential threat in your hotel room."

"I bet the mirror would be willing to stage an ambush if given a chance," I stated, making sure to keep my tone as neutral as possible.

"Oh? I'm not the only person with a healthy fear of huge mirrors? I keep imagining they'll fall on me and shatter into knife-like shards," he replied with laughter in his voice. "Someone will be bringing a laptop over to you in about an hour. I will ask for the hotel to provide a few extra keys to your room due to your current situation. Use the deadbolt and a note on the door if you will be unable to answer the door due to things like bathing, sleeping, and so on. If you become uncomfortable, I'll switch you out for one of the male officers."

"I'm not uncomfortable," I reported. "But I would like my files to go with the laptop."

"I'll have them brought to you. Is your door currently deadbolted?"

"Yes, sir."

"See if you can rouse your witness sufficiently to unlock the door so we can get in. I'll send someone over to serve as your hands and feet since you're at a temporary reduced limb capacity. I'll also have breakfast brought over for you so you can start working without having to deal with going out while handcuffed. I'm also going to make my uncle pay for your indulgences, as he's the reason you're handcuffed."

"If this lands me in court, I'm telling the judge that the Devil made me do it," I warned him.

"Honestly, I use that line every time I can, because it guarantees we get an angel for the trial. When the Devil made you do it is the truth, that's when the cases get fun. Nowadays, the judges don't even bother questioning me until they've called in an angel to confirm that yes, the Devil really *did* make me do it. And half the time, he'll show up because human courthouses amuse him. If your witness's family accuses you of kidnapping, I recommend you use that line."

"Wait, his family?"

"He does have parents and several siblings, and they're concerned."

Well, that just complicated my case. "Have they been questioned?"

"Not yet."

I frowned, wondering how I would question them without the handcuffs becoming a problem—or the curse hitting one of his family members. "I don't suppose you can ask the Devil if there would be any fatalities if his family were to be brought to the hotel for questioning regarding the matter of this curse?"

"Most of our cops take at least several months to get the nerve to ask if we can abuse the Devil in such a fashion. You're going to work out great here. As a matter of fact, yes. It won't cost me very much for that sort of peek, and it falls into a part of our job. Basically, we'll put your witness in our precinct's version of witness protection. You're his protection."

"I'm not going to be effective protection when handcuffed to him, sir."

"Well, he won't be escaping you while handcuffed. Be grateful for that. I tried to put my wife into protection once. She was eight months pregnant and viewed it as a challenge. I had regrets, but she had fun. She was officially off duty due to pregnancy and was not happy about it. She wanted to work until she burst at the seams. She hates being a freeloader. She did not view pregnancy as a job."

"I may regret asking this, but is she insane?" I blurted. Thanks to my various issues, I'd given up on the idea of becoming a mother, something I'd have to adapt to in the future. Until I'd been sucker punched by an archangel, children hadn't been a realistic option. "Another dumb question. How much do I actually owe that archangel?"

"You don't owe him anything, I promise. It's really precinct procedure to take care of health issues of all sorts if possible. Bailey is sensitive over it, and she's hoping to push broader health care awareness into the general population. I wish her the best of luck with that, but she's fixing what she can. Sick cops can't work efficiently, and we run into a lot of situations where angels, devils, or demons have to barter to handle mortal affairs. You came in at a good time. Mr. Mortan's situation has gotten a lot of attention."

"Really? But from whom?" I couldn't recall hearing anything on the news or on the internet about the man or his curse.

"From divines in general. I don't think it's directly divine in origin, but I can also tell you that you'll need to be on your toes. Someone is playing with magic they shouldn't be playing with, and I'm not sure what your witness has done to be the focal point of it. Everything we've gotten out of him and those who know him is that he's just a good guy and nobody can think of any reason why someone would target him." My chief huffed. "I'll be headed in as soon as I get the wife peeled away from her coffee maker. I'll call to get the wheels in motion on my end of things. Don't be surprised if you get a call from the commissioner. He gets cranky when his cops end up in the body shop for any reason. He tends to do personal check-ins as soon as he's notified about the situation. I have an hour to notify him before he drags my ass over coals for delaying on notifying him. I'll ask him to wait considering the circumstances, but I can't promise he'll listen."

"I'll be ready for his call," I promised.

"Good. Today will be busy, but I have every confidence you can handle whatever is thrown at you."

After having been sucker punched by an archangel, I believed him. "I'll do my best, sir."

"I'll pretend I didn't hear that. You can't do your best every day, as that would be your average and you'd never have the ability to shine when it's needed the most. Save your best for when it's truly important. The rest of the time, give a good effort but forgive yourself if it's not your best. Chew on that food for thought while you order breakfast—and get whatever you want, as my uncle will be footing the bill."

He hung up, and I contemplated how to handle my day. I began with shaking Alec's shoulder.

"Five more minutes," he begged, and he burrowed under his pillow.

"Can you wait for your five more minutes until after I order breakfast and we unlock the door so someone can bring my laptop and some files over?" I asked, grinning at his tone, which reminded me of my failed efforts to cajole my alarm clock into giving me five more minutes. "Once

I'm set up to work and can start reading over the case files, you can sleep in as long as you want. The Devil is handling your work, so you can enjoy an unconventional vacation."

While Alec grumbled, he got up, and after a little dance to figure out how we'd get out of bed while cuffed, we got the door unlocked, slipped the cuffs long enough for some privacy in the bathroom while maintaining a suitable distance, and otherwise prepared for a long day.

"Isn't it cheating if we take the cuffs off?"

"We'll go insane otherwise," I pointed out. "Mostly, we're cuffing ourselves so we don't forget, although considering who our informant is, we're being had, and I don't really understand why, but I don't care. I care about getting to the bottom of this case."

"Do you think he's trying to trick us?"

I eyed Alec and raised a brow. "I would assume so. That's his whole gig, isn't it? So. Breakfast. Apparently, the Devil is paying, and my chief feels we should run the bill up."

"Then it sounds like we should order a feast and eat ourselves silly." Alec narrowed his eyes. "Or sick. What do you think your chiefs will do if you get ill?"

"Bring an archangel into it," I muttered.

"Are you saying we could end the world through ordering too much breakfast?"

I considered the room service menu with interest. "You know what? Let's find out."

SEVEN

"Wait, Bailey is the one agreeing with the sensible theory?"

Alec and I competed for who could pack away the most bacon and pancakes. Several of my new co-workers, none of whom I'd met yet, watched in horrified fascination while we feasted, pausing only long enough to listen to my morning briefing, which boiled down to stay out of trouble and review cases until the chiefs had a chance to do more research into the curse.

I won on the pancake front while he dominated on the bacon front.

Alec maintained a relationship with consciousness for approximately five minutes before he passed out, and I decided as there was nothing realistically dangerous in range of the bed beyond a firearm that wouldn't fire itself when unloaded and some pillows and files, I freed my hand so I could work while he slept off his act of gluttony.

The amount of sugar-filled syrup I had consumed would send me into orbit for at least a few hours, and I meant to make the most of them.

"I thought you had to stay handcuffed," my new co-worker stated in a doubtful tone.

The poor guy, Officer Jacobson according to his name tag, would learn I bent the rules whenever I could as a matter of survival. Playing fair meant I needed to play hard, too—and I'd mastered the art of bending rules to keep my job. "The handcuffs are actually to make sure we stick close enough together. The Devil seemed to indicate if I stayed within a certain radius there wouldn't be an issue." I hesitated, and then I shrugged. "Mostly, I suspect it's more of a caution issue. If I'm alert and on my guard, then I should be able to dodge most unfortunate circumstances. The curse doesn't seem rigged to hurt or kill *him*. Unless you decide to shoot me, I'm perfectly safe where I'm at, and I can't control where you're at. And if something like an assault lamp tries to get me, I'm better able to defend myself. It's also much easier to type with both hands. This also lets him get better sleep, and he looks like he needs it."

"Yes, Sam was concerned about his physical and mental health. He's been through a lot the past few days. He asked me to let you know if you have any problems to give him a call, and he'll bring in a professional to help him. He's concerned because Mr. Mortan has not been nearly as distressed as everyone believes he should be." Jacobson ferried more of the filing boxes closer to the bed, taking care not to stack them too high. "I'm putting the oldest cases on top so you can start at the beginning."

"Thank you. I'm sorry you've been assigned to be my gopher for the day."

"I'm getting a hazard bonus for being in the same room with someone known to be cursed. Honestly, I don't think there'll be a problem."

"Why not?"

"Before you came, I got to handle some of the files, and everything I've seen indicates they were crimes already in progress; he was just an unfortunate witness. There were some freak accidents, but they're all things that would have happened even if he hadn't been present. Bailey agrees with my theory, but Sam doesn't. Sam is jumpy, though."

"Wait, Bailey is the one agreeing with the sensible theory?" I blurted. "She seems so…"

"Flaky? She's really not. She's wickedly smart, but she came to the force with some significant self-esteem issues. Honestly, I suspect Sam does agree with her, but she's *determined* to prove she's right."

Ah. I understood; if she suffered from self-esteem issues and her husband believed she was right, he might be willing to take the fall on being wrong to help her build confidence. "She seemed flighty, but I didn't really get a sense of self-esteem problems," I admitted.

"They're rampant, but you'll get used to it. She's a force of nature, and she's a huge asset to the NYPD, but she has her moments. Word on the wire is you can handle riding her at her worst, so you're going to end up doing a lot of extra training. Outside of Sam, most of us can't handle her for more than a single jump, and if we do, we get sick. Perky spends the rest of the day throwing up after a single jump, but he's intolerant to teleportation."

Well, I was grateful I hadn't gotten sick, but I worried for the other cops, who knew from bitter experience they couldn't handle her jumps. "What does she need a rider for?"

"Let's just say she's our resident explosives expert, but the lack of hands means she sometimes struggles with the payloads. Particularly, the removal of the disarmed bombs. If she detonates a bomb, she says it tickles nicely and asks for another one to play with. You would not be in the blast radius while she's playing with bombs, but you would be asked to help with those sorts of emergencies. You'd also handle recording and gathering evidence when she's a cindercorn, taking notes, and things like that. It'll be a good gig for you, because if you're working a case and need transportation, you have your very own cindercorn to take you to where you need to go in a hurry. Both chiefs will transform for emergencies now, which is nice, but having a good rider for Bailey will be a huge help."

"I know nothing about explosives," I warned.

"Trust me, you'll learn," he replied. "We've all learned. Where cindercorns go, explosions happen."

"That sounds rather alarming."

"It is." Grinning, he moved a few more boxes into place. "How can I help you get to the bottom of this case faster, McMarin?"

"Find me the oldest box of files, we'll split it in half, and we'll make note of everyone with any involvement, confirm the case's status, and see what we can learn about this supposed curse."

"Supposed?"

I raised a brown. "The Devil *is* the Lord of Lies, and even when people tell me he's rather honest, I'll search for proof while taking the route of most caution—and I rejected one of his incubi."

"Oh, that's definitely a way to get yourself tricked into marriage but little else," Jacobson replied.

"Pardon, but did you say tricked into marriage?"

"Think what you will of the Devil, but there's little he loves more than a wedding."

Heaven help us all, for we would need all the help we could get. "I got sucker punched by an archangel yesterday, Jacobson. I'm not sure I can handle even more insanity quite yet."

"Just be grateful it wasn't cancer. The cancer patients are usually partway through their battle by the time an angel gets a hold of them. The sucker punch is *far* better than the cancer treatments. The chiefs typically make cancer patients do traditional treatments first; if those don't work, the next treatment is a torture session at the hands of an angel. The cancer survivors at our precinct make it pretty clear you do not want the angelic treatments unless necessary *or* it is to make certain the cancer doesn't return. All of the cancer patients get that. It also takes an important owed favor to treat cancer. Your issues were minor in comparison—not minor in how much you were suffering, but it was minor to fix in comparison."

That I could believe. "Is that why nobody seemed to care about my issues?"

"Oh, we cared. We have just learned to not wince openly. It makes the newbies nervous. Now, the whole part about telling an incubus no? That'll go around the precinct in a hurry along with wagers on what sort of man will win you."

"I'm hardly a prize."

Jacobson chuckled. "I'm going to do you a huge favor and not tell either chief you said that. Let's just say I'm single, and there was a wager pool out on when I'll get hitched and whipped. I won it."

"You did? How?"

"I said it would be a cold day in hell first. The Devil brought in some snow for Christmas, so I won the wager. I have not been foolish enough to restart a wager pool. In reality, the right woman is never going to come along."

It took me all of three seconds to take the hint. "You're looking for the right man."

"Indeed I am." Jacobson shrugged. "So far, it has not been going well."

I tilted my head in Alec's direction. "What do you think of him?"

"I'd date him if he rolled that way, but he doesn't."

Interesting. "In good news, that doesn't stop you from admiring the scenery, right?"

"You got it in one, McMarin. Buckle up, this is going to be a wild ride."

No kidding.

WITHIN FOUR HOURS, I accepted the reality of the situation. It would take months to fully register the cases and discover the commonalities between them. Or, as the case was, the utter lack of commonalities.

Nothing matched, from murder method to cause of death to culprit. The only apparent common thread between them was the sole witness, one Alec Mortan. While location overlapped, I suspected it had more to do with Alec's presence than anything else.

I blamed the Devil for having inserted the concept of a curse into my head.

The subject of my thoughts sat beside me, working on

his laptop. I wondered what he did to fill the time, as he did his best to keep from interrupting me or Jacobson. I hoped he was able to do something fulfilling, something that let him escape from the reality of his situation.

In his shoes, I doubted I would handle the stress even half as well.

Then again, considering my promotion, I would find out how well I handled the stress soon enough.

I considered asking heaven for some help, but having met the Devil, I worried *He* might answer—and a brush with an archangel decided me. Divine intervention might seem like a good deal on the outside, but everything came at a price.

In my case, a fist to the gut and sore ribs.

Forcing my concentration back to my job, I ordered my growing spreadsheet by cause of death. "Until today, I didn't know there were so many different ways someone could die from a knife wound. A severed carotid. A severed jugular. A knife to the heart. A stab to the thigh. A punctured kidney. A punctured lung. Multiple lacerations leading to death through bleeding out. A lobotomy via steak knife. If anything, this case is the start of a horrific guidebook."

"101 Ways to Die?" Jacobson asked, holding up his notepad. "I've been making a list of causes of death, too, and while there are multiple counts during the same incident, I'm finding the same. If our lists fail to have any overlap, I'll be impressed. How many causes of death do you have so far?"

"Twenty-nine. You?"

"Twenty-two."

I handed Jacobson my laptop. "Input yours into the spreadsheet. It's worth looking into, mainly because the only connecting link we have is our primary witness. A lot of these cases are cold, too."

"Get used to that," Jacobson warned. "Our precinct is where cold cases go to languish in the freezer until a lead is discovered. Bailey doesn't care if the case is thirty years old. If we have the resources to look into it, we do. She's seen the anguish of cold cases, and she can't abide by it, so she tries to get closure for the victims whenever possible. Have you been given the speech yet?"

"About what?"

"How we are to handle cold cases."

"Considering I was just made a detective before being handcuffed to our witness, no."

Alec chuckled. "While I'm sorry you're having such a rocky start to your promotion, I am grateful I'm not handcuffed to one of the other detectives. Ignoring that we're not technically handcuffed right this moment. Hands are useful things."

They really were. "It'll be a little annoying when we have to go out, but I think we'll be able to cope. But if I have to drive, we will not be cuffed. It's too dangerous."

"That is reasonable. I wouldn't want you driving while cuffed, either. But if we were to get into a car crash, I'd be at a high risk of death right along with you. Maybe we should avoid cars altogether for a while? How much of this investigation can we do from this hotel room?"

That was a good question, and I eyed Jacobson with interest. "How much *can* we accomplish from here?"

"A surprising amount. We have the transcriptions of all the witness questioning, so unless we find something unusual with the work already done, we won't need to question anyone for a while. It's a matter of piecing together what we do have and figuring out how this potential curse ticks. Once we figure out how it ticks, it might be possible to identify who created the curse, and why."

"I really can't think of anyone I've angered *that* badly," Alec muttered. "I try to fly under the radar. I mean, I've annoyed members of my family over the holidays, but that's normal, isn't it?"

"Unless you have a major rivalry or are loathed by a family member, it's unlikely they cursed you," Jacobson replied. "Now, it's possible there is someone in your personal life behind it, but everything I've heard in my briefings implies that your family or closer associates lack the general resources or power to accomplish this sort of curse. The chiefs believe it is strong enough to on par with the divine, so unless you know some divines or have pissed one off, it's unlikely. We'll look into it, of course, but it's unlikely. You can interview your witness extensively if you wish, however."

Somehow, I'd landed in a precinct filled with matchmakers. While I read into Jacobson's comment, Alec seemed oblivious or immune. Either worked for me.

The last thing I needed was to break whatever ethical rules there were about becoming involved with a witness. If the curse broke and he proved available and interested, I could see myself diving over the line, especially after rejecting an incubus.

"But why the variety of deaths? What is the point of cursing someone so they witness the various ways someone can die? What's the point? That's what I don't understand." While Jacobson worked at inputting his information into my spreadsheet, I shuffled through the most recent papers, organizing them based on their general cause of death.

"And why multiple deaths of the same type in one incident?"

"Collateral damage," Jacobson suggested. "Or perhaps making certain us investigators are aware it's intentional. Someone getting flattened by a steamroller could, in theory, be an accident. Multiple people dying the same way is intentional. It removes the possibility of people interpreting it as a freak accident."

"That seems overly generous for someone laying a curse meant to make their victim miserable."

Alec chuckled. "I wouldn't call myself miserable, really. Concerned, baffled, and traumatized, certainly. But while I am saddened by the death around me, it also forces me to appreciate life more, I think. The therapy has helped." He handed me a notebook. "This is my journal, and it has notes on what my therapists helped me with. I don't know if it's useful, but I started it at their suggestion. I show it to them every session, too. I think I concern them because of how well I've adapted to my reality. I won't lie, however. I've grown almost numb to the death."

"It's not uncommon with people who see death often," Jacobson said. "It's common with cops, too, especially the homicide detectives. It's very common in hospitals. Nobody is truly immune to death—at least not somebody who is mentally sound. But people learn to adapt as a survival method."

I frowned, narrowing my eyes. "But that's another angle we should look at. Let's assume the curse isn't meant to harm but to help him adapt to death through exposing him to the many ways people might die. Why would he need that level of preparation?"

Jacobson blinked and stared at me. Alec raised a brow.

"You know," my co-worker said, and he fell silent, his expression puzzled. "I really don't know. Why *would* a forensic accountant need to be prepared to accept and cope with the realities of death?"

I stared at Alec, who shrugged. "Don't ask me. I never wanted to become a doctor or a nurse. Who else would need that sort of preparation?"

I had no idea, but if it meant getting to the bottom of the case sooner than later, I would find out.

EIGHT

The Devil might show up.

WHO WOULD NEED to be prepared for the realities of death outside of those in the medical field? While law enforcement had some need of resilience, especially among homicide detectives and medical examiners, Alec hadn't expressed any interest in joining those fields.

He enjoyed numbers. He appreciated the thrill of the chase, too. Those traits made him ideal for law enforcement. Working with financials would become a daily part of my life in the near future, once I learned more tricks of my trade and dealt with an investigation requiring me to examine every element of a victim's life—or a suspect's life.

Alec's financials might be in my future if I couldn't find the missing link in his case.

I hadn't even been promoted for a week, and I already understood the haggard appearance of the detectives in my former precinct. An easier case, one with fewer moving parts, possessed the potential to drive me insane. The requirement to keep company with our witness, who stood a high chance of witnessing even more death in the upcoming days, tested my patience, forced me to question my profession, and resulted in a rather strong dislike of the Devil's meddling ways.

A knock at the door offered a welcome distraction from the relentless papers also waging war against my sanity. Jacobson got up and answered it, and when he opened the door, the Devil strode in wearing a suit and masquerading as a human—mostly.

The diminutive horns peeking out of his flaming hair gave him away.

"You're not going to lose your virginity if you don't stay cuffed to your witness and get rid of the sidekick," Lucifer announced.

"If my virginity was of any importance to this case, I might be concerned, but as it isn't, I'm not," I replied, making a mental note to never again welcome distractions during a busy and stressful day.

The Devil might show up.

"She's already ahead of the game," the Devil informed Jacobson. "Imagine if I had said that to Bailey."

"She would have fainted from mortification, even after having kids," my co-worker replied with a grin. "Once she got off the floor, she'd remember she isn't a virgin thanks to her gorgon-incubus doohickey, resulting in even more chaos, as she would do her best to convince her gorgon-incubus doohickey to keep her around."

"Pardon, but did you just say gorgon-incubus doohickey?" I asked.

I'd heard the phrase before, but I hadn't thought anything of it. I'd been aware both chiefs could transform into cindercorns, but what did gorgons and incubi have to do with Samuel Quinn?

"Sam has diverse genetics," the Devil replied. "His primary shapeshifting form is a hybrid of a gorgon and an incubus. He needs every advantage he can get herding his cindercorn. Bailey is a genuine cindercorn, where Sam uses his shapeshifting talents from his incubus genetics to cater to her species. You'll get used to it."

"I will?" I blurted, horrified that I would adapt to the strange and the stranger.

"You handled my brother sucker punching you quite well. I see you have figured out the general loophole regarding the handcuffs. You're ruining my fun."

"Your fun was barring us from making any progress," I replied. "How can we help you?"

"I come bearing a gift of information."

After my first and brutal brush with an archangel, I'd learned gifts could hurt—or came at some price. "Is this information a double-edged sword?"

"Absolutely."

Damn it. "Okay. Is the double-edged sword lethal for anyone in this room?"

"Not necessarily, although you may find yourself inconvenienced and at risk of death if you decide to indulge in acts of blatant stupidity. As you're not the kind to indulge in acts of blatant stupidity, you should be fine."

"Should be fine is not the same as will be fine," I pointed out.

"Humans have an unfortunate tendency to indulge in acts of blatant stupidity, resulting in the deaths of others. As you aren't the kind to indulge in an act of blatant stupidity, you won't end up offing yourself as a result. I cannot promise that another human indulging in an act of blatant stupidity won't get you killed. This is humanity's nature—and its curse."

No kidding. "All right." I snagged a notebook, grabbed a pen, and prepared to take notes. "I'm ready."

"Before I begin, how familiar are you with continental drift?" the Devil asked.

"You mean the idea that the world used to be essentially one massive continent and drifted apart into the continents we know today?" I asked.

"Yes. For you to follow this, you need to accept that this theory is fact." The Devil shrugged. "It is, by the way. Just because *He* created the planet does not mean *He* created the planet in the time frame humanity prefers to believe in. *He* merely began the process of evolution and allowed nature to thrive. *He* is not a fan of unwarranted devotion, and *He* cares about deeds rather than any pleas for forgiveness. After all, someone who apologizes for a wrong but does nothing to change hasn't really apologized sincerely, right?"

Ouch. I'd believed similar things in my life, especially when it came to supposed believers claiming they were devotees. Without fail, they turned around and made snide remarks about people they disliked solely based on their appearance. "Right. I follow." I made a note about the Devil's observation and *His* general tendencies, curious to see where the information might lead us.

"Humanity did not pop fully formed from the ground as the sentients you know of today. Humanity had several stages. Before the first humans came along, whom society dubbed Adam and Eve, there were several species vying for superiority. One would become humans. The rest would become extinct without rising to their full potential. Unlike the whole snake in the tree with an apple nonsense people like to believe, sin has existed all along among mortal beings. Until I came around, sin among *His* divines wasn't possible. We didn't have free will."

"But mortals did."

"Somewhat. *He* did not feel like overseeing every last breath on the mortal coil. View the mortal coil as a giant terrarium, and the terrarium's owner prefers to observe unless something is going to break the whole ecosystem." The Devil shrugged. "*He* enjoys watching *His* creations grow. In reality, before my fall, free will was a future shadow. Everything had a set destiny. *He* knew every choice to be made, and *He* willed these choices to be made. My fall enabled true free will—or the ability for all things to fight the fate predetermined for them. Do all things fight their predetermined fate? No. But some can—and do. Your investigation needs to delve into the depths of predetermined fate and the requirements needed to fight it."

I jotted down notes on his commentary, reviewing what I had written while considering the implications of his words. "The requirements needed to fight it?"

"Yes. Essentially, the curse on your companion involves predetermined fate—events that have been decreed to happen, unless someone puts in a great deal of effort to change it. Then you will need to decide if the predetermined fate *should* be changed."

Having participated in the debate over fate versus free will before in school, far more times than I cared to count, I caught onto what the Devil meant, although the reality of the situation annoyed me. "Because not all predetermined fates are bad things. The consequences of those fates may be necessary." I guessed.

"No matter what you decide to do, there will *always* be a consequence. Sometimes, there are many consequences for a single action. For example, your decision to work without being handcuffed made you more efficient at your work. That is a consequence. Defying me also has consequences, although they are not negative ones. I appreciate when mortals think for themselves."

"But what does that have to do with Mr. Mortan's situation?"

"All of the deaths he has witnessed were predetermined fates; without major effort on the victim's part, their deaths were inevitable. The curse seems to implant either a compulsion or suggestion he should go where the death will take place. For example, if there will be a fatal car crash, he would unconsciously select the route that would put him in the wrong place at the wrong time," the Devil explained.

I narrowed my eyes. "I don't need to be handcuffed to him at all?"

"Technically not," he admitted with a grin.

I snagged my handcuffs from the bed beside me and flung them at the Devil.

To my amusement, he didn't bother to dodge, and I managed to smack him in the shoulder.

"For some reason, the women in my life keep throwing things at me. At least you're not like my secretary. She likes throwing vases at my face lately."

I scowled. "And the incident that landed me in the hospital?"

"Yes, the curse influenced that, in the form of the chosen hotel; it doesn't just influence him. That the curse can influence my nephew is impressive—and part of the reason I've decided I am interfering. It is not originated from my pantheon—or our allied pantheons."

"Christianity is allied with other pantheons?" I asked, frowning.

According to the Bible, the Christian way was the one true way, and no other divines were invited to the party.

"Yes, of course. You must remember, the Bible is a book by humans for humans—it is not truly *His* word. *His* words were twisted, corrupted, or mistranslated over thousands of years. Some of the stories are true—at the core. But outside of a few notable exceptions, the words are no longer *His*. Can you guess which ones?"

"I could make a guess at which one I hope is the truth," I replied. "But I'm not a Christian. I'm not anything, really."

"*He* doesn't care about that in the slightest. *He* is all about deeds. I don't care what religion someone was before they come to my hells. And my hells aren't just limited to the beliefs of one pantheon. It's all connected. Right now, the Greeks and Egyptians are leaving soul rehabilitation to me. They had their time in the sun and deserve a break—and I enjoyed my rest for the years they ran the hells. But, which words do you hope are true?"

"The ones about the walk through the valley of the shadow of death. Death is scary enough without having to go at it alone. Companionship seems like something that would ease the way."

"And that's why many cling to their religions. It is that fear of death that so often drives them. But yes, that part of the Bible is true enough. The curse is not originated from any of *His* religions, nor is it Greek or Egyptian in origin," the Devil announced.

"*He* has more than one religion?" I blurted.

"Humanity structures religion," the Devil chided. "*He* is the soul of quite a few religions. Humanity has just given *Him* a different name. They've also given me a different name. Really, it doesn't matter in the end. All souls go to the same places when they're done on the mortal coil. If I'm not sleeping on the job, I handle it. If I am sleeping on the job, the Egyptians, Greeks, or one of the divines handles it. Usually, I take care of it. Why waste the effort when my system works well for rehabilitation? There were a few instances I slept for a few months and nobody noticed I wasn't doing anything. I've organized my many hells to continue on without me as necessary. But things happen. Sometimes, a divine will ask for a soul for personal reasons. I'll often toss those sinners over to the requester. If one of the other divine comes out of retirement because someone offended them that much, it's not worth the fuss. I'll check to make sure the balance won't be disturbed, but as long as that criteria is met, the soul earned its fate, and penance can be done in many ways."

I would need a lot of time and copious amounts of alcohol to think through the ramifications of his words. "So, you're saying we need to look at other religions to find a divine who may have cast this curse on Mr. Mortan?"

"Precisely."

I eyed the man, who listened to the Devil with a raised brow. After a few moments, he said, "I don't think I have done anything to deserve the attention of a divine from any religion."

"You haven't, but one of your ancestors did. Or more than one. I'm truly not sure. I haven't looked deeply into it. What I have gleaned, I did to balance the scales on behalf of some of my devils and demons with the NYPD. It's a good arrangement. But long-term consequences happen. Take my little cupcake of a daughter. Everything she is is a consequence, mostly of those long gone. Her other father regrets some of the consequences she faces, but he has always done what was best for her despite the pesky predetermined fates surrounding their bloodline. Some of them were changed for the better, but some are predetermined for a good reason, so we let those continue unobstructed—and at times, we protected them." The Devil shrugged. "You aren't even an intentional target, although there are those who have taken notice of how death has changed you."

Alec turned to me. "Tell me something completely inappropriate but funny, please. I think I've reached my general threshold for this."

Inappropriate but funny? I considered his request, eyed the files taking over most of the bed, and replied, "I bet I could have the best closure rate for murders if I followed you around for a few months. I'd be able to chase down the killers right at the scene of the crime and have fresh material to work with—all without the crime scene being polluted before I arrived. I may not be an experienced detective, but I've heard that complaint enough to understand it's a problem I will face in the upcoming years."

Alec blinked, and his eyes widened. "That's brilliant. You *could* apprehend these murderers better if you happened to be there when the crime occurred."

"That wasn't funny, though. Useful, but not funny." I frowned. "I don't do funny all that well, I guess. I turned down an incubus to work. Now that's funny."

"No, that's just sad," the Devil muttered. "And, honestly, impressive. You really turned down one hell of a ride so you could work for somebody who treated you like shit just because you have breasts rather than balls."

Well, I could trust the Devil to be upfront with his thoughts at least. I shrugged. "I love the job but dislike the former boss. But my job is worth dealing with a bad boss. It seems I now have better bosses."

"I could hire you," the Devil said, narrowing his eyes.

"No, but thank you. I will take my chances with the unicorns, however crazy they may seem."

Jacobson snickered. "Wise decision, McMarin. Just wait until you get a chance to meet his secretary. It's a coin toss if she tries to murder him. She never succeeds, but it's a treat watching her try to eliminate him. She gives it her all, too. If Bailey tries to take him out, it involves ineffective flailing. Samuel tried once, but he got his ass kicked so Bailey could nurse him back to health."

The Devil sighed. "Why do I shower those two with favor? Oh, right. The one is my nephew, and I have to be nice to my nephew. He whines if I'm mean to him, and I hate the whining. He whined for a *month* after I reminded him who and what I am. The other is my prized cindercorn, and I can't just let my prized cindercorn suffer." Heaving a dramatic sigh, the Devil regarded me with a pout. "But I like feisty women working for me."

I understood Alec's desire for humor; a break from the relentless bullshit plaguing my life would be appreciated, but I foresaw many frustrating days ahead of me.

"I don't care," I informed the Devil. "I enjoy my job."

Well, I did when I was allowed to do it, rather than having to deal with hovering busybodies. It would take approximately ten years to go through all the files and start making sense of the crimes at the rate I worked.

Jacobson snickered. "I am telling Bailey you told the Devil no, and she's going to be delighted. She's going to make sacrificial offerings to you for months once she finds out."

"Just like my wife, she really does enjoy when people tell me no. She enjoys cultivating bad behavior. Your resilience is rare—and enjoyable. So, you want to ask me about why I'm interfering with your investigation," the Devil prompted.

I stared at the ruler of the many hells, blinking as it occurred to me he was being rather helpful—frighteningly so. "Why *are* you helping with this investigation?"

"I said interfering, not helping."

"I require help, not interference," I replied, adopting the neutral mask I used on my ex-captain. "Interference is typically not beneficial, and this investigation is warped enough."

"Would you accept ten percent malevolent and ninety percent benevolent?" the Devil asked in an exasperated tone.

"That depends on the nature of the malevolence." Did the Devil really believe I would accept any form of malevolence? I'd already landed in the hospital once trying to change a drug addict's fate. My tolerance for any additional negativity hovered at zero.

"You amuse me. Would it help if the malevolence was generally directed at criminals?"

"It would help a little," I admitted.

"How about ninety-nine percent benevolence? I could swing ninety-nine percent benevolence, assuming you don't tell my wife or my secretary. You do need a challenge."

I sighed and regarded my new co-worker with a scowl. "Is this normal?"

"Usually, we get told we're getting fifty percent malevolence, and if we're smart, we'll like it. One percent is a good bargain. The last time I had to deal with him, I got twenty percent benevolence, and I was told I'd like it. The next offer would be five percent. I decided twenty percent benevolence beat five percent benevolence."

The last time heaven had helped me, I'd gotten sucker punched by an archangel, and my ribs still protested the general abuse. "Okay. I accept ninety-nine percent benevolence," I replied, already regretting my decision.

The Devil laughed. "You'll be all right. It's only one percent malevolence. How bad could it be?"

As I didn't want to know the answer, I refused to ask. The damage, however, was already done.

How bad *could* it be?

NINE

Even the small steps mattered.

EVEN WITH THE various clues the Devil had left us, I couldn't figure out which divine could possibly be responsible for Alec's curse. The puzzle vexed me, although I took care to keep my frustrations to myself. A call from our chiefs sent Jacobson back to the station, leaving me alone with my thoughts—and with a mystery of a man determined to make the most of his situation.

In some ways, Alec handled the burden of the investigation better than I did.

I wanted to free him of his anguish while he learned to cope and adapt to it.

When I thought about it, I admired his general resilience.

"It seems I have two choices," Alec announced, startling me from my file review.

I put aside the latest of the cases, giving him my full attention. "What do you mean?"

"I was thinking about what Lucifer said, and I realized

something."

Well, at least one of us had realized *something*. I had a whole lot of nothing, although I thought I'd made some progress on a cold case. Nobody had questioned the victim's family *or* co-workers, likely due to a staffing shortage. It wouldn't help Alec's case, but I could try to find closure for one of the murders.

Even the small steps mattered.

"What did you realize?"

"It's really not my fault."

I admired Alec for carrying the burden of guilt for something he held no responsibility for. Some of the murders had been years in the making, although others had been crimes of passion, committed due to an opportunity rather than malicious planning. "It's not," I confirmed. "But witnessing so much death is hard on a soul."

"But what if I *could* make a difference for the victims? What if I did something like become a cop? If this curse is something that is going to happen no matter what I do, wouldn't it put me in a place to better secure justice for the victims?"

I stared at him. When I'd decided to become a cop, similar thoughts had rattled about in my head. I'd wanted to make a difference. I *had* made a difference, from the very first day I'd put on my new uniform and my badge. It had burdened me, but I'd shouldered those burdens with as much pride as I could muster. Making a difference mattered.

Could he transform his curse into a blessing?

How would he react if I hooked up with a patrolling officer and dragged him along for the ride? Would the reality of the beat change his mind?

I wondered if my new chiefs would let me test him on a

patrol to see if he took to the beat.

After several long, silent minutes, I said, "We could test that."

"How?"

"I don't know if it's legal or possible, but perhaps you could accompany me and a partner on a patrol for a few days. We did that as cadets when learning the beat. A pair would take a cadet along for the ride to see what it was really like. It doesn't take much to qualify as a cadet," I admitted. "Perhaps it's a little too easy, really. But I went out as a cadet my first day in the academy after hearing a long speech about expected conduct. The instructors wanted us to see the reality before we learned more about what it took to be a cop."

"I thought it would have taken a lot longer."

"Me, too. It was part of a pilot program to adjust how the academy trains cops. They wanted to sift through the washouts faster and get cadets promoted quicker. I think the washouts happening earlier did happen, but it didn't really help get the cadets promoted quicker. There's a lot to learn. Honestly, I don't think the training is long enough. I had to learn a lot while on the job."

Alec nodded. "So, you want me to accompany you while you work?"

"Ideally. If Lucifer is correct, all the curse does is put you where the crimes will happen—or draws the victim and the perp to where you are. I'm not sure which. I'm not sure it matters. We have to assume the curse is able to manipulate *someone* in this, otherwise is it actually a curse?"

"He could be lying about a curse," Alec pointed out.

"While possible, I don't think he's lying," I admitted. I eyed my laptop, which had evidence of my unsuccessful search for divines capable of creating such a curse without being involved with the Christians, Egyptians, and Greeks. I could only assume it meant some ancient divine held responsibility, one generally lost to history.

Without a few additional clues, which I suspected I'd have to wring out of the Devil, we returned right back to square one.

"Do you think my forensic accounting skills could translate well to police work?" Alec frowned. "I have a reputation of being a harbinger at work at this point, and there are a bunch of rumors spreading around."

I bet. People expected cops to deal with death often, where accountants were expected to wage war with numbers without literal bloodshed being involved. "Having an idea of how many financial files I'll be going through in my near future, if you otherwise qualify, I suspect your skills would be a good addition to the police force. We have interior officers, too. Not everyone works the streets, although it's part of the job."

"What sort of education do I need?"

"A high school diploma," I informed him.

"That's it?"

I understood; when I'd become a cop, I'd been horrified to learn I hadn't even been required to take a single college-level legal course to be able to wear a badge and enforce the law. "That's it. You go to the academy for a while to get your base education. I expanded my personal education so I had a better understanding of the laws I have to enforce. You'll be an asset when it comes to the financials; *you* know what crimes can be committed. We just look for connections in how money flows."

"That doesn't seem comprehensive enough."

It wasn't, and all I could do was shrug. "If you want me to inquire with the chiefs, I can do that for you."

"I think I would. My prospects aren't all that good because of my circumstances. I mean, I could move to another city and possibly get work, but I would feel better about it if I could turn the tables and do some good, despite my misfortunes. If I am really cursed, and I can do something to bring justice for the victims of these supposedly inevitable crimes, that's better than just bearing witness."

I'd witnessed my share of death as part of my job, but his circumstances reminded me that witnessing the end of a life truly became a burden one had to carry, often for years before time did its slow work. I'd grown used to it, although some nights I'd gone home in tears from what I hadn't been able to change.

There would be more of those days ahead of me without fail.

"Yes, working in the force would let you pursue justice, as would becoming an attorney. But you'd do more good in law enforcement. We give testimonies during the case and aren't penalized should we have witnessed the crime. Attorneys can't try cases where they are witnesses."

"I think I would prefer trying to be a cop first. I deal with enough attorneys as part of my job as it is."

He wouldn't escape the attorneys; the detectives from my former precinct dealt with attorneys on a daily basis, depending on how active their cases were and what was involved with bringing a criminal to justice. I'd let him discover that for himself, however. Rather than drag out a needless conversation, I grabbed my cell and dialed Mr. Chief Quinn, as he was the one more likely to give me a sensible answer.

"Is everything okay?" he asked, rather than give a proper greeting.

Somehow, I'd been transferred into a precinct full of worrywarts. "Everything is fine, sir. Mr. Mortan would like to know if he might be able to pursue a career in law enforcement due to his current state. We haven't been able to find any solid leads regarding the source of this curse."

"And he'd rather make the most of a bad situation?" Mr. Chief Quinn guessed.

"Yes, Samuel, sir. More specifically, it might be wise to allow him to accompany a patrol and shadow officers so he can get a feel if it is a suitable career for him."

"This is probably what my uncle wants. That's just like him. He'll give us just enough rope to hang ourselves with and expect us to do his bidding because he knows he's right." After heaving an exasperated sigh, my chief fell quiet.

"Does that mean we should pack up this hotel room and come to the station? You don't think it'll endanger anyone, do you?"

"No, I don't think anyone who wasn't already in danger will be endangered. My wife has been thinking about it, particularly about the predetermined fates element. I'll warn you now, things get sketchy when my wife starts thinking."

"I heard that!" Mrs. Chief Quinn complained in the background.

"You were supposed to. Now that I have your attention, go put your fur coat on. We're going to pick up McMarin and her witness. We also need to retrieve the files, so arrange for some vehicles. McMarin, that room will still be yours until we deal with your housing situation, and I'd prefer if you kept your witness close at hand. If you're comfortable splitting your time between investigating his cases and working on a patrol, I'll talk with the commissioner about the legalities involved with having him accompany you. If he's eligible to become a cadet, I might be able to sneak him into the current classes with an understanding he would not be graduating with the current batch *unless* he somehow manages to do the catch-up work. I can resolve some of the issues by having you babysit cadets through their on-patrol training. We're due to get a few new bodies. Our precinct also has no rules about couples working together as long as they agree to weekly therapy sessions. The sessions last half an hour and evaluate if the couple can continue working as a pair on duty."

"Do you attend these sessions?"

"Absolutely. The commissioner wanted Bailey in more therapy, so he concocted that. It works really well for us, so he's trying it with other partners working in the same precinct. Cops tend to marry cops in our neck of the woods for some reason."

I bet. "He's a forensic accountant, Samuel, sir."

My chief snickered. "You've been a detective all of a day, and you've already identified how useful he'll be for your investigations. We have a few trios in our precinct, so I expect that's what'll happen with you and your witness should he join the force. We'll be around to pick you up within an hour. I'll test Mr. Mortan's ability to cope with riding a cindercorn while Bailey delights in having a rider who won't throw up on her. Fortunately for everyone, Bailey is adapting to having coffee again at an appreciable rate, so hopefully she won't exhaust you through her general ability to bounce continuously."

Judging from the exasperation in his tone, my chief had found the end of his rope and might come unraveled with a few tugs. "Is she normally this hyper?"

"The freedom has gotten to her, and I'm losing hope it'll wear off anytime soon. She just ran into the wall in her hurry to go shift so she can run off some of that energy. I've been told it will be a week of this with intermittent periods of coma-induced quiet."

I laughed at the thought of the woman running out of gas and passing out, finally giving her beleaguered husband and partner a needed break. "And your children?"

"Lucifer has taken them to the conservatory he operates to help teach them how to care for animals, so they think they're on a glorious vacation rather than being evicted to spare my sanity. They also have several archangels as babysitters, along with an entire hive of gorgons, who have brought their fosters and children to get lessons. In reality, we're trying not to scar our children due to their mother's absolutely insane amount of energy. Apparently, it's a cindercorn thing, and it's good for her to have these episodes during a pregnancy. Something about the adaptive biology of hyperactive unicorns. Honestly, I stopped listening after I was told it's fine for her to be this hyper. I have been informed that you have your very own cindercorn slave for the next week at a minimum, as you'll be booked for CDC testing sometime in the future. Bailey has opinions about CDC testing, and she's overwhelmed with guilt, once her caffeine high wears off enough for her to remember she's a walking bundle of guilt and anxiety regarding general life and work performance."

"Does that mean Lucifer won't be bothering us for a while?"

"For at least ten minutes," my chief replied. "I'm sorry if he bothered you. I haven't figured out his ploy, although it probably involves your resilience to Bailey's teleportation. As he is unreasonably fond of cindercorns, he probably wants you to have many children who have your resilience so they can become friends with our children. He also has a tendency to plan matches, which is where your witness comes into play. You're likely compatible with him, and Lucifer does not joke around when he's indulging in one of his matchmaking ploys."

"Is this what a predetermined fate looks like?"

My chief sighed. "If you're not careful and assertive about what you want, yes."

I eyed Alec, who'd turned his attention back to his laptop. When honest with myself, getting naked and given more than an hour appealed, and I hadn't uncovered any habits I loathed from the short time we'd been thrown together. "I see. So, we'll have a ride in an hour?"

"Yes. I'll go get my fur coat on and herd enough vehicles over to clean the files out of your hotel room so you can use it as a proper room rather than an office. I'll make arrangements to ensure your witness can follow you around work. As Lucifer is the one creating all this trouble, I'll make sure Mr. Mortan's financial situation is not at all impaired due to this change of plans. By the time we pick you up, I should have an answer on your cadet questions, although I think it's a good idea. Psychologically, it'll be a great deal healthier for him if he's able to do something about what he's witnessed, and if he can't break the curse, working with it might make a big difference. And his accounting skills will be useful around here."

"I've seen those financial files. Useful is an understatement."

"And to think you haven't been a detective for long," my chief teased. "Hold down the fort until we get there, and I'll make certain everyone knows to be on guard. If his curse means we can get appropriate justice for victims, and he's all right with us taking advantage of that, we'll do just that. Lucifer told me these crimes would happen regardless, and I believe him."

"You do?"

"I asked an angel about it. She reminded me Lucifer tells the truth with alarming frequency, and that I would be wise to listen to what my uncle has to say on this matter. In any case, attempt to avoid any disasters until we arrive."

"It's okay to have a disaster *after* you arrive?"

"The disaster might be more manageable with us there, although honestly? I expect Bailey will be the cause of the disaster. Only time will tell."

TWO CINDERCORNS and three patrol cars turned the hotel into a circus. Determined to ignore the insanity erupting to life around me, I accompanied Alec and the bellhop, questioning everything about my current situation. No disasters happened, but if the gleam in the cindercorn's bright eye was any indication, some form of disaster would happen soon.

Probably to me.

Rather than complain about my lot in life, I handed my purse over to one of my new co-workers, accepted I would be riding the hyperactive cindercorn, and waited until I could hold her attention for two consecutive seconds to get into the saddle. As expected, Bailey pranced in place, but my fledgling riding skills handled her restlessness.

Samuel stood with picture perfect patience while Alec struggled to figure out how to get into the saddle, and I coached him on how to make use of the stirrup, promising no cindercorns would be injured if he struggled to scramble into the saddle. While rough and lacking even a vestige of grace, Alec got into position. One of the cops helped situate his feet in the stirrups and offered some tips, including the recommendation to grab Samuel's mane and hold on tight.

"No tele-port today," Bailey promised, and she bobbed her head. I suspected she wanted to bounce around and buck like a demented goat, but she settled beneath me in an effort to contain herself. "Make coffee when back to station. Enjoy stay with wit-ness?"

"He's good company," I replied, keeping an eye on Alec as he got a brief lesson on staying astride a cindercorn. Judging from the street, it would take an hour to reach our destination. "Is traffic bad today?"

"It bad," the cindercorn muttered. "If emergency we rider swap. I promise to be actual unicorn instead of trouble if we need to swap rider, but we can go fast in slow traffic if emergency. Otherwise, we plod with cruisers."

Plodding would help make certain Alec reached our destination intact. "That sounds like a plan. Is today better than yesterday?"

From what I'd gleaned from Jacobson, yesterday had been pure chaos.

"Better, yes. People behave better, time to breathe. No breathing yesterday." Bailey eyed her husband and turned her ears back. "Coma-inducing doohickey!"

"It's not my fault you drank coffee." Careful of his new rider, Samuel picked his way over to us and nipped his wife's neck. "You can nap on the couch after you settle our cops in McMarin's office and make them coffee."

"Okay. Nap good, but only a few minutes this time, not all eternity."

"I'll do my best to make certain you don't nap for too long. Just don't leave me behind."

Bailey snorted, and smoke burst from her nose. "Better go slow with new rider."

"I should say the same to you, lawbreaker," Samuel snorted back at her, and his included a few fingers of flame.

"Oh, feisty stallion. Me like feisty stallion."

"Bailey, it's not time to go home."

The cindercorn lowered her head and heaved a sigh. "Work so *rude*."

"You're the one who wanted a salary."

The gathered cops snickered before splitting up and heading for their cars. One cruiser took point in an effort to contain the cindercorns. To my amazement, it worked.

For a first-time rider, Alec handled himself well. After a few minutes of clutching the reins and Samuel's mane, he relaxed in the saddle.

"It's not bad when there's traffic," I commented, and to make it clear I wasn't angry at my chief for being rambunctious, I patted her neck. "It's safer to walk if they're in a hurry, though."

"I sad because true. Much safer. Much slower. Queeny make me behave until you get lessons. You impossible to replace, take much care."

Queeny?

Samuel snorted and bobbed his head. "Yes. I am making

you behave, because we've done how many test rides before finding *one* person who isn't me who can handle your badassery?"

"Many, many sick cops. So many sick cops. Cops now quake in terror if asked to come to our office and I a most beautiful cindercorn. They know doom comes for them."

"Or at least an upset stomach and a story to tell in the break room. You all right, Alec?"

"I'm fine," Alec replied, and he stared down at his feet, probably making sure he kept his heels down. "Is this what mounted patrols are like?"

Both cindercorns whinnied their laughter before replying, "No."

"This much worse than mounted patrol," Bailey announced with pride. "Cindercorns obnoxious, stubborn, free-spirited. View cars as objects to be destroyed. Horses just shy at things. Like plastic bags that might rise up and eat them. But not gunfire or cars. Trained not to. But plastic bags? Those dangerous."

"We've been working on the plastic bag issue," Samuel added. "But we also don't want to traumatize our patrol horses. Training them to not react to gunfire or cars is tough enough on them. Plastic bags might prove to be their greatest foe."

"And buckets," Bailey stated in a solemn tone.

"Leaves are also an interesting peril." Samuel maintained a safe distance from the back of the lead cruiser, and Bailey matched his pace. At each light or halting of traffic, she pranced in place.

I considered myself fortunate she restrained from bucking, as I doubted I'd keep my seat if she decided to bounce around in earnest.

After the first few minutes, Alec rolled his shoulders and asked, "Is it true being a cop is pretty stressful?"

"Yes," we answered, and I giggled at Bailey's exasperated tone.

"It's worth it, though," I added, hoping we wouldn't scare him off. "It's hard work, and it's sometimes thankless work, but it's important, and we make a difference every day. To me, that's worth the stress. We never know when a call might sour. We also never know when a call can lead to somebody's death. It's a part of the job, and I find it doesn't get that much easier despite exposure. We don't want anyone to die while we're on duty."

"You'd be a pretty bad cop if you did."

I shook my head. "I mean, there are times I've considered shoving my gun up an abuser's ass and firing, but I'm supposed to be one of the good guys, which means letting the abusers see their day in court."

Samuel whinnied a laugh. "We all have days like that. The next time a bad case blows through the precinct, you'll get to hear Bailey's thoughts on that. It's educational—and hilarious."

"Why laugh at my suffering?" the cindercorn complained. "Stomp and squish like grape, solve problem."

"Alas, we can't stomp and squish the worst of the lot like grapes, no matter how tempting it might be."

Alec stared at me with wide eyes. "Maybe you're the one who needs to be rescued, Josefina. Are you sure you're going to be okay if left alone with them?"

"I should be okay." I chuckled at his expression and shrugged. "You know that thing about cops and coffee and donuts?"

"I may have heard of such a thing."

"I prefer cookies over donuts, but she really makes the best coffee I've ever tasted. It's worth the risk."

"Yes. My coffee is the best coffee. You, too, get best coffee if you join force. Queeny, make it so!"

"He does get a say in whether or not he wants to be a cop, Bailey," Samuel replied.

"But why? I make best coffee, will give him best coffee, but he must live in our station on our floor."

Samuel heaved a sigh, reached over, and nipped his wife's neck. "We do not make cops live at work, Bailey."

"Oh. Right. He work on our floor, we send home at appropriate intervals. Pay therapy bills for putting up with me."

"You're so paying for that comment when we get home," Mr. Samuel Quinn warned, flicking an ear back.

Bailey lost hold of her little restraint and bucked like a bronco with a burr under her saddle. Somehow, I stuck onto her back, but after her third jump, I balled my hand into a fist and bonked her between her ears. "Bad cindercorn. Down!" I ordered.

It took three more smacks between her ears to get her to put her hooves on the asphalt where they belonged, and I somehow stayed on her back rather than crashing onto the ground.

Alec stared at me with wide eyes and his mouth open. Samuel's ears pricked forward.

I realized I'd just assaulted my boss repeatedly, and I bowed my head and sighed, wondering if the end of my career would happen within seconds, minutes, or hours.

Bailey swung her head at her husband, and the whites of her eyes showed. After a moment, she blurted, "Did you see?"

Samuel bobbed his head and whinnied. "I saw."

"I find best detective. I fight you to keep her." To make it clear she meant business, Bailey snapped her teeth at her husband, although she didn't land a bite.

"If you're not careful, she'll fight you, and you'll lose," Samuel replied. "Now, what have we learned here?"

"Buck at own risk."

"Detective McMarin, should she buck, do what you just did again but harder. She's got rocks in that head of hers, so she'll be fine."

Bailey whinnied. "Feel that burn long time. Encore, encore!"

"The last thing we need is you burning anything. Let's try to make it back to work without you giving our detective gray hair. One bucking incident is enough for today. Pretend you're trying to show an angel how they should behave."

Having seen an archangel in action, I appreciated Samuel's phrasing. "I swear I've never smacked a real horse like that," I said, fidgeting in the saddle.

Bailey turned her head so she could regard me with an eye. "Real horse no have rocks in head, so that good thing. My head? Many rocks. Deserve smacked between ears. If I buck you off, it hurt extra. Cindercorns buck much harder and higher than mere horse. Cop horse better trained," she confessed. "You stay on, you good rider."

I was? "I guess I did okay during mounted patrol training, but I was passed over."

"You pass over because captain idiot. Eat idiot captain."

Samuel heaved a sigh. "We've been over this before, Bailey. You can't eat the captains who annoy you."

"Stupid rules. Captains should be grateful I can't eat them when they annoy me."

"If you could eat the captains when they annoy you, we'd have no captains left. We'd probably have to promote your new detective due to the shortage of captains," Samuel stated in a neutral tone.

I marveled over how well he controlled his tone.

Bailey gasped and stomped a hoof. "Mine!"

"Not if you eat all the captains."

The cindercorn snorted. "Fine. I won't eat the captains. Or buck. Or prance much."

"Much implies you're going to prance."

"Ree-uh-liss-tic. Much excited, some prance. But less prance?"

"How about this, Bailey. If you manage to make it to the station without bucking or prancing, we'll leave work right at five."

Bailey flicked her ears forward. "Right at five?"

"Right at five. The kids will be with Lucifer or other members of our family for the rest of the week, too."

Somehow, I kept from laughing over the absurdity of the situation.

"House almost empty. Just doohickeys left."

"I may have planned a field trip for them. They're going to several museums and won't be home for a few days. The CDC is using it as a training experiment."

Bailey snorted flame. "No doohickeys, no children?"

"The house will be empty," he promised.

"I show angels how to be angels," Bailey announced, and she stood more like a statue than a living being. "I will be the best cindercorn."

I glanced at Alec and grinned before saying, "How does this compare to accounting, Mr. Mortan?"

"It's crazy, but I think I like it."

TEN

"I would have experienced horrified embarrassment."

HAD Bailey stopped to think about her shift for the day, she would have realized five was their scheduled time for departure. As I lacked enough information to appease myself, despite coming to the understanding solving the cases immediately wouldn't change Alec's circumstances, I decided to work late, maintaining the appearance I intended to leave at a reasonable time until the chiefs exited the building. As the cindercorn had managed to make it all the way back without prancing or attempting to buck me off, Samuel had taken her away from work temptations right at five.

That he had needed to toss her over his shoulder to get her to exit the building would amuse me for the rest of the night.

Either emboldened by the realization he held no true responsibility for the deaths surrounding him or he was simply tired of my company, Alec returned to his home, departing with one of the patrols heading in that general direction. Without an audience in my office, I could begin the real work, which involved sorting through the cases, populating my digital board, and prioritizing cases based on the probability of being able to solve them.

More than a few went into the cold case category, including the mystery of the disappearing steam rollers. Without the steam rollers or any actual evidence of what had happened, who the true target was, or even a why, I suspected the case would go into the unsolved mysteries file for years to come.

All magic came at a price, and according to the handy notebook of general rules detectives needed to follow, we faced strict limitations on what information we could peel out of angels.

"Peeling is so unpleasant. You could ask, but we'd have to say we cannot tell you," Sariel stated from somewhere behind me.

"If I put up a sign asking angels and archangels to please knock before teleporting in, would you heed it?" I asked once I remembered how to breathe.

"Probably not. It is quite interesting testing the little mortals for reactions."

As I couldn't imagine an archangel popping into my office without a good reason, I turned and asked, "How can I help you tonight, Sariel?"

"My brother is complaining that you are a free-willed being who has already overcome the aversions mortals suffer to test him. As he will complain for all eternity should he be thwarted, I informed him I would discuss the matter with you. I did not promise I would do anything more than discuss this matter with you. He seems to have forgotten to secure a more solid resolution for his current issue."

What sort of horrible things had I done in a past life to

deserve the attention of the Devil and his archangel brother? "Well, once it became clear that there was no real and substantial risk to those around Mr. Mortan, and that this curse is more of a magnet for these inevitable events, it seemed reasonable to allow him to resume as much of a normal life as possible while he decides how he wants to handle the situation. My job is to try to solve as many of these cases as I can—his is to decide how best to live his life. I can't make those choices for him. As I have no idea what I'm doing, I want to start with organizing everything before asking another detective for help learning the ropes."

"On that front, you will be fine." The archangel sat on my couch and relaxed. "My brother is a sentimental creature and dislikes when people he likes suffer through regrets, and he feels you will regret allowing Mr. Mortan to walk out of your life at this stage. In truth, a little regret will not hurt you and will make whatever future you decide stronger and brighter. In the end, the results are similar, but one is better. My brother can be an impatient soul despite having more patience than most for many of his plans. Then again, you make his precious cindercorn happy, and he takes that seriously."

"I smacked her between the ears today," I informed the archangel. "I'm not sure how that could make someone happy, but I wasn't fired."

"That definitely would have made her happy. She does not like the awe-inspired reactions some give her. By smacking her between her ears, you demonstrated you had expectations of her—expectations that don't involve you worshipping the ground she walks on. She still learns how to handle adoration. So, I am here to plant seeds of regret and curiosity. What *would* have happened if you had done something like ask Mr. Mortan on a date?"

I raised a brow at the archangel, wondering what his expression might be if he possessed a head. "I would have experienced horrified embarrassment."

The archangel's laughter chimed. "I was more thinking an abandonment of your virgin ways, but this is also accurate. While he is not an incubus and not gifted with an incubus's magic and skill, you will find him to be a considerate lover. He abhors the idea of hurting someone, which is what led to you meeting. For some unasked for advice, if you would like him to make it hurt good, you will have to do certain things, like beg. Sufficient begging will bring out his wilder side. Some spice is always good for a relationship."

What the hell? "Are you, an archangel, offering me advice on my non-existent sex life?"

"Absolutely. While I am an archangel, I would like to remind you that your chief is my grandson, and there are certain mechanics involved in such things."

Right. I had known that, too. "Forget I said anything. Wouldn't you say Alec deserves a say in his fate, Sariel?"

"Absolutely. That is why I only promised to discuss this matter with you. But I would like to remind you that you, also, deserve a say in your fate. But it is not your nature to take the offense when it comes to men, and you do not like aggressive men."

I shrugged. "You don't work as long as I have as a cop without seeing the darker side of humanity. And if anything, the men who are the recipients of abuse have an even harder time than the women. Society has told them they are failures if they admit they have been victims. Women are expected to be the victims, so there is less shame in that.

That's not right, but it's harder identifying when men are the victim. They work to hide the truth."

"Yes, they do. But since I am here offering free advice, your plan to get closure for those files on your desk is a wise one. You will reap the rewards for your hard work in the future."

Well, that was something. "Anything else I should know? Please consider that a request for additional information rather than a rhetorical question you simply answer yes to without elaboration."

"It did not take you long to learn the truth of that," the archangel replied in an amused tone. "There is something to be said for fresh starts, so I recommend you clear off as much from your desk as possible in a timely fashion. Most of these cases can be recorded and filed away, a few are good starter cases for you to get your feet wet in your new career path, and the rest shall be cold cases determined to thwart you for some time to come."

"I don't suppose you could sort those into the appropriate piles for me, could you?" I gestured to the mess of filing boxes taking over my office. "You could consider it making up for sucker punching me in the gut."

The archangel laughed. "That was quite rude of me. You are a bold human. It is easy to see why my brother likes you. But as for your question, yes. I can. I will even be considerate and label which are which. It is a small matter, and it does make up for my brother's meddling, so it balances the scales nicely. I will leave you with this: there are better days ahead."

The archangel snapped his fingers, and a flash of golden light enveloped my office. When it dimmed, Sariel had vanished. The boxes had also vanished, leaving neat stacks of files in sequestered piles across my office. Notes written on golden cards declared what was in each pile, offering me direction on how best to proceed with my time.

I began with the starter cases within my capacity to solve, as I understood I had a great deal to learn in little time.

Everything else could wait.

THANKS TO SARIEL'S masterful sorting of my files, I conquered the first few cases with relative ease, asking for help from several of the veteran detectives as I went through the process of questioning everyone involved and associated with the murders. The first one proved to be the easiest; cameras had caught the murder on tape, the woman's death had been witnessed by numerous people, and the culprit, once apprehended, caved under the first sign of real pressure.

Jealousy coupled with abusive tendencies had cost a woman her life, an unfortunately common occurrence that never failed to make my heart hurt.

In his twisted, selfish, and hateful mind, if the killer couldn't have her, no one could, thus leaving the world bereft of a bright soul many had cherished.

Solving the murder wouldn't bring her back from the dead, but acquiring justice might one day bring peace to those left behind in a senseless act of greed.

By the time I wrapped up the third case, which took a staggering two months following my promotion, I came to understand a great deal more about Alec Mortan's curse. While our quip of his life being a list of 101 ways to die remained accurate, I discovered it was less about the ways in which people could die and more about the nature of what drove people to kill each other. Society blamed passion for many deaths—murder most often occurred in the heat of the moment.

The first three cases counted, if I scraped at the surface of the mystery.

In reality, humanity harbored the capacity for violence and evil as much as we held the capacity to do good in the world. Like a spinning coin, every person could land on either face—or stand on its end in defiance of probability.

The deeper I delved into the mystery surrounding Alec Mortan and his uncanny knack for showing up where people would die—or cursed to witness humanity at its worst—the more I grew to respect the man for his indomitable will and determination to persist.

Death continued to haunt him, but after leaving my office to resume his life, he hadn't returned to my precinct.

Life had taken him to the far side of Long Island to a new job, and while reports of cases involving him as a witness hit my desk from time to time, other detectives handled the questioning, giving me paperwork to file into the collection in case I found some connection leading to the source of his curse.

It amazed me how a short, frantic time could make such a difference, but I found I missed his quiet company. It took time to understand what Sariel had meant about having regrets in a way. However, I found an appreciation for what I might have gained but had chosen to lose.

I had met one man I could see attempting to form a

relationship with, which offered the hope others were out there.

I also learned remaining a virgin drove the incubi and succubi involved with my life absolutely wild, as I refused their advances and enjoyed luring them to the end of their ropes. Of the people I worked with, Bailey had caught onto my ploy, and she laughed every time my status as mostly young, available, and virgin got the best of the nosy divines, demons, and others known to prowl the precinct.

I enjoyed the game, inciting the Devil and his crazy family just from living my life as I wanted rather than to their expectations.

Sometime when the summer began to creep into spring's turf, Bailey bounced into my office armed with one of my travel mugs filled with coffee, which she presented with a flourish.

"How did your checkup go?" I asked, accepting her gift with a pleased sigh. The coffee would make whatever she needed of me easier to handle, and if she thought it would sour, the drink would be laced with some pixie dust so I could make the most of the situation.

She grinned at me and flopped onto my couch. "The tiny terrors are doing well, and I won't have to give up the ambrosia of life until two weeks before delivery, and I get to be weaned off it this time in a sensible fashion. I also won't be off it too long. The busybodies want them on pristine milk for the first month, then I can start exposing them through second-hand joy."

I chuckled, as my chief's entire family went to extremes making sure their cindercorn and her foals all made it through pregnancy without major mishap. "And how is Sam?"

"He's strutting like a peacock as usual. He is inflicting his peacock ways on his grandfather at the moment, who was this week's examiner of developing troublemakers known as babies."

"I will sucker punch him in the gut if he even thinks about invading my office," I warned her with a grin. It'd taken me a full month to realize the archangel enjoyed when the lowly cops got rowdy, so I'd taken to joining Bailey in her futile efforts to launch surprise attacks on Sariel.

"He is planning on invading your office, as he enjoys honing your self-defense and offense skills."

"Is that what we call this? Honing my self-defense and offense skills?" I pointed at my digital board, which was all of three weeks old thanks to having successfully chucked an archangel into its predecessor. "Honestly, I'm more impressed Sariel replaced it after I broke it."

"I've been trying to throw him for months without success. You nailed him on your first try after completely catching him by surprise. You earned his adoration for life with that stunt."

"Along with an office full of feathers." As I'd been warned I'd be entertaining a feathery foe soon, I set my coffee in its safe spot, a present from the Devil's wife, who insisted I needed a place where my coffee would never spill. I reached into my drawer for the latest trick in my arsenal, which was a foghorn meant for a boat. I also pulled out two pairs of earplugs still in their protective packaging, and I tossed a set to Bailey. "Thank you for informing me that angels have auditory sensory organs in the vicinity of their shoulders, by the way. I have chosen my weapon in my latest attempt to prove to the archangel he sucker punched the wrong woman."

"Are you trying to earn an invitation to a triad, Josefina? That sounds like you're trying to apply to become the human member of a triad."

"No. I am not confident I can handle one man. Two of them would take me to the brink and push me over. Engaging in a relatively harmless prank war with an archangel seems like a good way to test my fortitude, however. How long do I have before he shows up?"

Bailey checked her watch. "I would say no more than two minutes."

"If I break any of my hardware this time, I'm sorry."

"I'm sure Sariel will end up replacing it with something better, and you've put your coffee in the safe place, so it's fine. We all need a little excitement in our lives today. Well, you don't need any more excitement in your life today. We have been given cadets, and Queeny has decided you are being bequeathed with a cadet. When I left, he was digging through our closet looking for a bow."

In so many ways, moving to Manhattan had been a huge step up in life, as long as I recognized both of my bosses were a little crazy. I couldn't even call them a few cans short of a six pack; they needed at least one can to qualify between the two of them, and I held serious doubts they could manage that much.

That Samuel, the saner of the two, searched for a bow for some poor cadet meant one thing: they'd both lost what little grasp they had on reality.

How had I become the sole bastion of sanity in our precinct?

"You owe me," I informed my chief, and before she could argue, I put the ear plugs in, held my foghorn under my desk, and eyed the woman in challenge.

She decided wearing her ear plugs beat having her ears ringing all afternoon due to my ongoing war with an archangel.

On the two-minute mark, the archangel popped in. He said something, which was muffled by the earplugs. I stood, pointed the foghorn at him, and let rip.

As expected, feathers flew everywhere, and the archangel abandoned my office in a flash of golden light. Smiling, I removed my ear plugs and placed everything on my desk. Bailey hooted her laughter, kicked her feet, and fell off my couch, rolling as her mirth got the best of her.

A few moments later, a rather rumpled archangel teleported back into my office. "That was evil of the highest order, and I commend you for having won that round."

I loved how honest archangels tended to be, especially in the face of defeat. "Archangel feathers are worth at least a thousand a pop on the internet, and I have an office full of them now. All I need to do is get a statement from you about their authenticity, and I'll have enough money to date a man for at least a week. I've heard men are expensive, but I wouldn't know because I keep foisting the available men on unsuspecting co-workers."

Sariel's laughter chimed. "Did my brother send over some incubi again?"

When wasn't the Devil sending over incubi for my amusement? The last batch had resulted in a lively run of the Game of Life during a break, and while I'd lost the game, I hadn't lost any clothes—and I'd made a few suggestions on which co-workers would enjoy a visit from an incubus along with the reasons why.

At least one couple would be getting a welcome addition

to their household thanks to my distribution of sex demons around the precinct.

"I do appreciate having people to play board games with during breaks." I scooted back in my chair and opened the cabinet that held my fledgling game collection. "I almost thought about Monopoly, but I play by house rules, and I'm not sure my bosses would have appreciated fifteen hours of profanity laced play coming from my office."

"I would have forgiven you, but Sam would sulk that he hadn't been invited," Bailey reported, climbing off the floor and brushing off the archangel feathers sticking to her clothes. "Shed a few extra feathers as compensation for having to deal with Lucy's idiocy. Last week, he sent over twenty-three incubi. Then he sent over a succubus just to make certain which team Josefina bats for. We've determined she prefers team incubi, but she admitted team succubi offers a lot of damned fine incentives."

"We went for a manicure and pedicure, Bailey. This is not a hint that I want to start dating succubi. Well, unless the dates are for manicures and only manicures. She'd starve within a week of being in a relationship with me, but her nails would be beautiful."

"I feel my brother has bitten off more than he can chew, but it is so much fun watching him try to crack her shell. At the rate he sends his demons over, she will be immune to their magic by the end of the year. She will have even more resistance than you do, Bailey," Sariel teased.

"Resist an incubus twice, and you're flagged for life," Bailey complained. "I have the only incubus doohickey I need in my life, and that's that. But if you could talk to Lucy and tell him Josefina doesn't need the attention of twenty-plus incubi a week, that would be nice. At the current pregnancy rate in this precinct, half our staff will be on paternity or maternity leave within eight months. We do not have enough cadets to cover half the precinct being out for leave due to incubi spreading the love, correcting formerly unknown conception issues, or generally helping couples become pregnant. And no, I don't care if they were helped with permission! Do you know what I have on my hands, Sariel? I have a staffing problem on my hands, all because Uncle Lucy can't keep his sex demons at home."

"But everyone is so happy," the archangel teased.

"Everyone except Josefina," Bailey grumbled.

I stared at the pregnant cindercorn with a raised brow. "I'm very happy, thank you. I have a good job, it turns out I'm not utterly shabby at being a detective, and I've only had to go out four times so far this week to add new cases to my count." Two of the cases would be easy; the evidence pointed at an obvious culprit, and all the work I'd done yesterday led towards an easy conviction. Between the camera footage, the DNA evidence, fingerprints, and everything else I'd meticulously gathered from the site, I would be closing those cases and adding them to my tally by the end of the week, assuming the results came back as expected. The other two would be tougher, and I expected the one would go into my pile of cold cases.

I had nothing except a single partial fingerprint, insufficient to narrow the pool of culprits down to something sensible, and a hair without the blasted root tissue needed to become sufficient admissible evidence. Without the tissue attached to the hair's root, the best I could hope for was some mitochondrial DNA evidence from the interior shaft of the strand.

Mitochondrial DNA evidence wouldn't get me the conviction I needed.

I moved my mouse so I could check the time on my computer. "Of course, that's partially because I'm scheduled for desk work this week, as I hadn't been informed there'd be new cadets coming in. I've only been taking cases when the other teams couldn't take the calls right away." For whatever reason, I still lacked a partner, but it worked well enough; when I went to a crime scene, an established pair went with me. They handled everything I couldn't, and I focused on investigating.

One day, I would get a partner. One day.

Bailey grinned. "There is a cadet. One cadet. This cadet is for you. We've decided you're keeping this one as a present. Thus the bow. Technically, this cadet is a while off graduation, due to a complete lack of practical experience, but he's solid on the book smarts. Since we're going to be losing staff like crazy in the upcoming months, Sam wanted to get cadets working with us as soon as possible. Our staffing budget is fucked, but we're going to see if we can crank performance through cutting the number of street hours and spreading the high-stress workload. If it works out, we'll get a better budget to work with. A safer public is a happier public, and a safe and happy public means we get a better budget." Bailey wrinkled her nose. "Your cadet passed the knowledge portion of his exams already, so we're going to be trying a new training system. You'll show him the ropes, teach him how the streets work, and educate him on the general nature of detective work. You'll be on rotation to work a patrol with your cadet once a week. We're currently planning an eight-month trial with him before he's issued his badge. The commissioner wants to test this method. If it works out, assuming the cadets pass the knowledge tests after two months at the academy with a minimal error rate, they'll be assigned to a pair to get further education while in the field."

I could see the ploy working—assuming the cadet was partnered with a knowledgeable and patient pair of cops. "We're going to end up with a quartet if I tag along with another pair," I pointed out.

"It's your fault for being so efficient and just dragging out a pair when you need to investigate a crime scene. If you weren't so damned good at it, we would have forced a partner assignment on you already," my chief complained. "But you keep performing well, and Sam hates breaking things that aren't broken. He's going to cry if the cadet breaks the working system."

Cadets could make a mess out of things in a hurry, especially if they were the kind who wanted the prestige and power of being a cop. Those tended to wash out early in our precinct.

If Samuel didn't catch onto them, Bailey did. If by some miracle those two didn't, the rest of us sniffed out the dangerous, unwanted behaviors and either sent them packing or kicking them back to the academy until they figured out they served the people and not the other way around.

"All right. As you don't want Samuel to start crying, I have to evaluate and make certain this one doesn't wash out."

"Correct."

"Is this a bad time to remind you that I'm a jackass with the cadets and have one of the higher washout rates? It took all of three weeks working with the cadets to figure this out."

"If he survives you, everyone will know he is quality material."

I couldn't argue with that, so I didn't. "All right. Send him in, and warn him I'm tough on a good day, and he doesn't want to see me on a bad one."

Bailey chuckled, got up, brushed herself off, and headed for the door. "You do love making the cadets squirm."

"If they survive me, they turn out to be better cops, so let them squirm." I waved, got up, and began to gather my collection of archangel feathers. "Thank you for your contribution to my dating fund, Sariel."

The archangel laughed. "As *He* did not tell me I could not, I will even authenticate your feathers to maximize your reward for having landed yet another surprise attack upon me."

"It's nice to see angels aren't assholes all the time," I replied.

"It keeps you mortals on your toes."

ELEVEN

"Just wait until you see the body."

It took all of twenty seconds to clue in on Bailey's behavior when I caught a glimpse of the cadet with Sam in the hall. A rather nervous and fidgety Alec Mortan, who did justice to his cadet's uniform, pattered down the hall. Judging from his posture and the wringing of his hands, he'd enter orbit if I subjected him to the foghorn. To prevent an incident, I put the foghorn back in my desk and decided to kick back and relax in my chair, propping my sock-covered feet on my desk.

I waited for my boss to enter my office before raising a brow and saying, "I understand why you would want to put a bow on him now. Thank you for not humiliating him."

Chief Samuel Quinn revealed a red bow from his pocket, which had seen better days. "This was the only one I could find, and he was already nervous enough. I haven't let him take the practical test for investigating financials yet."

"The one test I'm guaranteed to pass, and he is making me wait to take it," Alec complained.

I chuckled. "You'll appreciate that after you go through the rest of the gauntlet. Have you been given the speech on the precinct rules?"

"For some reason, most of the speech involves appropriate fraternization among officers. Otherwise, I've been told I shouldn't steal Chief Quinn's coffee."

"Which Chief Quinn?"

"Both of them," he replied with laughter in his voice. "I even got a mug with my name on it to make it clear how the coffee works here."

Once the customized travel mugs were brought out, the hiring was as good as finalized, and as a general rule, cadets didn't get their own mugs until they'd done a few weeks of work—and had survived at least one patrol with me.

After what he'd been through, I couldn't blame either of my chiefs for laying off and giving him his mug early. "You better have secured an agreement from Chief Bailey to make you some of her coffee in that cup."

"He gets ten because she yanked him out of the academy early. We're losing another one to your wicked ways," Samuel complained.

"I'm not the one being wicked," I reminded him. "I just refuse to take my clothes off for the packs of incubi Lucifer keeps sending over. It's not my fault people talk to me, and the wise men and women of this precinct inform me when they wish to have a child and would not mind if an incubus assisted them with their problems. Otherwise, fertility clinics are expensive. I'm helping as I was helped, if you please." I paused, shrugged, and added, "Even if you don't please, honestly."

"That's what I figured. It's fine, except we really don't have enough cops or cadets to handle the surge of pregnancies around here. Please stop helping everyone get pregnant. Please. I'll remind people to ask me if they need help on that front."

"I'm more approachable, I have the contacts, and the incubi like playing board games on my breaks. You'll break so many hearts if you ban them from the precinct. Look on the bright side; it's never been easier to get small favors from Lucifer and his demons. All you have to do is give them a board game with me for half the shit we need them for."

"I hate how true that is. Alec, she's all yours. She needs coffee every hour and a half or the beast emerges, and not even Lucifer is willing to tango with the beast when she hasn't had her coffee. If the beast starts foaming at the mouth, swing by my office for a packet of pixie dust. Fortunately, she doesn't froth often, but you know it's bad when the frothing starts. Honestly, you're here to learn and be her gopher. If you survive that, you'll be set. I'll leave you two to get reacquainted. Oh, and McMarin?"

"Sir?" I asked.

"I just got tossed a murder case with a financial file about ten miles thick. Please make use of your new cadet and find out if the suspect would have just cause for murder based on the vic's financials."

Ah. Everything became clear. "Let me guess. You received this file approximately twenty minutes before you plucked this specific cadet from the academy."

Samuel snickered and waved his hand. "While that may have happened, I refuse to admit it. Just wait until you see the body."

I hated seeing the bodies, but it was an important part of my job. "What's so special about the body?"

"Death by goldfish," my chief answered before leaving my office.

"Death by goldfish? What the fuck is death by goldfish?" I blurted.

"I don't know, but I'm afraid to find out," Alec admitted.

I NEEDED to brush up on animal abuse laws and find out if goldfish were protected by any of the acts barring animal cruelty. The goldfish, which numbered in at fifty-two with possibly more crammed deeper in the corpse, deserved a better end at the very least. Until I learned more about the victim, a middle-aged white male, I would reserve judgement about if he'd deserved his fate.

The goldfish, ranging in size from a quarter up to a ten pound monster that had been forcefully shoved where the sun refused to shine, would result in at least one therapy session. The last thing anyone needed to see involved fish fins sticking out of someone's ass.

The coroner and our precinct's primary forensics medical examiner held a conversation in hushed whispers, probably trying to come to terms with the gruesome job ahead of them.

"This is not the sort of evidence collection any of us wants to participate in," I informed Alec. He, as the new gopher of the precinct, held three cameras, and someone had given him the basic rundown on their use. With an admirably neutral expression, he photographed the body and the poor fish.

"Chief Quinn really wasn't joking about this one. It is

death by goldfish. And to think I thought I had seen everything when I'd gotten up this morning."

"I would say it's nice that you can be surprised still, but it's really not. What did those poor goldfish do to anyone?" I sighed and shook my head. "If the doctors in the corner could come join us, we might get out here sometime this week."

Dr. Harrins, the poor bastard who would be extracting goldfish carcasses from the corpse, eyed the body before shrugging and strolling over. "If you could have your forensics people come up with a better strategy for the fish, I might be able to have an autopsy done sooner than later."

Wait. He needed a *better* strategy for the fish? I scratched my head and regarded the corpse with a frown. "Is there a reason you can't just pull them out?"

"We aren't sure what species of goldfish this is. Goldfish do not usually have pronounced spines like this. We don't know if we're dealing with an endangered species of fish or not."

The instant the word 'endangered' left his mouth, I realized I'd been tricked and given a hell case. "The fish are already dead. Just don't damage them when you remove them until you get an identification on the species. If they're endangered, offer the scientists some of the bodies for study. Isn't that how this should work?"

"The fish themselves might have contributed to his death," the coroner replied.

"Well, that seems likely, as the victim obviously has been impaled with numerous goldfish. At the very minimum, it appears he choked on a few. Call somebody who knows about fish and find out if the fish are venomous or poisonous. Both may apply." I bit my lip so I wouldn't laugh at the reality of the fish possibly being both venomous and poisonous. "From your initial look at the body, does it appear as though the fish bit him?"

"Considering we had to remove several fish from his genitalia to move the body without damaging the corpse further, yes."

Oh. Oh my. My eyes widened. "I see. In this case, I'm grateful I haven't seen."

"There are pictures," Dr. Harrins promised.

Wonderful. Not only would I have to get a close-up look at the corpse with a bunch of poor fish still sticking out of him, I would have to look upon the body in its original state, with even more fish. "I'm assuming I'm going to get a complete look at our victim, including toxins?"

"The first thing we did was grab a blood sample and send it off to the lab for the initial toxicity report," Dr. Harrins promised. "Then we removed some of the fish making it difficult for us to handle the body."

"Such as the ones attached to his genitalia?" I asked.

"There were two sturgeon. They were attached to his nipples. The sturgeon survived their experience and are currently being held for questioning. They're definitely endangered, but we got them in the appropriate water in time. The aquarium helped with that."

No matter what, I couldn't afford to laugh at the thought of fish titty tassels on the victim. I had no idea how I would question a pair of traumatized fish, but I would cross that bridge when I got to it. In the meantime, I would concentrate on maintaining my professionalism. I cleared my throat, circled the body, and questioned everything about my life. Would staying at my old precinct have spared me from beholding the horrors of death by goldfish? Well, fish, as it hadn't just been goldfish responsible for the man's death.

I would wonder about that for a long time. I drew in several deep and calming breaths before I asked, "Where was our victim found?"

"Fortunately for the sturgeon in question, in a bathtub, which was filled with river water."

That explained a few things. "But why didn't the fish let him go? Or swim away?"

"Magic. They were, well, stuck. It took a practitioner trick to remove them, and they were the only fish survivors of the incident. They did not contribute to his death, as the species in question is neither venomous nor poisonous." Dr. Harrins winced and pointed at the victim's mouth. "We're still trying to figure out how to unravel the magic holding those fish in place. After we remove the magic holding them in place, we'll be able to surgically remove the remaining deceased aquatics."

Poor fish. "Okay. Contact the CDC regarding the fish removal, tell them the case involves at least two fish of an endangered species, and encourage them to offer help getting that magic off the body so we can get an autopsy report." According to Samuel's commentary, we already had an identification of the corpse and access to his financials, which would simplify matters for me. "I'll leave you gentleman to your job, as us hovering isn't going to help you with the extraction of evidence."

Dr. Harrins cracked, bowed his head, and snorted a laugh. "You said that with a straight face, McMarin."

"I work with Chief Bailey Quinn, Harrins. If you want to crack my professionalism, you're going to have to work harder at it than that." At least once a week, the cindercorn went out of her way trying to get me to break and dissolve into helpless laughter, but thus far, I had contained my mirth until back in the safety of my office.

One day, she would break me, but I intended to hold out for as long as possible.

The sturgeon titty tassels might be the event to break me, but I would do my best to restrain myself until in the questionable privacy of my office.

"Right. You're her rider. I keep forgetting that—and I keep forgetting to give you the condolence card I picked up a few weeks back. I saw it, and it was perfect."

I allowed myself a smile at the thought of the coroner getting me a card. "I appreciate the thought. I've been dodging the CDC testing they want me to do, but I've been told it's coming, like it or not. A card is appreciated at this stage."

"I bet it is. I'll call the CDC and play the endangered species card, and I'll give you a ring as soon as I have any concrete evidence for you. I wish I could give you a solid cause of death right now, but I honestly don't know if he was dead before the fish became involved. I won't be able to find out until we are able to remove them."

I wished him and his team the best of luck. "Anything else I should know before I head back to my office?"

"Wear gloves when you go through his possessions."

"I always wear gloves. I don't want my fingerprints on the evidence."

"Double them up, or you will regret everything."

AS THE CHIEF Quinns preferred the evidence remaining pristine, always under lock and key, and consistently under video surveillance, the precinct's detectives shared a floor with the evidence vault. To access the evidence, I needed to punch in a code at the vault's entry, which would identify the location of the evidence I wished to handle. At the same time, I received a room announcement, a reminder of basic protocols for evidence handling, and a stern order to wear gloves. Depending on the evidence I was handling and if it was deemed potentially dangerous, it would instruct me on other safety gear as needed.

According to the evidence log, the goldfish victim was named Mr. Thomas Hardy, he had been thirty-seven at the time of death, and worked as an upper manager at an advertising firm. The three pages of known associates, potential suspects the initial responding officers had tossed together, and a flag warning me the gentleman had a history of playing women warned me I had one hell of a case on my hands.

Oof.

The last thing I needed was a murder case including a page and a half of jilted women with motive.

To complicate my day, the evidence machine warned me to wear a mask and scrubs to go with my gloves.

The scrubs worried me. Unlike in hospitals, our version of scrubs came courtesy of the CDC and used practitioner magic to make sure we didn't come into contact with potentially dangerous evidence. Once I made certain the system understood there were two unfortunate bastards stuck on the job, I began running Alec through the safety regulations.

"Why would his possessions be contaminated?" Alec asked, observing as I dug out all the required safety gear so we wouldn't have the wrath of our bosses raining down on our heads the instant they found out about a single cut corner. "He was killed with goldfish. And sturgeon."

"I don't know, but we are about to find out. The scrubs suck. They emit magic in pulses, and for most people, those pulses tend to tingle or itch. In my case, it tickles, and I hate them more than anything else I've encountered at this job yet. If someone had warned me about the tickling scrubs, I would have refused the promotion and dealt with my former jackass boss. Without fail, every two weeks, I have a date with these damned things. The life of a detective is not full of prestige. It is full of tickling misery."

"I will hope for a tingle," Alec stated, and he went to work ditching his personal items from his pocket and putting them in the holding bin, which would be held in the vault until we finished with the evidence. Considering that we needed the scrubs, I was grateful my phone would be safe until I finished going through the items that couldn't leave the vault and its hive of sterile offices.

Unfortunately for us, the system notified me there were six boxes already checked out and likely waiting in my office, and we had four more to pick up when we finished going over the evidence.

As expected, every thirty seconds, the scrubs pulsed, and the pulse translated to a nefarious tickle destined to put me in a crabby mood for the rest of the day. Retrieving one of the carts, I headed for the section of the vault holding the registered evidence.

Instead of being on one of the countless racks with a tag, ours was in a CDC safe, one of twenty we had, meant to hold dangerous evidence or something we needed to keep particularly secure.

"Fuck," I announced, eyeballing the safe. Every safe had a pair of phones next to it. One allowed for calls out. One contacted the CDC for help if we needed it opening the damned thing.

I had been registered for each of the sets, which meant I could place my hand on the panel while staring into a retina reader. The panel would jab for a blood sample, chew through my DNA, and then confirm a match with my magical signature and my retina scan. So far, nobody had been able to crack the safe without having the living body of a person registered in the system.

Somehow, the device could detect the difference between live bodies and corpses.

I picked up the phone for the internal system and stabbed the extension for Mr. Chief Samuel Quinn.

"What's the problem, McMarin?"

"I would like to take the rest of the day off to recover from this terrible idea of a joke, sir," I complained. "Why is the death by goldfish case locked in the secure safe? Your answer is going to determine how much effort I put into trying to go home. I have incubi on speed dial. I could get one of them to come in and help me out."

Alec snickered.

Damn. I hadn't realized the accountant-turned-cadet possessed a sense of humor capable of withstanding me at my worst—and the safe plus death by goldfish would put me at my worst within an hour, guaranteed.

"Ah, the glorious sound of my detective finally locating the end of her rope. What got to you?"

"It tickles," I groused.

"Ah, the scrubs. Sorry. I forgot you had that reaction. I will see if the CDC can adjust the magic on it while still being safe. I shouldn't have forgotten that. I'll tell Bailey to make you coffee as soon as you're done, and I'll have her up your grade of pixie dust before sending you home for the day. I'll get your cadet to take you to your place. He lives next door."

Wait. I'd gotten a place in one of the complexes landlords worked with the city on to provide affordable housing for cops. I'd expected a tiny studio with the bare necessities and had gotten a four bedroom suite I could afford on my budget. While I hadn't gotten any pets yet, I'd joined the queue to get a working dog to help with investigations and protection.

The last I'd checked, I was scheduled for evaluations within the next month to see if I could be trained to handle one of the police pups.

Unfortunately, as I worked with Bailey often, I needed a special pup, one who could deal with the cindercorn at her worst.

I frowned, wondering what my chief was up to. "What sort of next door are we talking about?"

"Your building, but on a different floor. He has a studio, as he's ranked as a cadet, so a lot of his stuff is in storage, but he's in the queue for a good apartment if he shakes out. We'll see in a few months. And don't feel sorry about the studio; it's the equivalent of a two-bedroom in floor space, it just doesn't have enclosed rooms except for the bathroom, which is a good one."

"Do you know how much these apartments cost if we were to rent them normally?" I complained.

"Yes, I do. I also know why cops are getting them at the rate they do," he replied with a chuckle.

Hm. As he'd cultivated me to push my luck, I asked, "Why do we get them at the rate we do?"

"Lucifer's daughter and her husband own the building, and the rent rates pissed her off. When she made the acquisition, she had an anxiety attack because apparently she can't handle making too much money. She ended up asking Bailey for help. Bailey's form of help involved the suggestion she renovate the entire building to be spacious apartments and rent them out to the police. We also house some folks in witness protection there until we can get them moved to somewhere safer."

Well, that explained a few things. While I hadn't met Lucifer's daughter yet, I heard about her exploits often.

She meant to change the world for the better, and at the rate she was going, she would take over the world before reforming the damned thing. "Ah, okay. That makes sense. Please thank her for me."

"I'll do that. Is there an actual problem beyond the itching?"

"Yeah. Were you aware our victim had goldfish attached to his genitalia and there were a pair of still-living, endangered sturgeon attached to his nipples?"

My chief made a sound suspiciously like a giggle. "I had not heard about his genitalia, but I was aware of the sturgeon. They went to hell for some tender loving care from Lucifer's wife, who has become an undisputed master of caring for fish. They were in rough shape. They'll be fine, although there is currently a dispute over who will get the fish and what their fate will be. One is male, the other is female. I expect they will be bred, and the babies will be released into the wild once they're old enough to have a decent chance of survival."

Well, at least someone would get a happy ending from my hell day. "I would appreciate some warning about why we're in scrubs, Samuel."

My chief sighed. "Items in his bathroom, which were registered as evidence, were covered in some form of caustic slime. The gloves you checked out are impervious to it, and the scrubs will make sure it is neutralized if it gets on you. It self-replicates, and we haven't identified what is causing the replication. Your room on the floor is already treated in preparation for the crap, and there are special boots inside for when you open those containers. It will get on the floor, and the practitioner magic we have going in that room only cleanses it every minute."

"You mean it's like hagfish slime?" I asked. Only a few weeks ago, someone had decided it had been a good idea to transport a bucket of hagfish in his car, resulting in a slimy mess and the shutdown of an entire street. "I don't think we have had sufficient time to recover from the hagfish incident, sir."

"There will never be sufficient time to recover from the hagfish incident, McMarin. Bailey cried for a week because she couldn't get it all out of her coat even with the help of fire. She only stopped crying when I informed her I would have to sacrifice myself and brush it out of her fur."

The pregnant cindercorn kept the precinct topped up on amusing incidents, which helped me deal with the insanity my life had become. "We'll be careful, sir. Thank you for the warning regarding the replicating caustic slime."

"You're welcome. If you need help, give me a call. Do not ask for Bailey. Her solution to all problems today involves fire. The commissioner isn't letting her up the budget for public relations and working with shelters. She wants more budget."

When didn't she want more budget? "Good luck with that, sir."

"Thanks. I'll need it. I'll give her credit, though. She goosed the commissioner out of a budget upgrade for cases involving kids, so she might even let this go for a change."

Nothing riled up the precinct more than the cops wanting to help needy kids and not having the budget to work with. "How did she pull that miracle off?"

"Don't ask. It involves statistics you won't appreciate."

I read behind the lines: she'd done research into domestic violence issues and in-need families. "The budget is for making sure kids get into the foster system and are properly monitored?"

"Bingo. We'll have more resources to be able to make sure we can work with the social workers—and we are going to be able to better evaluate if children actually *should* be removed from a household. We're getting an on-call angel for these cases for minimum wage, around the clock. Our angel is also going to be staging interviews with all parents who have lost their children into the system. If it is determined there was not just cause, they will be reunited."

Damn. "Think the angel would be willing to answer questions outside of the custody cases?"

"As a matter of fact, yes. The angels are being paid to be available around the clock, and you know how they hate being paid for work they're not actually doing."

I snickered. "Congratulate Bailey for her masterful acquisition of an angel."

"I'll do that. Be careful with that evidence. I've already sent one person to the hospital today for acid burns, and I'd rather not have to send someone else. We hadn't realized it replicates, and we hadn't upgraded the danger rating yet."

"Nobody really expects self-replicating acid," I replied.

"Precisely. So, if you can figure out what's going on with that slime and why they're trying to erase evidence, let me know."

TWELVE

"But were you given an appropriate paycheck?"

THE NEXT TIME someone warned me an acid self-replicated, I would be more prepared for the reality of the situation. Within five minutes, the light coating on the non-organic materials the caustic fluid hadn't eaten through yet had tripled in volume and spread out over the steel table. Given time, I expected the fluid would eat through the table. The victim's credit cards already showed signs of deteriorating, although I hadn't realized some caustic fluids existed capable of breaking down even plastic.

"Remind me to do research into caustic fluids, Alec." I held up a deteriorating credit card, which was intact sufficiently to pull off the important details, including the card number, expiration date, and security code. While I handled the evidence, he took photos of everything. "It's even eating through the plastic of these credit cards. Maybe we have to use glass to store it? Nobody warned me becoming a detective involved a solid knowledge of chemistry."

"Is this practical chemistry?" Alec asked with a frown. "I

took more math than science in school, and I can't remember if chemistry was the acid test section of my education. It went by in a blur, honestly."

"I'm fairly sure this is chemistry," I replied, grateful the CDC had provided fancy gloves capable of withstanding the hell fluid dripping off the credit card. "I am noticing a trend, though."

"That everything here is somehow financially related or identity related?" Alec pointed at the pile we'd already dealt with, which ranged from the soggy pulped mess of life-insurance papers; we'd dealt with that first, and we'd managed to get the policy numbers off as many of the sheets as possible along with some names. That information would turn into warrants for the original copies. "Insurance, taxes, credit—it's all here. And covered with this slime."

The slime did remind me of the hagfish incident, with a goopy consistency and a tendency to stick to everything. "I'm getting the Blob vibe out of this, truth be told."

"I hope you won't think less of me for saying this, but I want to go home now."

I laughed, as I wouldn't mind heading home, especially now that I knew he lived in the same building I did. "Thanks to a bunch of incubi showing up in an effort to seduce me, I'm the proud owner of a bunch of board games. When I refused to take off my clothes but their boss said they had to spend time trying, we came to a suitable alternative: we play board games during breaks. As the inconvenienced party, I get to keep the board games." I narrowed my eyes. "I also just realized my apartment is large enough to host gaming parties, and I'm thinking I need to have gaming sessions over the weekends. I may not be accepting the advances of incubi, but there is no reason I can't invite them over for gaming." My eyes widened. "Well, shit. I've been trained to have fun by my bosses. But then they make me do shit like play with dangerous acids while on the job."

"There are no shortcuts we can take on this, are there?" Alec continued to take photographs of everything I handled from every angle, and every now and then, he made use of our digital tablet to make a notation about something we wanted to remember that wasn't immortalized in image format. "Is this what you do daily?"

"Fortunately, no. I mean, there is a significant amount of tedium, but I usually don't have to wear a partial hazmat while handling evidence. Usually, I have to deal with blood or other bodily fluids, especially if I'm being sent to a homicide scene. The chiefs don't tend to send me out on the rape cases. I have earned a reputation."

"What sort of reputation?"

"I will work myself to death on a rape case, even though the odds of getting a successful prosecution are low. My success rate for a prosecution is pretty good, but they only put me on the cases they think we have a decent chance of winning. Otherwise, I overwork on them."

"I'm confused. Isn't it a good thing to work hard?"

"No, working to death is never a good thing. Working hard in a sensible fashion is a good thing, but I am not sensible on those cases. I'm usually assigned theft or homicide cases, as I work hard without working myself to death. We'll have to test your tendencies, too. That's a thing here. The chiefs want to put people where they shine, but they need to shine in a healthy fashion. I get too involved with the rape cases, so it's not as good of a fit as you might think."

"You may as well classify me as the same way," Alec stated.

Interesting. "I'll tell the chiefs. If you're like me, we'd be powerhouse detectives on the rape cases with good odds of securing a prosecution. But we have to be perfect on our end to get them. Most rapists walk."

"That disgusts me."

I understood, and I appreciated we stood on the same ground on the subject. I'd seen detective pairs split up due to differences of opinion in how cases should be approached before, although the chiefs took care to handle those situations with grace for all parties involved. "It disgusts me, too. Also, when we are tasked with domestic violence cases where the woman is the perp, we need to take extra care with the victims; men often withhold the reality of the situation because society has declared, foolishly, that men shouldn't be the victims of rape. They are. They're just far less likely to tell someone they're a victim, so prosecuting their rapist is that much harder."

We processed five more credit cards before I blinked, went to the pile we'd already checked, and began counting cards, confirming each one was unique. "Make a notation that this is an abnormal number of credit cards, Alec."

"Oh, I already did that. I noticed the high number of cards after we hit card number ten. Most people only have an average of four cards."

I had one card, and I obsessively paid it off on a weekly basis, terrified it would grow teeth and bite me. "I guess my one card is unusual?"

"It's smart. It gives you access to a credit card without giving you too many routes to enter debt. I wouldn't have any credit cards, except they're convenient for paying the bills and some stores, especially online." Alec shrugged. "One seems smart and sane to me."

"Can you tell if these are real credit cards or if they're prepaid?"

"There are names on the card, so they're not prepaid cards. These are real credit cards. Now, they might be *secured* cards, but that is a different kettle of fish from a prepaid card. I can't tell if the card is joint with someone unless we get access to the financials, however."

I nodded, and as my curiosity threatened to take over, I sorted through the remaining items, separating the cards into various piles. Ten credit cards went into an expired pile. Twenty-seven went into the active pile. He had a passport, a passport card, a driver's license, an insurance card, and four library cards. The library cards puzzled me, as he had one for the New York Public Library system, one in Delaware, one for a county system in Maryland, and one for Chicago. "Make a note to look into the legalities for library cards in places you don't have residency, Alec."

"Noted," he reported after fiddling with the tablet.

In the box of personal items, which included the soggy ruins of three pairs of shoes, a mess of deteriorated clothing, and a bunch of knick-knacks, I located a wooden box showing zero signs the caustic fluid bothered it. "Hello. What do we have here?" Setting the box on the table, I cleared away space so we could photograph it and make notes. Like everything else, it secreted the slimy substance, although it seemed impervious to harm.

Alec pointed at something engraved on the top of the surface. "That's a practitioner working."

I blinked, squinted, and sure enough, several symbols were etched into the wood. At first glance, I'd missed them, as they bore resemblance to the box's natural grain. "Excellent eye, Alec. How much practitioner magic do you know?"

"Not enough to identify what that does," he admitted.

"Okay. Did Chief Quinn give you a phone for work yet?"

"Yes, but it's in storage with my personal belongings. I thought it'd be wise to avoid ruining my phone on my first day."

Good call. "Use the phone on the wall, call Mr. Chief Quinn, and ask him to send someone who is familiar with practitioner magic to review this before we proceed. The last thing we need is setting off some trap playing around with magic we don't understand."

"Sounds like a good idea to me." Alec obeyed, and after referring to the extension list posted beside the phone, he used the end of his stylus to tap the numbers on the phone. "Hey, Samuel? It's Alec, and we found something fishy in the evidence."

I pressed my lips together so I wouldn't snicker at the man's ruthlessly used pun.

"It is not an actual fish in this specific case." The man grinned and winked at me. "When I scale it down to the bare minimum, there is a box with a practitioner working on it. Otherwise, we would have already tackled this task."

Oh, hell. If Alec leveled any one of those wordplays at Bailey, she'd lose her mind. Not only would she lose her mind, she'd go out of the way to make sure he never left our precinct.

The more painful the pun or zinger, the more she loved it.

"She's staring at me. Why do you ask?"

Right. Our boss had matchmaking tendencies almost as

bad as any angel, and I would need to remind Alec he was under no obligation to form any relationships with anyone unless he wanted to. Shaking my head at the insanity, I set aside the box and pulled out the next item.

Grabbing a live and angry hagfish had not been in my plans, and with a shriek, I flung the slime-producing eel-like creature across the room, where it hit the wall with a sickening splat. It stuck and began a slow, squishing descent towards the floor.

"I think we may have located the source of the slime, sir. It is approximately a foot long and resembles some form of strange eel."

"It's a hagfish," I informed him in a whisper, staring at my gloved hands, which had at least an inch of the slime clinging to the plastic. Between the gloves and the other protective clothing, I'd avoided getting any of it on my skin. "I need to be decontaminated, and if you could tell my boss I think I am done for today, that would be appreciated."

"I think Josefina has reached her general tolerance for slime, as she has a rather amazing amount of it all over her hands. She requests a decontamination. I also think she may want to go home, judging from additional commentary." Alec hesitated before saying, "He says you can't go home early. Once you're decontaminated, he has to hover protectively while Bailey makes you coffee and profusely apologizes."

While I expected something along those lines, I sighed and glared at the hagfish, which continued its extended journey down the wall to the floor, adding to the slime problem. "He wants me to go to the hospital just in case, doesn't he?"

"If it makes you feel better, he is expecting me to be checked, too."

It didn't, as I would have preferred neither one of us needing to be checked over due to exposure to abused wildlife involved with a murder case. "He's going to need a bucket for the hagfish. And a mop."

"He's already called for the CDC. He is also questioning where the hagfish came from, as there were no hagfish when the box was packed."

"It's just yet another mystery that needs to be solved," I complained. "When I was promoted, nobody warned me about the hazards of actively solving mysteries, Alec. I was not given full disclosure!"

"But were you given an appropriate paycheck?" he countered.

"Right now, it's questionable."

Alec chuckled and said, "Instead of sending her home, how about a raise? Because I don't think anyone makes enough to deal with the caustic slime of a possibly undead hagfish."

Was the fish an undead fish? I eyed it warily, wondering if hagfish could come back from the dead. I questioned how it was still alive.

It wiggled on its otherwise languid journey to the tiled floor.

"It could be an undead hagfish," I conceded. "And if it is, I am definitely not paid enough for this and request a raise. I will accept my raise in a form of the best pixie dust we stock and some new board games for my collection. Since this is something Lucifer would come up with just to torment me, he can pay for it."

Laughing, Alec relayed my commentary. "He says he is

coming down with our resident hazardous materials expert. She's changing into her fur coat now. The other expert, who will purify us using the fires of heaven and hell, apparently, will be here within twenty minutes unless we start showing symptoms."

"What the hell does he mean by showing symptoms? Of insanity? Being in this room is a symptom of insanity." I inhaled, counted to ten, and exhaled. "Okay, I feel better now."

"Understood, sir." Alec hung up the phone. "We are to stay near the door but remain in the room unless the hagfish makes any dangerous moves, in which case we sneak out of the room and lock it in until someone deals with it. As for symptoms, I think he means burning and itching."

Thanks to frequent exposure to incubi who enjoyed testing my limits, I often suffered from a different sort of burning itch, and my preferred candidate for the removal of said itch had taken the idea of joining the force seriously.

I needed some time to think about the various fraternization rules, which mostly boiled down to avoiding personal conflicts from interfering with work, attending mandatory couples therapy, and otherwise spending an excessive amount of time with my potential partner.

The hagfish seemed like an easier problem to deal with. "Is wiggling while stuck to the wall dangerous? This is definitely among the more disgusting of the cases I've been assigned."

"Honestly, I'm impressed it's still stuck to the wall," he admitted. "At the rate it's going, the chiefs will get here before it actually hits the ground. At least it doesn't seem to be burning through the paint."

"Yet. It doesn't seem to be burning through the paint

yet." I joined Alec near the door and kept a close eye on the hagfish. "I can't even blame your curse on this one. Samuel likely used the case as an excuse to pluck you out of the academy."

"He's been looking for a reason for weeks. My instructors put me on notice I'd end up with a lot of on-the-job training. They shuffled my education schedule so the fraternization course was part of my introduction to the academy."

I snorted a laugh at that. "That's not just sending hints. That's bludgeoning you with them. Let's start with a friendship, Alec. If you can handle being stuck with me for three weeks at work and then come to my place for games every evening for the same period of time, and we haven't tried to kill each other, then there might be something to their matchmaking ways. Be forewarned, however. The precinct is loaded full of busybody matchmakers. There is no escaping. If you aren't being matched with someone, you'll end up being sucked into the matchmaking ploys. It's contagious—and prone to leading to surprisingly happy relationships as far as I can tell. I'm the precinct's most stubborn woman at this stage."

"So I have been warned. When I suggested they just let you decide how to handle things, they stared at me like I'd grown a second head or something."

I gestured to the hagfish, which concluded its adventure to the floor and writhed around in a puddle of its own slime. "Do you think it's a magical hagfish, Alec? It's produced at least ten times its body size in slime so far, and it hasn't died yet. Do hagfish need water to survive? I'm concerned." While I hoped the hagfish survived its misadventure and use in someone's murder, someone else could sacrifice their body and sanity dealing with it.

I had lines.

Handling the hagfish crossed those lines.

"I don't know what it is, but honestly? I never thought I'd say the fish scares me more than the magical teleporting steamroller."

I thought about it, and I nodded my agreement. "Insane caustic mucus fish are definitely scarier than the magical teleporting steamroller. That one went in the cold case pile, by the way, in case you were wondering."

"I was, actually. Do you think that was the perfect crime?"

"You know what? I'm really not sure. Think we'll get hazard pay for this?" To my relief, I heard footsteps outside of the door, and I took the opportunity to escape the room and its many horrors. I decided Chief Samuel Quinn deserved most of my wrath, as his cindercorn wife would be handling the cleanup jobs she abhorred. "You are a horrible person, Chief Samuel Quinn!"

"Middle name Le-vit-i-cus. Use, diss-uh-prov-ing-ly," Bailey instructed.

As the cindercorn would heave sighs until I obeyed her, I dutifully altered my scolding and said, "I am going to need therapy for what happened in that room, Chief Samuel Leviticus Quinn!"

"What happened?" he asked with a raised brow.

"I reached into the box and got a handful of hagfish. Then I threw it, it stuck to the wall, and oozed down. Now it's writhing on the floor. I'm going to feel guilty if it dies. I even screamed before throwing it. It was an instinctive reaction."

Perky, who got saddled with the precinct's odd jobs thanks to his education as a doctor, strolled down the hall with a sloshing bucket in hand. "We will attempt to assuage your guilt, McMarin. Did any of the evidence survive?"

"I don't know. Ask me after you find out if the hagfish makes it. It's evidence now." I wrinkled my nose. "We got a good number of photographs before I located the hagfish, but I don't know if the box with the practitioner working survived under all that slime—or if it's responsible for the appearance of the hagfish."

"We're naming this the Fishy Case," Perky informed me.

"And I'm guessing you're expecting me to tackle it, bait in our perp, and balance the scales of justice while I'm at it," I replied in my driest tone.

"It's like you work here or something." Without bothering with any safety gear, he strode into the slime-filled room and headed for the rogue fish.

"Safety gear is a thing, and I don't care if your wife is around to pull her damned tricks," I hollered at him.

"I was actually the one who pulled the tricks this time," Samuel admitted. "It would have taken twenty minutes to gear him up, and the CDC likes yelling at me that I need to justify my paycheck through practical usage of magic. He's basically wearing an invisible layer of hazmat clothing, and I'll dispel it once he's detoxed. He just wants the hazard pay so he can buy more toys for his kids."

As Perky had four kids with another one on the way, he needed all of the hazard paychecks he could get his hands on. "Maybe I should give him my share of the hazard pay."

"You need your hazard pay to pay for the board games we all know you want, and we also know you're eyeballing a gaming computer. If you don't want us to know what you're lusting for, you shouldn't sigh wistfully at it in the break room while hoping you catch Bailey and you can guilt her into making you coffee."

Damn. At the rate he was busting me, I would need to hand over my badge and ask to be escorted to the nearest holding cell. "Four kids is enough to rattle somebody, but he's going to have another in a few months, Samuel."

"You're fretting, McMarin. Perky is only half of the puzzle that is the Perkins household, and they're perfectly capable of handling the next kid to come along."

According to Perky's snort, he did not agree with our chief's statement, and even the cindercorn whinnied her laughter.

"Next time, you re-mem-ber you need birth control, silly Perky."

"You say that like there was anything accidental about the decision to take leave of our senses in the hopes of another kid. I'll remember that the next time you get stars in your eyes and want more kids under hoof." Perky came back out with the bucket, which housed the hagfish. "You may as well call the CDC again, Sam. This is not a standard hagfish."

"Well, shit," the chief muttered, heaving a sigh and grabbing his phone. "If this damned thing is endangered, do you know what's going to happen, Perky?"

"We will either have to agree to house it or find some poor bastard to house it for us," the doctor dutifully arrived. "We could set up a tank in the lobby. As long as we ward it against any unexpected ruffians and rowdy criminals resisting arrest, it can be a good talking piece or something."

"There will be no talking hagfish in my precinct," Sam grumbled.

I raised a brow and stated, "It's a hagfish, sir, not a nagfish."

Bailey tossed her head and whinnied. "For that, I make you coffee. Perky, salvage the evidence you can with other bucket, then we lock box in box, then purify office. Then you get clean and get coffee, too."

"I do like when the hazard pay comes with good coffee," Perky stated before doing as our chief ordered. "Since you're still kitted, see what you can salvage in the time it takes me to hand over the fish, McMarin."

"You got it." I waded back into the office and aimed for the pile of credit cards to discover the fluids had finished them off. Of the evidence we'd already sorted, only the box remained intact. The hagfish had also taken out the contents of the other box, leaving us with a sodden mess. "It's all ruined," I said, shaking my head at the lengths the perp had gone to remove evidence we'd be able to trace through the victim's financial portfolio and identification records. "I fear we have a stupid criminal on our hands, sir."

"I'd say we have a criminal capable of erasing evidence. Why do you feel this one is stupid? I mean, most are stupid, but what has this one done to be stupid?"

"All of the destroyed evidence, outside of this box, is data we can pull out from the financial records, sir. That's pretty stupid."

"Maybe they wanted to make it a little harder on us?"

Both chiefs sighed, and I recognized the moment when they realized I was right.

"I *hate* stu-pid crim-i-nals," Bailey wailed.

We all did. "I'm sure the criminal believed there was a good reason to go through all that work," I said to appease the woman. "If we're particularly lucky, we can close it out after a review of the financials, and you'll have extra justification to keep your new cadet."

The cindercorn pricked her ears forward. "Yes, yes. Good idea. McMarin, clean up, take your cadet upstairs, do fi-nan-cials. It not paper goo; we smart, not put with goo fish."

"Time to earn your paycheck, Alec," I said, heading for the sterile room we used to decontaminate if any of the evidence proved to be more hazardous than we preferred. "I hope you weren't hoping to escape math with your job choice, because if so, I have bad news for you."

THIRTEEN

"The hagfish needs a home."

The hagfish survived.

According to a marine biologist, the hagfish belonged to some new species, and it would need to be observed and studied for more information. According to a remote scanner, the hagfish was female and pregnant, ending any discussions of dissecting her for the sake of science.

As hagfish had not been extensively studied or bred in captivity, nobody understood how they reproduced—and nobody could tell me if the hagfish normally became pregnant or were an egg-laying species.

Our specific hagfish would have at least a hundred baby hagfish to care for, assuming the marine biologists could figure out what to do with her.

Bailey wanted the hagfish to live in my office, and she was willing to fight every single government agency on the planet to make her dream of me having an aquarium happen.

As such, a war waged in my office. Alec lounged on the

couch, laughing his ass off over the heated dispute between the marine biologists and the cindercorn determined to become caretaker of every odd species to cross her path.

"The lobby has space for a large aquarium, and we can put a donation jar for the costs of care, and everything over the hagfish's cost of care would go to public services," I suggested, hoping my commentary might put an end to the yelling destined to give me a headache. "The hagfish needs a home. Nobody is disputing that. Make the home useful. In the lobby, she can be accessible to the public. A donation box for the hagfish can make sure it doesn't hit our budget, and anything over can be flagged for specific funds. Add it to a fund for working with schools and education or something. If the hagfish needs a specific owner, you can put my name on the paperwork, but she needs more space than my office provides. The lobby has a large chunk of space we can dedicate to the fish. Practitioner magic can protect the aquarium from the rowdy crowd, not that our lobby typically gets rowdy."

We had a second entrance where we took the truly dangerous folks who might put up a struggle. I hadn't known about the entry until my third week on the job, as my chiefs had gone out of their way to keep things quiet while I learned the basics of being a detective.

My former captain had neglected a lot about my post-hiring education, which I rectified through evening studies and shadowing detectives on difficult cases.

The marine biologist, a woman named Alicia, considered me with a scowl, but she nodded. "With the right protections to keep the environment pleasant, that would be an acceptable housing arrangement for the animal."

"Make it so," Bailey commanded her husband, pointing

at the door and snapping her fingers. "Our magic hagfish must be properly housed by the end of the day."

"We have no evidence it's magical, Bailey," Samuel replied.

"Hagfish don't mass produce slime on their own. It requires water. The hagfish is creating water so it can slime everything. This is evidence of magic," the cindercorn announced.

The marine biologist blinked, her brows furrowed, and she regarded the scanner in her hand, which also doubled as a giant encyclopedia and knowledge databank. "She actually makes an excellent point. Known hagfish species excrete protein and mucin, that when exposed to water create the slime. It takes very little of these substances to create a rather startling amount of the slime. The fish is producing its own water, as otherwise, it won't react. Did you use saltwater or freshwater when putting the hagfish in its temporary habitat?"

"Saltwater from the ocean here. We keep several large tanks on the first floor in case of aquatic incidents, so we just fill the bucket with the appropriate water type. This isn't our first dance with hagfish." Bailey giggled. "Our hagfish is a lot more dangerous, though."

"Yes, the caustic nature of its protein and mucin is a concern. We'll need to evaluate slime samples to identify if the hagfish has been modified to produce this variant of the slime."

"Can you handle the housing and evaluations of the hagfish in someone else's office, please? I still need to get some work done, and I would like to go over the financials of our vic before I head home for the night. If you actually need me, bring coffee and a good excuse." I stared at Mrs.

Chief Quinn and pointed at the door. "I'm talking to you. Out, demented unicorn. I need to work."

Bailey giggled. "She called me demented, Sam."

"Yes. Your training has borne the results you wanted. She is now willing to tell you when you are indulging in your typical insanity. Move it my beautiful and demented unicorn. We don't want to find out what happens if McMarin becomes truly cranky we're interrupting her productivity."

The herd of people left, and I breathed a sigh of relief, getting up and closing the door behind them. "I apologize for them. Bailey cannot handle when animals are in trouble. If she can save them, she will—and she doesn't want the hagfish to be dissected for science. It's not a problem if the animal dies of natural causes or is already dead, but if she sees a stricken animal, she loses her fucking mind. We have very strict rules on how we're to deal with animals while on duty. If the animal can be legally saved, we will save it, and we do not euthanize unwanted beasts. We also only work with no-kill shelters, who are compensated by the city to take in displaced animals. In our contract terms with the shelters, no-kill shelters only euthanize animals who cannot be rehabilitated from injury or illness. Extreme behavioral problems that cannot be resolved through training and appropriate handling are handled on a case-by-case basis. Usually, they're sent to the Devil's many hells to join some form of rehabilitation program—against animal abusers."

Alec chuckled. "Yes, I had been warned about the animal issue in the academy, as it was clear early on I would end up in this precinct. I'd been flagged the day I enrolled. Apparently, Mrs. Chief Quinn had told the academy if I enrolled, I was hers, and she would fight them for me. They did not want to fight the cranky, pregnant cindercorn."

"Does anyone want to actually fight the cranky, pregnant cindercorn?"

"Not particularly. So, how do financial investigations work on an actual case? I did not get any education for this at the academy."

"You won't; detectives are expected to learn this after receiving their badge. You just happen to have the appropriate education already. Essentially, we will go through the papers we've been given from the various financial institutions associated with the victim, and we look for anything suspicious. We identify the victim's patterns, looking for changes or anything that might be linked with the murder. It's complicated, so you should like it. I expect you'll be teaching me a lot of tricks of the trade."

"It'll be a two-way street," Alec replied, getting up from his place on the couch and heading for the pile of boxes containing the financial records. He grabbed one, hauled it back to the couch, and plopped down, setting it between his feet. With the same general enthusiasm as a child at Christmas, he took the lid off and snagged the first envelope of records.

I dug through my desk, grabbed one of my tablets and a stylus, made sure it had sufficient battery for him to work with, and brought it over. "I usually take pictures, load it into a note program, and jot digital notes all over the pages so I can refer to the records later. These tablets do not leave my office unless they're checked out with the chiefs. We have forms for it, since they contain evidence."

"We don't have to take our work home with us?"

"It is strongly discouraged. You'll appreciate that after a

while. The only time we're supposed to take work home with us is if we're assigned a police dog *or* if we're high enough up in the ranks to be on call. I'm on call if there is an important break in one of my cases, but I'm only contacted if it needs to be addressed immediately. The dogs go home with their handlers, and they're taught when they're on the job. I'm in the queue to receive a dog, but I don't know when that'll happen."

"I was warned there would be a canine in my future, and I have been going through training to help handle a dog."

Damn, the chiefs were out for the accountant. "No is an allowed word. If you become uncomfortable at any time, please use the word no."

"They're fine. I think it's nice they care about you enough they're going to these lengths. I appreciate your approach, and honestly, the stories about the incubi are hilarious. You have some serious street cred for your general ability to tell sex demons no. I've seen pictures of some of the incubi, and it's generally agreed even men find them attractive."

I chuckled. "You don't have a problem with living in the same building with me?"

"I don't, and if you want to spend time together outside of work, I'm game. I suspect we're both more interested in making a friendship work prior to establishing any additional benefits. Honestly, at this stage, I'm also interested in yanking on the chains of nosy busybodies, as your dating life really isn't any of their business."

Of all the things I'd learned while working under the Chief Quinns, the concept that romance was more about the relationships rather than the sex stuck with me.

Without the relationship, the sex meant less than nothing to me. I'd lived without it my entire life, and I could live without it in the future without issue. However, with the right relationship, I expected sex would become something truly special.

I wanted to capture that special moment.

I considered Alec with interest. "The relationship is more important to me than the sex."

"I generally feel the same way. And the only way we'll find out if there is a relationship to be had is to give it a shot. Honestly, if we survive each other for a few weeks on the job and still want to see each other in the evenings, that's probably a good indication there might be something to the matchmakers and their busybody ways. And if there's no interest, it's no skin off either of our backs. We'd be better off as just co-workers."

"Agreed. I have a few rules," I announced.

"No cheating should be one of the rules if it isn't."

I chuckled. "It is. If we both agree we are interested in trying to make a relationship work, then I feel we should stay dedicated. If you want out because you want to go have a fling with a succubus, just give me a heads up so I'm aware. The same applies to me. My second rule is to be honest. That's about it. I mean, beyond condom and safe sex rules. No children unless we actually want them. Once you're on the force long enough, you'll see the consequences. People like to say that pregnancy mystically transforms a mother into a caring entity who will do anything for her child, but that simply isn't true—and it often falls to us to try to rescue these kids from abusive family situations. And worse, there are times where we can't do anything at all."

Without fail, I ended up with a session or two on a shrink's couch trying to come to terms with the reality of my job—and that there were parents in the world who would kill their children because they were in the way of their life's ambitions.

"That was in the first week of courses, so we understood what we were getting into. We got both sides of the picture when we were being taught what to expect while on the job and how to handle an investigation involving child abuse. Or worse."

"We'll end up with those cases now and then. The chiefs try to rotate the detectives through those cases, because they're among the hardest we have to handle. And we get therapy sessions afterwards. Nobody handles those cases well."

Alec nodded, and he shuffled through the papers on his lap. "What do you think killed our victim, really?"

"If I had to make a guess, I'd say greed. If it is greed, we'll find some evidence in the financial records. Honestly, the financials are often where we learn most of the story, especially when we have a silent victim."

"A silent victim?"

"It's when we have no witnesses of the crime, the victim has no close associates, and we haven't found anybody to help offer insight on what happened and why. The cases with silent victims are often the hardest, as we have to piece together their life from the little evidence left behind, usually in the form of financial documents and physical evidence. Right now, I have no idea if we have such a victim on our hands, but we'll find out soon enough. My job, while you're digging through the financial records, is to figure out where he worked, who he was associated with, and find out if we have anyone to question. Once we know who we need to question, we'll hit the streets and start work on solving this case. If you're expecting a quick process, brace yourself for disappointment. It took me a few weeks to come to terms with the idea that solving crimes is nothing like what is portrayed on television or in the movies. Sometimes, the pieces fall together, but when it can take five to ten days, at a *minimum* to run fingerprints, things tend to stall for a while. Our current average processing time for fingerprints on non-critical cases is two months."

"That's *average*?" Alec blurted. "But why two months?"

"The fingerprints have to be manually confirmed. It's as much an art as it is a technical skill. There are a lot of factors. For example, how well was the lift on the fingerprint? How clear is the print? How many people have similar prints? The last case I got prints back for, there were fifty people with similar fingerprints. It takes an expert to interpret the prints, and they can get it wrong—or can't tell who the print belongs to. Sometimes, we can get lucky with the computer systems; every criminal's fingerprints are registered in a special database that can be compared against the prints we have on file. It's when we have to do new fingerprint registrations that we have issues."

"When you have a first-time criminal or a suspect who is yet to be fingerprinted?"

I nodded. "It's a process." Gesturing to the stacks of financial information, I said, "Given the volume of financial records, I suspect our victim is going to have a lot of associates, which means we'll spend a lot of time questioning people on why someone might have murdered him with a bunch of fish."

"And whatever other fish they might find when they

autopsy him," Alec muttered. "Do you think the CDC will be able to get through whatever is holding those fish in place?"

"I hope so, else this case is going to be even nastier than it already is. What are your thoughts so far?"

"I think someone with a high amount of creativity, a grudge, and ready access to magic is responsible. If they didn't want to be caught, they wouldn't have killed him in such a flashy fashion."

Okay. I reevaluated my stance regarding taking the long and slow approach to dating. A smart woman didn't allow a smart man to wander off without at least attempting to catch his attention. "Anything else?"

"The criminal is also stupid. By using endangered species, they've brought in a lot more investigative power. It's possible they thought the use of endangered species would hamper the investigation, but that's not how things work. It elevates the type of crime, meaning we'll receive additional resources and personnel."

"I see someone has been briefing you regarding some of the quirks of law enforcement."

"While I'll admit ignorance isn't stupidity, drawing so much attention to the crime *is* stupid. It's almost as bad as writing down your crimes for somebody to find." Alec smiled and patted the financial records on his lap. "Or in this case, having someone else conveniently write the crimes down for us so we can discover them one line item at a time."

I foresaw needing to drag Alec away from the financials of any future case. Usually, someone had to drag me *to* the financials, as it was my least favorite part of being a detective.

Some matches truly were made in heaven—and in hell.

I needed to have a talk with the various divines with a tendency to come to the precinct to create trouble for me, and every other single person who dared to seek out employment with the Chief Quinns. Rather than complain about it, I allowed myself a chuckle at the absurdity of my day. "Before you get lost in those papers, care to make a prediction on the case?"

"A prediction? You mean guess who did it and why?"

"Yes. I always brainstorm a list of motives, suspects, and so on, mostly to get it out of my system. If I'm having trouble with a case, I'll ask another detective to review the case first and then refer to my brainstorming session. I've actually cracked one or two cases that way. How? Because you're absolutely right—criminals *can* be stupid. They often are."

"My bet is on money laundering or embezzling—or both. The high number of credit cards implies he's spreading around a lot of purchases in an effort to hide his buying activities. A quick way to launder money is buy illegal things with legal money. Using credit cards to make the purchases, especially if spread around to a lot of lenders, is a good way to hide the activity. If he owed someone money, he could be removing his debt through buying stolen goods or massively overpaying for common goods. This transfers money to the other party without drawing suspicion. It's a fairly common tactic. If you've ever seen a common enough novel selling for a few hundred bucks, I'd give it high chances of being part of a money laundering gig. Nobody with common sense will purchase the book, but someone paying off a debt or laundering money digitally will."

I chuckled, grabbed a notepad, and jotted down his theory. "That's better than what I have, which is basically nothing."

"Basically nothing isn't the same as nothing. What's your guess?"

"The killer hated him and also hates fish, and they decided to get revenge on the fish *and* the victim at the same time."

"Okay. I can understand why you would think your idea is basically nothing, although I will admit it is frightening plausible. I have a question, though. Why would anyone hate fish that much?"

"The first time you smell someone reheat fish in the microwave, you will understand."

WHILE MANY PEOPLE believed in the concept of karma, I was more of the kind to deal with consequences. While some argued karma *was* facing consequences, I lacked the general belief the universe had anything to do with the process of someone getting their dues.

Our victim, Thomas Hardy, made me rethink my stance on karma and its role in the universe.

"Can you repeat what you just said, Alec?" I asked, hoping the accountant-turned-cadet would tell me something other than the first of the secrets he'd discovered in the mire of Thomas Hardy's financials.

"After separating all of his credit card statements by month and reviewing matches by type of store, it appears Mr. Hardy was operating some form of aquatic operation.

There is over three hundred thousand dollars of charges to fish stores in the past three months alone."

Who would spend that much money on fish? Why? The information provided a clear link to the man's death, however, which meant it moved up the priority list to the top. "I'll request a warrant for the receipts," I replied, already regretting the amount of paperwork required to get the information, especially if the stores were outside of our jurisdiction.

"No need. Whomever pulled together the financials had copies of the receipts."

What? I stared at the man. "Impossible."

"Why do you say that?"

"No case ever goes that smoothly. There is no way we have the receipts we want to review right in the box of first financial evidence. It's impossible. That's divine-level magic. I don't even know if the Devil could pull off that trick."

Speak of the Devil, and he might appear applied to my life, and I cursed myself for having drawn the attention of my chief's uncle. "You rang?"

"No. I said your name, and I regret I forgot I should never do that unless I want you to show up." I scowled. As Bailey encouraged bad behavior often, I reached for my coffee mug, determined it was empty, and held it out. "Please make your niece make us coffee."

To my amusement, he took my mug. "As I need to talk to her and check in on the babies anyway, I will do this for you. What do you think I can't do?"

"Didn't peek?" I challenged.

"It's more entertaining when the mortals tell me I can't do something to my face. It makes witnessing their astonishment all the more enjoyable."

When I thought about it, I couldn't blame him. I pointed at the boxes of financial information. "Someone got their hands on the precise receipts we needed with a strong tie to the murder method in our case. I won't have to call a bazillion fish stores after securing a warrant to get the information. That's miracle-level work, Lucy."

"Oh. That. Your victim is meticulous and kept his receipts. That evidence was removed, fingerprinted, and copied before you were notified. As you're generally correct otherwise, I'll give it to you, but just this once. How are you liking your cadet so far?"

"I am doing the things he isn't precisely fond of, he is loving the things I hate. We are developing a functional work relationship."

"An agreement for five dates with your cadet, and I will make sure everyone stays out of your hair about it for a month. I will convert everyone in this precinct to prime examples of how angels should behave."

"You want to accept that bargain," I told Alec. "He is offering us the Holy Grail in this pit of matchmakers."

"Shouldn't we ask for more details about dating first?"

"No. That way, he can't dictate what counts as a date. We can decide, and as long as we label it as a date, we meet the terms of the agreement."

Lucifer chuckled. "The dates may not happen during work hours."

Well, I wouldn't argue with him on that one. "That is fair and reasonable. Alec?"

"I'm fine with that."

Some chance was better than no chance, and five dates would give us both an idea if we could tolerate each other outside of work. "Bargain made. You will have better chances of succeeding at your various schemes if you don't annoy us and leave appropriate gift cards and board games where we can easily find them, with our names clearly labeling them as ours."

Lucifer snickered. "You just want me to send over more incubi with board games for your new collection."

"Until you sent them over, I had no idea I enjoyed board games that much, but yes. Your schemes have a higher chance of success if you include a variety of two-player games in the mix."

"Hint received." The Devil disappeared with my coffee mug.

"Do you deal with him daily or something?"

"Not quite, but he adores his niece and nephew, so he comes around often doing his best to make certain everything is perfect in their world. He is good at scheming, but if you give him an inch, he'll take a mile. The instant you start actually negotiating with him, you've generally lost—unless he likes you and you want a little more out of him. He's surprisingly relaxed about people asking for a little more. As he didn't leave any stipulations on what it means to date, we decide, and if we like the arrangement, great. If not, he'll try to figure out why his initial ploy didn't work."

Alec laughed. "Can we pretend like we hate each other outside of work just to screw with him?"

"I'm calling that a date," I informed him. "Nothing improves my day quite as much as yanking on the Devil's tail and getting away with it—and I know the perfect accomplice in our dastardly deed to drive him to the edge of his sanity."

"Not over the edge?"

I shrugged. "I don't know what it says about me, but I

love the Devil. I don't think you could make a worse enemy or a better friend than him. And let me tell you, there are a lot worse things in life than having the Devil angling for your general happiness. It definitely beats the alternative."

"That's one way to put it."

FOURTEEN

The public adored seeing the cindercorn in action.

THOMAS HARDY'S receipts implied he owned and operated an entire aquarium. With hundreds of huge fish tanks and other supplies unaccounted for, it fell to me to do some more thorough investigation of his life. Fortunately for us, his financial information did a good job of telling us where he often went.

He paid a rather hefty mortgage payment once a month for a property in Pennsylvania, deep in the country, a prime spot to commit a large-scale crime of almost any sort. While it took some work, the chiefs got us jurisdiction to make a visit to the place. While I disliked the idea of taking a green cadet to a completely unknown location in the woods, I held back my complaints.

The Pennsylvania State Police joining us for the ride helped convince me we probably wouldn't be murdered and dumped somewhere, never to be seen again.

"Do we normally get to take field trips like this?" Alec asked, eyeballing the line of cruisers escorting us across the state to our destination. My cruiser, which proudly declared my status as a member of the NYPD, drew more attention than I liked.

"No, we don't, but since it's our case and the CDC wants to get down to the bottom of it, they asked Pennsylvania to play nicely with us. Normally, we hiss at each other from the state lines like angry cats in a territory dispute."

"Is that true?"

I laughed at his skeptical tone. "Not really. We try to get along. Investigations can go to hell in a hurry if there are jurisdiction issues. This is one big jurisdiction issue. The CDC handling the jurisdiction issues makes things easier. In reality, nobody wants this case."

"Now that I can believe. He had how many fish crammed into him?"

"Too many." By too many, I meant hundreds, and the total species count had come out to fifty-three, with a collection of endangered or threatened species to go with the four unidentified species removed from his body. Excepting the precinct's new pet hagfish and the two sturgeon, none of the other fish had survived.

The sturgeon were headed to an aquarium to become permanent and spoiled residents in an effort to help preserve the species.

"Do we have a count of the actual number of fish?"

"I can't remember offhand, but it's in the hundreds. I made a notation in the case file. Honestly, when the morgue called with the autopsy results, warning me they'd be sending an entire box of records over, I did my best not to think about it. Let's just say the prosecutor is going to have a field day assuming we can lock down a solid suspect."

We had more suspects than we needed and insufficient

evidence to do anything more than question people about their relationship with the deceased. My current favorite subject was a woman Alec had located through the financials.

She was listed on four different life insurance policies along with some of his credit cards, all of which had been opened within the past three years. According to the court documents flooding my office, they had filed preliminary documents to be married a little over a month ago.

None of those cards had been used for suspicious aquarium store purchases, which threw a wrench in the investigation. Was she aware of his fishy activities? If so, could his involvement have been part of the motive? The lack of overlap counted as a major red flag and implied he hadn't wanted her to be aware of his activities.

In some ways, his financials had asked far more questions than answered, although that was fairly standard during an investigation.

While we had already questioned the woman about her fiancé, we hadn't gotten much out of her. If I judged solely from appearances, she hadn't had any idea he'd been killed until we'd notified her. Unfortunately, I'd already encountered several instances of loved ones having killed their family and doing a damned good job of putting on an act, so I no longer trusted my eyes.

Some people put on an act. Others reacted to their stress over having been questioned. Some genuinely grieved for the death they'd caused.

The lesson would remain a painful reminder my personal experiences and reactions to grief rarely matched another person's, and I could not judge life based on what I felt or understood to be the truth. Once I had stepped away from my narrow field of experience, I had learned the world was a far larger place than I had imagined, and people were more varied than I'd believed possible.

When I stopped viewing problems with how *I* would approach finding a solution, it became much easier to come up with other possibilities.

So far, I had at least twenty viable reasons someone might want to kill Thomas Hardy using a wide assortment of aquatics, and his fiancée's access to his wealth after his death was only one of them.

"Do you think his girlfriend did it?" Alec asked.

I shrugged. "Right now, I don't really have any idea who did it. Do I think she has motive? Yes. The life insurance policies we know about are worth half a million. A few weeks ago, I dealt with a case where someone killed someone else over twenty dollars. There are too many unknowns in the case. It could have been something dealing with all these aquarium store receipts, it could be involving the life insurance policy, or it could even be using the life insurance policy to clear off her credit card debt." Getting a hold of the fiancée's financials had taken submitting the mutual cards and life insurance policies to discover a mess of debt the life insurance policies would cover with a nice sum left over. "There is a lot of financial backing for the crime to be related to her and her debt."

"But the fish?"

"If she found out about his fish operations, why not? The CDC has already submitted a lot of information to us regarding how the crime could have been committed. The level of practitioner magic required is within the grasp of most."

"That surprised me. I would have thought it would have taken a lot of schooling and skill to commit the crime."

"It surprised me, too. The hard part would have been getting those rare fish."

"But if he had a fish operation going on, couldn't she have gotten them from him?"

"Yes, it's possible. But unless we are able to find evidence, this is only speculation. This is the hard part of the job."

"Hard, yes, but someone needs to do it. I've come to learn if I'm not willing to do it, why would I think someone else is going to be willing to do it?"

In my time in the force, I'd met a lot of people who'd come to that same conclusion, choosing duty over comfort. Those cops tended to be the best, putting the job and service to community over their personal securities. I counted as one, although I hadn't realized I fit the mold until after I'd gotten saddled with my current chiefs and being required to, at least once a week, ride a stubborn and psychotic fire-breathing unicorn while on duty.

For some damned reason I still failed to understand, the public adored seeing the cindercorn in action, and they liked it best when they got to see *me* right along with her husband or stallion, depending on the day of the week.

"I've asked myself that from time-to-time, and the answer is always the same. If I won't do it, who will? And so I do. I serve the public, even when the public wishes I wouldn't serve. The public generally does not appreciate when we bust them for speeding and reckless driving in particular."

"But they appreciate when we bring killers to justice, except for the killers, of course."

I nodded. "The killers really don't appreciate when we bring them to justice for some reason."

"Well, if they were better at committing crimes, they wouldn't get caught."

"Let's not encourage the criminals to be smarter and do better. It's hard enough catching them as it is."

EVERYONE HAD SECRETS, and Mr. Thomas Hardy owned an entire aquarium. Unfortunately, his operations included involuntary labor involving missing people from a collection of six states. Some had been victims of criminal dealings gone wrong, taken from loved ones to send a message. Others had owed debts to the wrong people and hadn't been able to pay.

I could understand why someone might want to eliminate the man using his passion.

Within five minutes of stepping foot onto the property, it had gone from a fairly unusual murder case to a disaster. If I had been given my way, I would have tossed the entire case to the FBI and CDC to deal with, but no.

They wanted me to continue heading the investigation.

I wanted to go home, make a cup of hot chocolate, and hide for a few weeks.

"This wasn't supposed to happen," I informed Alec in one of the brief moments we weren't being bombarded by CDC or FBI agents out to squeeze every detail they could out of us. "There are countless endangered species here being successfully bred along with a human trafficking ring Hardy used to care for his millions of fish. And that is not an exaggeration. *Millions* of fish. There are millions of fish here, Alec."

He offered me his coffee cup. "I think you need this more than I do at this point. When the CDC agent realized I was a cadet learning investigations, she added some pixie dust to it. Apparently, cadets should be gently pampered rather than thrown into acid baths."

I accepted his cup and took a sip. Sure enough, the CDC agent had laced it with enough pixie dust to make sure neither one of us would be suffering from an anxiety attack after a single mouthful. "Was that when I was getting grilled by the FBI on being in Pennsylvania in the first place?"

"It sure was. Did they give you any problems?"

"No. They just complained I complicated matters. The Pennsylvanian cops backed me up on it, and they had all the appropriate forms with them."

"I think it was the girlfriend now," Alec said, and he stared at one of the nearby aquariums. "She works in humanitarian rights, and the one thing that would trip her trigger would be the enslavement of people. She likes animals, and she'd appreciate the conservation efforts he's putting in this place, but if she found out he used slave labor to care for these fish? Yeah. I could see her shoving a bunch of fish up his ass and hoping they'd eat him alive from the inside."

I nodded, aware of the underlying reasons the woman would go so far. "Her little sister was trafficked. It was one of the few stories with a happy ending."

"There are going to be a lot of happy endings now, but also a lot of pain and struggling. Stockholm syndrome is going to be commonplace. While captive and unable to leave and required to work, these people *like* the fish and caring for them." Alec gestured at an elderly couple. "Their son is heavily involved with a crime ring, and they were taken as leverage. They handle feeding a lot of the fish. It gives them purpose and meaning, and they don't want to leave."

Alec had a tendency to listen, and not only did he listen, he took the time to think about what he learned. "I have no idea what will happen to this place," I admitted.

"It will become a rehab center for the victims and a proper aquarium," Lucifer announced from behind me. I screamed, but before I could fling Alec's coffee halfway to the moon, the Devil rescued it. "A little jumpy today, aren't you?"

"Well, you did appear behind her and gave no warning before talking. Most would react in a similar fashion. But thank you for saving the coffee. We need the dust in that coffee to get through today."

I rescued the coffee from the Devil, took another swallow, and gave it back to its owner. "Thank you. Especially with him here, I definitely needed that."

Alec chuckled. "He's not that bad."

"Alec, he's the Devil. He *is* that bad."

"I'm so bad, I'm good," Lucifer added with a grin. To keep the general peace, and to keep from freaking out the men and women who would need a lot of time and help to come to terms with their freedom, he had opted to show up as a white man dressed in a suit, although he had a pair of flaming horns peeking out from his hair, which did a good job of warning people some prime evil lurked among them.

"I don't lurk."

"You most certainly do lurk," I replied. "Why are you here?"

"Your cindercorn has separation anxiety, so she called me."

I rolled my eyes and let out an exasperated sigh. "Are you serious?"

"You left her for the entire day, maybe even *two*, Josefina. Then she realized she left you with a cadet. You might be doomed or something."

"Doomed?" I asked, raising a brow.

"Stuck with a cadet without any form of birth control or condoms."

I slapped my forehead. "What is *wrong* with that woman?"

Alec tittered and sipped his coffee. "Do we only have to pick one thing? I have a list. It adds to her charm, though."

"What charm? She sent the Devil here to do what?"

Lucifer laughed, snapped his fingers, and manifested an overly full bag from the pharmacy down the street from my work. "She bought all of this stuff for you. She put in so much effort trying to secure your happiness."

As I couldn't tolerate the thought of rejecting the crazy cindercorn's help and thus hurting her feelings and adding more chaos to the general insanity at work, I accepted the bag. "Please remind your niece I am perfectly capable of handling my own birth control purchases as they're needed, should they be needed. Virgin doesn't mean ignorant or stupid. It just means I am more stubborn than you are."

"I'm going to feel that burn for a while. I'm going to tell my wife that, and she's going to reward you. She might even take pity on me for a change."

"I wish you the best of luck with that, but don't hold

your breath, Lucy." I braced for the worst and peeked inside the bag. With at least six boxes of condoms, if I decided to end my days as a virgin, I'd be set for a while. "Did she buy the entire selection of condoms?"

"I think so. My nephew actually went with her and attempted to contain the insanity, which is why there is only one bag of items."

"Remind me to thank him for that later." I held the bag out to Alec. "I think this hint is directed at you."

Alec headed for the nearest fish tank setup and set his coffee on one of the lower shelves before taking the bag, crouching, and investigating the purchases. "You mean beyond the hint I received when I came into work this morning? She cornered me and said I had a chance because she'd booked us a special room at a nice hotel not too far from here."

The cindercorn would drive me insane. "Even if we were to make use of any object in that bag, we will keep our status secret," I informed him.

"That's going to drive her right off the edge into the realms of madness," Lucifer warned.

"But will she be bringing us coffee while she's going mad?" I replied with a wicked smile.

"I'm telling my wife you are a flirt," the Devil complained. "That's just evil, and I love it."

"I have no interest in flirting with you, Lucifer."

The Devil clutched his chest, fell to his knees, and reenacted a death scene. While he went about his slow and agonizing death, I angled for Alec's coffee, drank down half of what was left, and offered the rest to him, which he guzzled. "Now that I have felled one source of great evil, let's see if we can get some actual evidence about this case, Mr. Mortan."

"That sounds like a good idea. Good luck with your heartbreak, Lucifer," Alec replied, chuckled, and set the empty cup beside the Devil. "Once you're done there, if you could throw that out for us, that'd be great."

EIGHT HOURS after discovering the aquarium, we had gotten some substantial evidence regarding the kidnappings of those forced to care for the millions of fish in residence. The credit card purchases all fell in line with the operational costs of his facility. With the awareness of the number of custom tanks, ponds, and various other habitats, we were able to pinpoint all associated transactions. We had no idea where he'd earned the money for his projects, but I suspected the crime lords had paid him off to make the victims disappear.

For a rare change, the victims were worth more alive than dead.

In an effort to ease proceedings, someone had gotten the idea to bring in experts from around the United States to check in on all of the inhabitants. It didn't take long for them to acknowledge the expertise of those who operated the aquarium.

The setup amazed the professionals, as did the number of successful breeding projects other aquariums had tried without luck for years.

We even found an entire huge pool dedicated to the

toxic hagfish, and they shared space with some coral, clown fish, and a few unidentified species of fish.

According to the caretakers of the hagfish, one had gone missing. At last count, they had over a thousand of them, and they bred early and often, which made tracking them, even with magic, rather difficult. They'd only noticed because the missing hagfish had a reputation of being the first to show up for dinner and the last to leave after their meal had been served.

The sturgeon had come from a breeding program meant to reintroduce the endangered species back into the wild. Most of the aquarium's residents, many of them highly illegal to own without a permit, were slated in some shape or form for conservation and population recovery.

Lucifer followed me around like a demented puppy, but I tolerated his presence because he understood the importance of coffee and kept bringing us fresh cups when we ran out.

"Why haven't you left yet?" I finally asked the Devil.

"I'm waiting for the CDC to swallow their pride and admit they want to ask me for help running this place. And they will. It's hugely entertaining watching you try to do your job while the CDC and FBI hover. I've been asked to give a performance report. I will be forced to give you a most excellent grade. You haven't tried to throw me into a tank once, and I'm far more annoying than any of the agents bothering you."

"You're supposed to be the Lord of Lies, Lucifer."

"It's so much work keeping the lies straight," he complained.

"So, about Alec's curse," I prompted, gesturing to the cadet, who had been thoroughly charmed by one of the stingrays, who lived in a pool not far from the hagfish. Upon learning he could pet them and they loved to be petted, I'd lost the cadet to his love of wildlife he could pet.

There was a lovable shark in the neighboring room who lived to be cuddled, and I had been forced to retrieve Alec several times so we could get work done rather than play with the friendlier aquarium residents.

"He has come to terms with the reality he may never know its source or why he drew the short straw. His decision to make the most of his circumstances will ultimately be why he one days frees himself from its burden. While I have learned the source of that mystery, solving the mystery is not what will ultimately break the curse. His choices and decisions will be. While I could tell you who has done it and why, I won't. That is part of the journey. I can say if he truly wants to discover the truth, it is within his power to find out. But will he want to?"

I could make a guess or two, but I settled with my favorite, and I asked, "Will his willingness to pursue justice be the deciding factor?"

"Yes, but it is a lesson he must learn on his own. It's not much of a curse if he loves the work he does pursuing justice, is it?" Lucifer shrugged. "It's not that I don't want to help you. I don't enjoy making the undeserving suffer, but I also understand that helping you now would hurt you even more later. It is because I like you and your cadet that I will hold my silence."

Upon reflection, I realized the Devil had the right idea, and that we could live without knowing the full and complete truth. "If anything, his curse would become a blessing, if his life's mission *is* to secure justice for the wronged."

"You will give voices to the silenced in ways you never thought possible." The Devil gestured to the collection of aquariums and pools filling the massive room. "This changes the nature of the crime substantially, doesn't it?"

"It really does. And it's not a crime we will solve neatly, with every string tied and every clue isolated, confirmed, and used in the pursuit of justice. It might take us years to come down to the bottom of this." At last count, three hundred people had called the aquarium their home, held hostage with a potent form of practitioner magic that would take an angel to safely break. "I don't know if we'll ever solve every element of this case."

The practitioner, one Thomas Hardy, could no longer undo the chains binding them to their prison. Once freed, I expected the victims would need a great deal of time before they would willingly leave the complex.

Almost all of them had found purpose in their projects, and they didn't want to abandon the aquarium and the work they'd done over long years separated from their friends and family.

"Hardy's murder opened a flood gate. But at least his murder can be explained and justice can be found. The murderer will have regrets by the time you finish." Lucifer looked me over and chuckled. "How do you like your first taste of large-scale crime?"

"I spent all day hoping some kind FBI agent would send me home," I confessed.

"That will not be happening. Every piece of evidence in this place needs to be catalogued, and as the murder victim is your jurisdiction, you will be in charge of everything. But, think about it this way. You have access to the FBI and the CDC. Help is only a request away if you do not know how to handle something of this scale—and handling something of this scale will teach you many lessons of use down the road. You might say this is part of your fate, just like it is the fate of your cadet to face his curse and its many deaths, none of which will be his own."

"Well, that's something."

"I am slightly concerned with how much enjoyment he is getting from petting that stingray, though."

I regarded the cadet, chuckling at his open delight. "I'm worried about if I ever have to take him to a zoo. He might want to start petting the big cats. They won't be nearly as charitable about being touched."

"My wife becomes a snow leopard, and she isn't very good at hiding how much she enjoys when someone scratches behind her ears. Arrangements could be made. My daughter becomes a lion, and her husband is a kelpie. If he wants to pet dangerous wildlife, I can provide."

"Did you just call your family dangerous wildlife?"

"They're wild, they're alive, and they're dangerous, so yes."

"I'm doing you a favor and not telling your wife you said that."

"I appreciate that. Thanks."

As the Devil wouldn't do my job for me without a bargain, I would spare us both the hassle and avoid asking any questions I would be able to find the answers to in time. However, he tended to drop hints if he felt something would be a waste of time—or he wanted to get his selfish hands on a sinner. "The girlfriend?"

"Has more than earned her visit with me at a later date. Dig deeper with that one."

Excellent. "I'll pursue other leads as well. This is not a one-woman or one-man job."

"The murder or the enslavement of innocent bystanders?"

"Both."

Lucifer smiled. "I knew you were a smart one."

"Not all of the enslaved are innocent, though." I shrugged. "But I suspect unless any of the crimes were particularly dastardly, things like petty theft will be written off as fully punished in the eyes of the law."

"You're catching on. And to think Bailey was getting so upset her precious rider would crack when the darker realities of being in law enforcement came crashing down. I tried to remind her you'd already seen the realities of it, but she was wearing her blinders while sticking her fingers in her ears."

"There is nothing dark about accepting somebody has paid a far larger price than they should have. And anyway, if you ignore the human rights violations at play here, isn't this like community service, but worse? It shouldn't be hard to suggest to the right people that adding to their hardships may not be the right choice."

The Devil patted my shoulder. "For that, I'll make sure you have a nice dinner brought to your hotel so you can attend to your cadet properly. And I'll even live up to my name of the Lord of Lies and make sure all of my devils and demons know to tease you about your virginity long after you've ditched it for more pleasant pursuits."

I snickered at that. "Even your nephew?"

"Especially him. I'll ask him to keep his mouth shut. He'll cooperate because his wife becomes exceptionally entertaining when she realizes he's played her. He so rarely plays her like that, and it revs her engine. Tell me, do you like fish?"

"Apparently, I do. Why?"

"Some of these fish are better off in loving homes where they won't show back up in the environment, and they would not thrive in my many hells. Their natures are simply too gentle, and it would be difficult to buffer them from the miasma. Most beings can adapt, but not these gentle spirits."

Ah. I'd heard about the Devil's soft side for animals, something that created many problems, as mortal animals tended to shy away from the Devil until they had a chance to adapt to his devilish energy. The work dogs all needed a week or two to get used to him, and while he tried to hide it, I'd noticed his distress.

At heart, Lucifer remained an angel, albeit a twisted one.

"You understand. They would be sickly in my care, but as neither you nor your man have devilish ancestry, you will be good caretakers for them. I'll help set up their habitat for you, and I will mask my energy when I come to see them with some help. My secretary has been practicing for when we have to handle delicate species."

"You've been avoiding their section of this aquarium, I take it?"

"I have all but smothered my presence here."

I nodded. "I don't mind taking care of some fish as long as I'm taught what I need to do, especially if they can't go back into the wild."

"They would not live for long. Their habitat is long gone, and there is no place for them in the wild. But, perhaps with time they can be a beloved species bred in captivity, a beautiful jewel of the waters humanity can enjoy, thanks to the compassion of an evil man."

"I wouldn't normally associate evil and compassion," I admitted. "But at least he isn't yet another psychopath with a history of a poor childhood and known to hurt animals."

"He didn't have a bad childhood, and he's always loved animals more than people. But that's what led to here. People never had value to him. Animals did. Humans are delightfully varied. I will give you some free information, however."

"Oh?"

"If you don't tell someone you are going to your hotel, you will not be leaving from here. The FBI and CDC will bring in the evening shift to help deal with this place, keep it running, and learn what is needed to keep all of the residents alive. Oh, and when they ask about the otters, shrug."

"Otters? What otters?"

"The ones on the other side of the complex that I will be stealing."

"Lucifer, you can't steal the evidence," I scolded.

"Like hell I can't steal the evidence!"

"No."

"I'm taking the otters."

Arguing with the Devil wouldn't result in anything, so I grabbed my phone, dialed his wife's number, and listened to the ring tone.

"Hello?" Darlene answered, which warned me something held her attention.

"Please tell your husband he cannot steal my evidence, Darlene. We haven't even registered them as evidence yet, so he can't steal my evidence."

The Devil's wife laughed. "Did he find some otters at the crime scene?"

"Apparently."

"Tell him to come home and fill out the paperwork to adopt the otters properly. The CDC will play ball with him, as he has no sense and an ever-growing love of otters, but I'll make him follow protocol this time. Thank you for the warning. Ask him how many new residents we'll be getting, please."

"How many otters, Lucifer?"

"Fifteen," he announced.

"I heard him," Darlene said with laughter in her voice. "I'll have some of the fucking assholes get to work on their residence. In the meantime, tell him he is to compensate you for being a pain in the ass and bothering you while you're working. I've also been notified you'll need a second safe space for coffee for your cadet."

"Yes, considering how today has gone, I expect Alec will need a safe place for his coffee. While you're working miracles, tell my bosses they are mean, mean people, and that I will be crying myself to sleep tonight because I have to pretend I'm qualified to wrangle the FBI and CDC. They're all up in my investigation!"

"Made you stand around and just confirm if you're okay with how they're proceeding?" she guessed.

"Basically. I get to investigate after all the evidence is carefully gathered. I don't know anything about pulling evidence off fish tanks, so I've been watching Alec pet a stingray."

"Enjoy the view?"

I chuckled at her well-aimed tease. "They're both

adorable, but I don't have space to house any stingrays, so he can't take one home with him."

"Miniature stingrays exist, and some of them are cuddlers."

"Repeat that, please?"

"Miniature stingrays exist, and some of them are cuddlers."

I heaved a sigh. "I'm surrounded by animal-obsessed freaks, aren't I?"

"You absolutely are. Don't worry. You'll get used to it. And once you get used to it, you'll join us. This is your fate, wolf wrangler."

"I'm getting a police dog, not a wolf. And I'm just in line."

"That's what you think," Darlene said, before hanging up on me.

I bowed my head and heaved a sigh.

"She told you about the wolf, huh?" the Devil asked.

"You will follow proper channels for the adoption of your otters, and you will not ruin *any* of my evidence. You ruin any of my evidence, and I will give you a taste of hell you will never forget, Lucifer."

"I'm telling my wife on you," he muttered.

I held out my phone. "Go ahead and try me."

The Devil stared at my phone, narrowing his eyes. After some hesitation and a sigh, he took my phone and called his wife. "I was just tricked, my darling. She's making me try her, and she's going to win, because she's going to make me use filthy words again."

I rubbed my temple, wondering if I could ask for hazard pay for babysitting the Devil. "I don't have all night or nearly enough painkillers for this headache you're making, Lucifer."

"I said I would tell on her to you, my darling. She said if I ruined her evidence, she'd give me a taste of hell I'd never forget. She shouldn't be flirting with me when her cadet is nearby."

Alec glanced up from playing with the stingray to raise a brow. "You aren't even competition, so why are you posturing? We're not even in the same league. I'm a bachelor of sterling reputation. You are not."

Oh. My eyes widened. Would Alec survive? If he did, would I need to nurse his wounds when the Devil snapped at the implication of being inferior to a mere mortal? I could handle caring for him while he recovered from whatever evils happened to him in the next ten minutes.

Lucifer sighed. "Darling, her cadet's joining in, and I feel it is unfair I'm being goosed by a pair of mortals. The one keeps rejecting my incubi, and the other keeps rejecting my succubi, and they are being absolutely rude."

I turned my attention to Alec. "You've been rejecting succubi?"

"I figured if you could tell a bunch of incubi no, I could tell a bunch of succubi no. It was a challenge to see if I had the emotional fortitude to handle daily temptation. He's been sending succubi over daily since the day I joined the academy. I made them dinner, and when they discovered I'm barely capable of cooking, they gave me daily cooking lessons. I'm no longer a scourge upon this world—or at least a scourge upon any kitchen I step into." Alec gave the stingray a final pet before joining us. With zero evidence of caring, he faced the Devil, and stole my phone. "Hey, Darlene. How are you tonight, sweet angel?"

Lucifer's shoulders slumped. "I can't even get mad at him, because whenever he does that, she becomes so damned happy."

I patted his shoulder. "It's okay. She is a sweet angel, and it does not appear he's flirting with her."

"Her favorite hobby is torturing fucking assholes in my many hells, and you two think she's an angel."

I grinned at Lucifer's disgruntled tone. "She protects my coffee. This is important. I have never seen her be anything other than an angel."

"Haven't you learned angels are assholes yet?" the Devil asked, scowling at me.

I had, although I appreciated Sariel's asshole tendencies, and I made a point of sending him a card once a month thanking him for sparing me from a living hell within my uterus. "But she's a nice angel."

"Sorry about that, Darlene. I suspect Josefina is hungry, so she's getting snappy at your husband. This sort of entertainment can't be purchased for any price. At what point should I save him?"

Lowering his head, Lucifer muttered something and sighed. "Outdone by mere mortals."

"She says you should come home so she can tend to your mortal wounds. She is offering to kiss it all—"

The Devil disappeared in a faint cloud of sulfur, and I coughed, waving the fumes out of my face. "Well played, Alec. I thought he'd never leave."

"Darlene hasn't fed in a week, she's hungry, and he's been busy with really important matters, so he's hungry, too. The chiefs texted me earlier and asked that I make sure he headed home for some attention before one of them snapped and killed somebody. While you two were verbally sparring, she confirmed there will be dinner at our hotel along with a few presents in the form of gaming laptops. We're children who need toys. I have no idea why she thinks that, but I'm not going to argue, not when I get a free gaming laptop. Our salary does not allow for gaming laptops without a lot of preplanning."

Damn. Alec had played the Devil. "Has anyone told you competence is sexy?"

"I may have heard something like that, from the incubi determined to figure out how you tick. For some reason, demons keep showing up and dropping hints when they aren't teaching me important life skills, like how to cook, clean, and not bring shame to my household."

"They made you be domestic?" I rubbed my brow above my eyes, questioning everything about my life. "I don't know if I should be sorry on their behalf or concerned you needed lessons—or disgusted at myself to understand how much I appreciate someone who can handle half the household chores."

"Honestly, I expect to do most of the chores. I do my best thinking when I'm cleaning, and it only took a succubi a few weeks to teach me how to clean effectively *and* mindlessly so I could think while I work. And cooking is like math with food, and I really like math *and* food."

I picked up the pharmacy bag, gathered everything I had brought with me, made certain I had my cruiser keys, and nodded my satisfaction over my checks. "I am finding those FBI and CDC liaisons, and I am telling them we are going to the hotel, where we will be inaccessible for twelve hours. I've been told there will be food at our hotel, and I'm sure I can figure out a math problem you can help me solve."

"What sort of math problem?"

"It's a very complex algebra equation."

Alec snickered. "Algebra, is it?"

As I wore the ugliest sports bra on the planet, he'd get to witness my bra vanish and become a mystery. "Chemistry is science, so we'll have to play with that after we explore the mathematical possibilities of algebra."

"How long does it take to ditch the FBI and CDC?"

"Good question, but if they know what's good for them, less than five minutes. I'm hungry."

"Are you, now?"

I smirked at his tone, which implied he'd caught onto the double nature of my comment. "Starving, even, and I have plans on enjoying dessert tonight."

Afterword

Dear Reader,

I hope you enjoyed 101 Ways to Die! The short novel remains much as it was in Dirty Deeds 2. The four primary stories found after this afterword are slices of life snippets, things that wouldn't be included in a novel like this but are fun snapshots of the characters' lives.

I hope you enjoy this fun foray behind the scenes.

If your version of the book has a fifth story beginning with "Pilot," I hope you enjoy that as well! The instructions at the start of the story will be valid for the months of June and July of 2023.

If your version of the book does not have the "pilot" short story, it is due to one vendor's aggressive error-reporting policies; that vendor does not receive the bonus short story.

I do ask, if you find a mistake in one of my books, that you remember my books are worked on entirely by living, breathing people. Vendors do not have, nor should they have, creative control over an author's work. As a courtesy to those who wish to be helpful and have a place to report typos, I maintain a form on my website, which you can find here: https://www.thesneakykittycritic.com/found-a-typo/.

FIFTEEN

Interlude (During Chapter 10)

WHILE I HAD the hotel near work until the police-hired real estate agent could find me a closer place to live, the day after Alec Mortan returned to his life and I was given the keys to a shiny new police marked SUV, I headed for the questionable comforts of home. In reality, the hotel beat my apartment in all ways. Before leaving the parking garage, I put my new city-issued cell phone to use, hooking it into my vehicle's sound system.

After my old banger, driving something unlikely to abandon me at the side of the road counted as a novelty. I put the SUV into gear and began the tedious process of escaping Manhattan.

Once on the road, I pressed the voice-command button on the steering wheel and said, "Call Mom."

The vehicle complied with my wishes.

Nice.

"Hello?" my mother answered, her tone a blend of puzzled and concerned.

"Hey, Mom. It is the most beautiful and elegant of your children. I have been given a work phone," I announced, rather proud of my status as the owner of two phones, one of which would work reliably. "Is it too late to impose for dinner?"

While my parents could retire if they wanted to, both worked, and they preferred staying up past their bedtime and eating dinner at a horrendously late hour. I suspected they had adjusted their schedule so I could impose on them, as I tended to work the morning or afternoon shifts and often hadn't been able to go home until well into the evening.

"It's not too late. I haven't even started cooking. Is everything all right?"

"I got transferred."

"Oh." While she only issued one word, I understood how she ticked. With my asshole of an ex-boss in the picture, she assumed the worst. Reality was a strange and cruel mistress.

I giggled at the awkward silence. "I would say I have a brand new cruiser, but it's actually an SUV. Apparently, as I don't have four legs and hooves, I have to be able to haul saddles, bridles, and other equine junk for my new bosses."

My mother sucked in a breath. "You got moved to the mounted patrol? I knew you wanted to, but you'd gotten passed over because of your captain."

"I deserve a celebratory feast, Mom." I got stuck at a light, and I tapped on the navigation panel, delighted to find my new phone had pulled out their address from my contacts as a possible place I might wish to go. I pressed the button to make the system give me the fastest path.

Traffic would only cost me an hour and a half.

"I'll make something nice. How long will it take for you to get to us?"

"An hour and a half. I promise I won't abuse my sirens or lights getting there faster."

"Good. I'd hate to have to break another slipper on your hard head."

I laughed, as my mother's method of discipline often involved flinging one of her house slippers at me when I did something worthy of punishment. One slipper had connected with my thick skull, bouncing off to end up in the fireplace. "I wasn't the one responsible for the loss of that slipper. I still don't know how it managed to fit between the grate and the fireplace."

"I still blame your father for not having put the grate back into place properly after stoking the fire and adding a new log. If you had behaved, you wouldn't have gotten the slipper."

"I still question how you have such good aim, Mom."

"Long years of practice. That, for the record, is entirely your responsibility."

I had an entire herd of little brothers, all of whom were members of the force on the mainland, careful to avoid the Bronx in case they got pulled into the insanity that was New York City. "I had you fully trained before those cretin brothers of mine got a chance to help you improve your slipper-throwing skills?"

"Precisely. I will summon your brothers, and I will make certain they bring you presents appropriate for your good news. Do you have a horse yet?"

"Not precisely." When my mother found out about the cindercorns, she would lose her mind. "When you summon my brothers, tell them to check my record first, that way they know what presents to bring me."

"Again?"

I grinned; I had made my brothers find out I'd become a cop through that method. I had been a little slow to the chase due to my decision to go to college before applying to become a police officer. They'd gone straight into the academy as soon as they'd been eligible, making the decision to avoid everything to do with New York City. "Again. It's more fun this way, Mom. I need a little fun after the week I've had."

"All right. I'll let the other brats know they need to snoop on you before coming over. An hour and a half should be enough time to summon everyone. I'll get your dad to run to the store for a treat."

"Strawberry shortcake?"

"I think he can manage to swing by the bakery to see if they have any left. Drive safely, and call if you'll be delayed."

"Will do."

She hung up, and I grinned, wondering what sort of inane things the Chief Quinns had put into my police record. With how things had gone, I expected chaos in the form of the cindercorn laying claims of ownership upon my person.

I'd find out soon enough from my brothers, who would go out of their way to rib me, for that was what my family did when given a single opportunity.

A COLLECTION OF SIX CRUISERS, older ones like the piece of shit I'd traded in, littered my parents' front yard. My family, to honor me, had left a spot sufficient to park the SUV in the driveway. I took it while laughing my ass off, as my SUV could handle the grass better than their vehicles, all of which likely needed some tender loving care from me.

I killed the engine, got out, and used the fob to lock my new baby, and as she was all of a day old, I gave her roof a kiss and a loving pat.

My brothers, still in their uniforms and fresh off work, piled out of our parents' home to swarm me. Before they could get a hold on me, I made a sweeping gesture and showed off my new SUV. "Behold! Some other bastard now must deal with my junker. Look at her. Look how beautiful she is. She had eleven whole miles on her when they gave me the keys."

My brothers, aware I might turn into a banshee should they not indulge me, spared a few moments to admire my new ride.

"It seems your cruiser has a strange shape," the youngest of my brothers, Ricardo, stated, and he circled the vehicle. "She is oddly tall. There is very little dirt upon her. Every letter is crisp and clear." He paused at the questionable logo showcasing my status as a detective on the back near her gas cap. "She also seems to be a detective's vehicle."

I pulled out my badge and beamed, showing off my new and shiny picture, rank, and number, as the Chief Quinns had given me free rein to pick my new identification number. I'd selected 06660 because it cracked me the hell up with the bonus of potentially summoning the Devil every time I used it.

"06660?" Ricardo swiped my badge out of my hand

and read it over, laughing before grabbing me, hugging me close, and spinning me around. Once he set me on my feet, he said, "We have not told our parents about your promotion, but I'm afraid we have done something truly terrible to you."

"Cindercorn plushies?" I guessed.

"There is a real, live horse in their living room."

I regarded my brother, who had come out of the parental mixing vat looking just like the rest of us, although I carried the burden of feminine beauty rather than handsome masculinity. "There is not a horse in their living room."

"She's a year old, and she should make a good cop horse for you down the road. She's a flaxen liver chestnut."

I did the math: I had six brothers who had been given a budget of an hour and a half, and one of them worked with the mounted police in New Jersey. The probable culprit, named Henry because my mother loved the name and felt at least one of her sons should be named after a king, grinned at me.

I snatched my badge, plowed through the pack of brothers barring my way, and stormed into the house.

Sure enough, there was a young horse with a dark coat and a pale mane and tail standing pretty as a picture in my parents' living room, accepting treats from my mother.

"I am *so* sorry, Mom," I said before claiming the yearling's lead line. "Where does this horse actually belong? I would *never* let those jerks bring a horse into the house!"

My mother laughed at me. "I allowed it because your brothers wanted to surprise you. Apparently, you are receiving a gift of a horse, which your brother will raise until she's old enough to ride. You'll be expected to visit her when you can. He will also take care of training her so she can be used on the job. She is a legitimate candidate to become a police horse. Her name is Marigold."

The filly regarded me with bright eyes, her ears pointed forward. I let her sniff my hand, and once she satisfied herself, I rewarded her with a petting. "I'm still taking her outside."

"Let her loose in the back. You know your brothers have basically turned it into a paddock for horses anyway, in case work comes home with Henry."

I clucked my tongue to catch Marigold's attention, and she followed after me willingly enough. Henry must have taught her how to handle steps, as she descended down with admirable grace. I unclipped her lead line, checked to make certain nothing would cause the animal problems, and spotted my brother's trailer and truck parked in the neighbor's driveway across the way and in the back. Henry's wife, Kelly, who was standing in the bed, grinned and waved at me.

I waved back, and as I loved the woman for containing my brother's wicked ways, I blew her a kiss before heading back into the house.

My brothers joined me in the living room, and they grinned at me.

"A horse, Henry?"

"Your other mounts are temperamental, inclined to forget you may require sane and reliable transportation, and rather chaotic," he replied, winking at me. "Now, tell Mom the real deal, as she's convinced you're part of the NYPD's mounted police."

I showed my mother and father my new badge. "Detective third rank!"

My declaration won me a round of applause, as was our way whenever we jumped another hurdle in our careers. My father eyed my badge number. "06660?"

"As I was being transferred out of my original precinct, they let me pick my badge number. It amused me."

"What's this about having temperamental, chaotic mounts?" my mother asked.

My brothers went for the lumpy, paper-wrapped packages taking over the couch, and because my brothers were jackasses, they threw their gifts at me. I shrieked, defended my face, and dealt with being pelted with the inevitable cindercorn plushies. Once the assault ended, I grabbed one, tore off the paper, and laughed at the soft and floppy stuffed animal, which did a decent job of mimicking the red and black mottling of cindercorn fur. Displaying the toy to my parents, I said, "I don't know which one of you gifted me with a tolerance for insanity and odd magic, but thank you. Because of you, I can ride cindercorns. My other ride is a unicorn, and she's pretty crazy."

My father's expression betrayed his worry.

My mother gasped, clapped a hand over her mouth, and turned to my brothers.

Her foot came up, she grabbed her slipper, and held it aloft. "You *fiends!*"

My brothers wisely scattered, but it was too late for Henry. My mother took aim and flung her slipper, which smacked into his head. "You're celebrating your sister being in a life-threatening situation?"

She went for her other slipper, and Henry almost made it to the door before it connected with the back of his thick skull.

I did the only thing I could. I pointed and laughed at my

brother, who fell to the floor and attempted to enact a death scene to avoid a proper whacking with her shoe.

"We're celebrating her promotion!"

As I did love my brothers, even when they ambushed me with a horse, I caught my mother in a hug and cuddled with her. "It's a really good promotion, and I get to move closer to work. And if I save Henry's life, he'll buy my new horse tack and help me figure out where she'll live closer to my new job."

"I'll call your bosses and inquire if they have spare space in the police stable, especially since I'm working with training police horses," Henry promised, and as he was wise, he crawled over to grovel at our mother's feet. He wrapped himself around her legs, which helped make certain she couldn't reach any more shoes.

After giving my mother another hug, I retrieved my fallen cindercorn plushy and showed it to her. "I will definitely be keeping this on my bed with me. Henry, did you all get me one?"

"They're all cindercorns. We thought you'd like a herd for your room."

"See, Mom? My brothers are demented, but they give good gifts. I'll even stash one in the cabinet in my office and see how long it takes someone to notice it's there. It's not really any more dangerous than what I was doing before."

Henry snorted at the blatant lies coming out of my mouth.

I kicked him.

"Why are all of our children cops?" my father complained.

I pointed at myself, as did Henry. The rest of my brothers pointed at me, too.

"It's true, Dad. All during their youth, they heard me whine and cry about how I *really* wanted to be a cop. I put on all those cop shows, and I made you take us to where we might see the mounted police doing their jobs."

"That's what got me. The first time I saw a cop on a horse, I got it. Josefina has always preferred mysteries and investigative work, but I wanted to work with the horses. The others are just copycats."

I laughed because it was true.

My work phone rang, and silence fell. Retrieving the device and checking the screen, I came to the conclusion my boss had tried to ambush me at the hotel and had not found me where she expected me to be. As the cindercorn called on her cell, I foresaw chaos if I refused to answer. I swiped my finger across the screen. "Ma'am?"

"You're not at your hotel," Chief Bailey Quinn whined. "I was going to drag you to an apartment to see if you like it. But nobody has seen you, so we investigated. You weren't even spotted in the lobby!"

A giggle bubbled out of me. "I'm sorry, Bailey, ma'am. I went to have dinner with my family. I do have a question for you, though."

"What do you need?"

"Where do our precinct's horses live? Is there room for a personal horse? My brother works with the mounted police in New Jersey. He trains horses, and he gave me a filly as a promotion present. He's going to train her to be a police horse, but I need to find a home for her. Would owning a dedicated police horse be a problem?"

"Considering we were thinking about getting you one for when we have two feet instead of hooves, it's definitely not a problem. We have available stalls. I'll make certain she has one, and we'll find you a horse for when you need one until she is old enough to be trained. We don't train horses until they're five at the earliest, but we can handle a freeloader. What's her name? Age? Breed?"

"Her name is Marigold, she's a yearling, and she's a flaxen liver chestnut."

"That's a color, not a breed, but that's a very pretty color, so that's now her breed. Her breed has been accepted."

I nudged Henry with my foot. "What breed is Marigold?"

"She's a Morgan," he replied.

"My brother tells me she's a Morgan."

"One sec." My chief howled for her husband and relayed the information, demanded that a stall be made available immediately, and that she was going to steal a truck and trailer to retrieve me and my beast.

"Ma'am, we can transport Marigold. My brother and his wife are here with their trailer. I have the SUV you gave to me earlier today. I haven't been kidnapped. I took the vehicle *you* gave me and went to see my family for dinner. I'm sure I can even find my way back to the hotel."

The Chief Quinns bickered, and after a moment, my chief protested and the sound changed, implying someone had stolen the phone. "McMarin?" Nilman asked.

Later, I would have to thank *somebody* for a sensible officer having claimed the phone. "Hey, Nilman. Please try to contain the insanity. I went to a family dinner, and my brother gave me a filly to be trained up later to be the most sensible of my equine companions. She's a yearling, so she'll need some time to grow up. I need to find a home for her, and I'll need to schedule time to work with her. I need a sensible animal."

"Well, you're not getting sensible with the Quinns, that's for certain. Considering Bailey is willing to fight Sam over it, your horse will get a spot at our stable. It's not too far from here, and she'll get field trips to the pastures. If she doesn't pan out as a work horse, we can train her for parade work easily enough, and that'll justify the feed and housing bill." Nilman sighed. "Between episodes of snarling at her husband, she has requested I investigate this brother of yours, and I seem to have uncovered a mystery. Why are there seven McMarins in the force within a few hundred miles?"

"I'm a bad influence on my little brothers," I replied.

"They're all your brothers?"

"Yep."

"And they're all younger than you?"

"Yep."

Nilman grunted. "That idiot captain. Hey, gas guzzler. I have verified that McMarin has a brother who works with the horses in New Jersey, and his file marks him as a talented breeder and trainer. If he says the filly will be good, she'll be good. Want me to inquire if they have a horse ready for her to ride?"

"Yes, please," Mrs. Chief Quinn replied, her voice muffled. A moment later, she squealed.

"Sam has thrown her over his shoulder, and he's apologizing profusely, promising he will contain her so you can enjoy the rest of your evening with your family. Please ask your brother if he has any trained horses he can sell to the NYPD for your use."

I rolled my eyes at the fuss but relayed the message.

Henry huffed but nodded. "I'll schedule a call with New York City tomorrow, and I'll bring the candidates to their training stable along with Marigold."

I informed Nilman of the plan, and he promised to make certain everything was taken care of on his end. "I'm sorry. I had assumed once off duty that I could just wander off."

"Oh, you can. Bailey is just excited because she has a line on a place for you. She has forgotten you haven't been home since this started and might like to have your own clothes."

That, too. "I will be swinging by my apartment to gather some things."

"Just let us know if you end up having a long commute in the morning, that way the gas guzzler can make you a proper cup of coffee when you get in."

Well, in that case, I would be staying the night at my apartment or with my parents. "I'm going to do that just as a final reminder of why this promotion is one of the best things to happen to me in a while."

Nilman chuckled. "Enjoy the rest of your night, and I'll see you tomorrow."

I returned my phone to my pocket and regarded my brothers through narrowed eyes. "Has Marigold been given her supper yet?"

Henry laughed, got up to his feet, and kissed my forehead. "She's been fed, so don't you worry about a thing. I'll probably sell them that chestnut bastard you like watching from the fence but never scrounged up the courage to ask if you could have. He likes you because you always feed him treats. And if you fed them any bullshit about not being able to ride a horse because your boss was a piece of shit,

I'll make sure they're corrected—and I'll be correcting you."

I gulped and made a warding gesture against evil. "If I was that good, I wouldn't have gotten passed over for the mounted patrols!"

My entire family snorted, and my mother pointed at the dining room. "I think it's time you sat down and told us what's going on, Josefina."

I widened my eyes. "I heard a rumor at work this week that I have a name that isn't just McMarin. Is this what they meant?"

My brothers snickered, and Henry held up his hand for a high five, which I gave him before grabbing my collection of cindercorns and heading to the table, where I took my usual seat next to my mother. At my mother's curt order I was to keep my ass seated like a good girl, as the newly promoted did not ferry food, I stayed put while everyone else invaded the kitchen.

In true McMarin fashion, my parents opted to argue through food, which featured my father's attempt to convince my mother the Irish had plenty of culinary offerings worth writing home about. Unfortunately for my father, my mother won, as she brought out a taco feast along with a roast.

I waited long enough for her to sit down and offer grace before grabbing the corn tortillas, which were still warm from their adventure in the oven. Rather than sticking to traditional fare, she'd catered to my special needs, which involved the sharpest cheddar she could find and a layer of peppers between my tortillas to make sure I cried with every bite. Whooping my delight, I stole the grilled peppers and went to town in an effort to light my tastebuds on fire.

My mother smiled sweetly at my father, who raised his fist in acknowledgment of his defeat. A bowl of his potato soup made its way to me, and I waved my first taco his way in acknowledgment of his contribution to my dinner.

"While she tames her stomach, why don't one of you boys tell your momma why it's taken so long for your sister to get the rank she clearly deserves if she's been bumped to Manhattan?"

Of my brothers, Tomas was the one most likely to give our parents a straight answer, as he hated my ex-captain. I pointed at him with my taco before taking a bite, careful to make certain everything that escaped made it to my plate so I could fill another tortilla with it.

"Her ex-captain is a prejudiced dick who hates women," my brother announced. "She asked us nicely not to worry you about her work woes."

My phone picked that moment to ring again, and I sighed, relinquished my taco, and checked the display to discover Mr. Chief Quinn wanted to speak with me. Rising, I said, "I need to take this."

I stepped into the hallway, which was the minimum distance to be counted as not staying at the table while on the phone, and answered, "Yes, sir?"

"My wife is convinced you need to be rescued, McMarin."

"From my parents and brothers?"

"She did not anticipate you having six brothers, all of whom are police officers."

I burst into laughter. "Hold on a second." After muting the phone, I said, "Mom, can I put the phone on speaker so everyone can talk to one of my new bosses?"

"Of course. Clean a spot, and if any of you get food on that new phone, you buy it."

With that taken care of, I unmuted the phone and said, "I'm putting you on speaker, sir. I'm the oldest, but I was the last to make it through the academy because I detoured to go to college first, and I was in for six years. After that, I stayed on the bottom rung."

"Because of Captain Frankson," my chief stated, and he huffed. "Well, that problem is officially resolved—and if he doesn't walk the straight and narrow, well, he'll find out I'm not nearly as nice as everyone thinks."

I blamed my mother's tacos for bursting into laughter at the thought of Samuel being nasty to anyone.

My mother raised a brow at me, and I scarfed my first taco down and went to work assembling the next one before the tortillas had a chance to cool.

"Is it true she's going to be your primary rider?" Henry asked.

"My wife's, but she'll get me when my wife is on two feet rather than four hooves. Which McMarin are you?"

"Sergeant McMarin with the mounted unit," Henry replied, "But you can call me Henry."

"You're the trainer. Excellent. What's the real situation with McMarin's riding ability? She seemed to imply she was not all that good, but my wife went into orbit, and she sat the ride pretty as a picture, so I'm suspicious."

"She's good. Mom got me my first horse when I was five, and Josefina was responsible for keeping an eye on me. I was born in the saddle, but she took interest in the mounted patrol once she was assigned her precinct. Things didn't work out, so she lost a lot of confidence. I've got a bastard of a horse she loves and can handle that would make a good patrol horse. He's fifteen, and he adores Josefina. He'll set any other rider on their ass if they don't ride just right, so you can use him for training whenever she doesn't need him."

"How much for him?"

"He's worth about twenty-five thousand as is," my brother replied.

"Sold. We'll negotiate the final price to account for any extras I'm missing but assume he's as good as sold at that price. Now what's this about the flaxen liver chestnut that's got my wife bouncing off the walls?"

My entire family laughed, and I got up to check on the horse to discover my brother's wife was working her on a line. I opened the back door and ordered the woman to get her ass inside, wash her hands, and have some tacos before the gluttons ate everything.

Kelly laughed, released my filly, hugged me on the way in, and did as told. Rather than grab one of the spare chairs, she decided the only place for her was on my brother's lap.

"I picked this filly for my sister out of last year's babies, hoping she'd either get a promotion finally or decide she can have a horse. I got tired of waiting for those circumstances, and I decided she was getting Marigold at the first sign of good news. She's a good horse, and I think she'll pan out to be an excellent police horse. She's patient, she wants to learn, and she's smart."

"McMarin, the gas guzzler will trot you over to our stable at least every other day to work your horses, and it's not a far drive to get to from the place we found for you. We'll make a contract for the filly and your other horse, so they'll be your animals but earning a salary for being work animals."

"Shouldn't I be paying for the horse then, Samuel, sir?"

"No."

With one curt answer, Samuel won the adoration of my brothers. I smothered a giggle through taking another bite of my taco. "This won't be a problem?"

"It's not a problem. You have to put up with the gas guzzler at her worst, so frankly, that sort of bonus is something the commissioner will agree with the instant I tell him. You want a sane horse when we're on set patrols and for parade circumstances."

I didn't look forward to the parades, but I would do my job with a smile. I considered my brothers, and I pointed my taco at Tomas again, hoping he could spare me from being the center of attention.

My little brother laughed. "My sister has sacrificed me to be the one to interrogate you, sir."

My chief chuckled. "I'm ready. What are your questions?"

"Is it true she was passed over for promotion due to her captain's prejudices?"

"It's true. I needed a new promotion for a case, and Detective McMarin met all our criteria. So she was promoted out of Brooklyn to Manhattan. As we bar long commutes, we're going to be moving her to the Manhattan area, although I think you'll find she's readily available for family dinners. Just let one of us know you want her to have dinner with you, and we'll cut her loose. We are aware of her workaholic ways."

My brothers whooped, and I decided the only thing that would save me from my family would be another taco. I delayed long enough to fall upon the bowl of soup to make my father happy before seeking out the hottest peppers on offer, snagging the carnitas, and overfilling my taco, sprinkling diced onion, cilantro, and some lime crema on top. Any other day, my mother would have skipped making the crema, but she catered to my special, non-traditional needs. "Thank you, Samuel, sir."

"Is she always this formal?" he complained.

"Yes," my family chorused.

I joined everyone in laughing and said, "I'd say I'm sorry, but I'm really not."

"Carry on, McMarin," my chief replied. "I'll see you tomorrow. If you're going to be late after celebrating, just text me. I can probably contain my wife."

He hung up, and my entire family stared at me.

"Did your boss just check in with you after hours?" my mother asked.

"Yep."

"And he's a cindercorn?"

"He can become a cindercorn, and I've even ridden him," I confirmed. "I've also ridden Mrs. Chief Quinn. Her name is Bailey, and I'm going to reserve using her name when I want out of trouble."

My brothers grinned at me, and I had to put down my taco to exchange high fives with the entire lot of them. Henry ordered, "Tell us what happened, from the very beginning."

"Well, everything began with one irritated Captain Frankson wielding a piece of paper declaring I had been promoted…"

SIXTEEN

Meeting Josefina

I'D BEEN to enough police stations in my life to have grown numb to the presence of cops. In my search for a silver lining, I wasn't wearing any blood, the cops seemed nice, and the office I waited in beat a sterile interrogation room. If I judged from appearances, I'd be dealing with a stern detective. However, I'd been assured and reassured Detective McMarin would take good care of me.

As every other detective I'd dealt with in the New York City area had been a man, the woman who swept into her office, dodging her fellow cops, stole my breath. With dark hair and skin closer to brown than white, I pegged her as a mix of some sort. I wondered if she had a drop of American blood in her, although only citizens could be issued a badge.

I settled with a probable second-generation American with some form of South American ancestry blended with something European.

I really needed to stop trying to figure out where people

came from based on their appearances alone. Without fail, it got me into trouble, although I'd learned to keep my mouth shut about my speculations.

When those speculations included a beauty like her, with warm brown eyes, a serious expression she worked to gentle, and a proud bearing, I needed to stay on my toes so I wouldn't make a fool of myself.

Once I started telling her the truth, she'd either pity me or join the ranks of detectives who found my predicament impossible.

"According to the meteorologists, we will be wise to bring umbrellas with us in the afternoon, but I wouldn't hold your breath. We are in New York, after all. Mr. Mortan, I'm Detective McMarin, and it's a pleasure to meet you." She held out her hand to shake with me.

Her hand warmed mine, a welcome change to my cold state.

Witnessing death always brought along a chill nothing eased.

Her expression softened further. "I asked someone to make us drinks, but I think I'm going to get away with that exactly once."

Despite everything, I found myself grinning at her, as she'd already stepped away from the usual behaviors of detectives determined to get to the bottom of my misfortunes. They failed, always. I lacked hope the woman could change my circumstances, but I would cooperate, especially if it might help bring justice for those who'd died. "We'd been talking about how you'd just been promoted and transferred to this precinct. I'm just going to apologize now for the trouble."

"You're no trouble, Mr. Mortan." Unlike her fellow cops, when she said I wasn't any trouble, I believed her.

Over the years of being questioned by the police, I'd gotten good at identifying when a cop put up a front or showed me their true colors.

Detective McMarin struck me as the type who disliked sacrificing her honesty and integrity.

After regarding me for a moment, she said, "Be advised that this conversation will be recorded, and if you would like legal advice from an attorney, you may request it at any time."

In some ways, I found comfort in the usual script, which offered us both some protections—and consequences, should we step out of line. "I'm used to the routine. I don't need any legal advice. I'm just the world's most unfortunate witness. Honestly, this office is a lot nicer than the interrogation rooms."

If I could be questioned in an office every time life twisted sideways on me, I'd be a much happier man.

She considered me before nodding, and I wondered what she thought.

I'd seen better days, and unlike my other stints being questioned, I became painfully aware of my myriad of shortcomings.

Of all the cops I'd dealt with, I wanted her to think better of me than most. Her looks played a part; I was only a man, and such a beauty didn't cross my path every day. That her beauty came bundled with intellect and a kind demeanor?

Such things didn't happen every day. In my life, such things happened less often than my tendency to be at the wrong place at the worst time.

"I was brought in to provide a fresh perspective, so I'd like you to introduce yourself and tell me when the trouble started," she stated. While she maintained a mostly neutral tone, her body language remained relaxed, even when she got up from her seat to turn on and work with the digital board taking up a great deal of her office space. I questioned the presence of the whiteboard beside it, but if she wanted to tell me why she had two, she would.

I knew better than to rock any boats or push any buttons.

"My name is Alec Mortan, I'm thirty-four years old, and I work as a forensic accountant. I'm currently employed by a corporation on Wall Street to expose any internal fraud, embezzlement, and so on. My job is to investigate questionable accounts at the company, identify any suspicious money movement, and learn who might be behind the transactions."

My career choice hadn't impressed most of the cops I'd met, although Detective McMarin eyed me with interest. "When did you start working as a forensic accountant?"

As knowledge could make or break a case, I started at the beginning. "When I was twenty-six, I decided I wanted to get out of marketing to work as an investigative accountant. Or a forensic accountant, whichever you prefer. I like working with numbers. While marketing involved a lot of number crunching, I didn't find it engaging enough. There wasn't much mystery to the numbers to me. The only problems I had to solve were making sure my equations were correct and that I showcased my data in an easily understandable fashion."

It had taken me a few years to realize I'd wanted more. I wondered if the lure of solving mysteries had made the woman want to become a detective. Wrinkling my nose, I detailed how I'd gone from being a marketer to earning the appropriate qualifications to work as an accountant. I'd then blitzed my way to becoming a forensic accountant.

"And that's when the trouble started." I sighed. "It was during lunch on my first day, and my new boss took me to a restaurant down the street. It was a nice day, so we ate out on the patio. A driver decided to use the sidewalk as the road and killed ten people and injured a bunch more. I still don't know why he did it. The guy didn't seem drunk, especially not after he got out and made a run for it. Nobody told me what happened to that guy, but he took off down the street at a sprint."

According to her expression, the woman loathed and abhorred cowards who would hit someone and run, and she made a notation on the whiteboard.

She used one to register specific cases, and the other to take notes to deal with later, and I admired her inclination to keep everything neatly organized. To help her, I pulled out the date, time, and case number I'd been given.

Then, without any sign of the pity I usually dealt with, she inquired about my relationship with the victims.

Most nights I lost a lot of sleep wondering what might have been, if only things had been different. Rather than tell her that, I stuck to the verifiable facts.

Feelings wouldn't help her solve any of the murders I so often witnessed.

Rather than discount my experiences, Detective McMarin took the time to look up the case numbers I gave her, telling me of the case's resolution if it had one.

None of the other cops, before her, had bothered.

For the first time in the years following the first death I'd witnessed, I wondered if the beauty with the brains might be able to do something about my circumstances.

I could only hope.

SEVENTEEN

In Training

I REMEMBERED the first few weeks of wearing a uniform declaring me to be a cadet. Like Alec, I'd been ready to jump out of my skin, determined to make the cut and receive my badge. Unlike Alec, the pressure of success and failure had threatened to break me.

Everyone welcomed him with open arms, doing their best to make him comfortable.

The fish case had something to do with that, as no cadet deserved the horrors of that investigation right out of the gate. To make it up to him, I'd snagged Perky and Nilman to accompany us, and we went out for a more traditional beat, patrolling Central Park. The regular patrol remained on duty, although we warned the pairs in the area that we had the murder magnet out for a stroll.

Alec might regret dubbing himself a murder magnet, but all cadets needed to be ribbed a little to test their fortitude. "So, Murder Magnet, what do you think we're going to encounter today?"

He eyed the park and pointed down one of the many trails leading into the shadier, wooded sections. "Is it just me, or is that a prime place to hide bodies?"

We all laughed, as Central Park had more than a few spots good for such things. Before marrying Bailey, Samuel had been one of the driving forces behind cleaning up the park. After marrying her, most people in the area strived to keep the park clean and safe, as the cindercorn tended to make an appearance when someone made a fuss in *her* park. "It used to be, but crime rates have plummeted since we started running consistent patrols. During the busy parts of the day, there are usually ten pairs out and about, and that's excluding the mounted patrols that cover a lot of ground around here. That said, if there is a body, I'm sure you'll help us find it. It might be a little fresher than we appreciate, too."

"And McMarin will end up being the apprehending officer, as she's the fastest of us," Nilman added, taking the time to check his bulletproof vest and his various accessories. "All right, Cadet Mortan. What are you supposed to do before starting a patrol?"

"Turn on the body camera, make sure the microphone is turned on, and do a complete check of my gear, including my weapon should I have one." As cadets didn't carry firearms, we had him armed with a baton and a stun gun, both of which he'd already been taught how to handle. He went through his check while we watched, and outside of Perky giving him some advice on making the vest a little more comfortable to wear, he passed. We all went through the same prep, and I wondered what evidence the body cameras might record.

It would be our first time out and about together, as the

fish case had kept us busy in my office for three weeks. Outside of the station, Alec spent most of his time in my apartment, where we did everything other than work.

I owed the Devil a thank you card and a present.

My morning took a turn for the absurd as Lucifer picked that moment to pop into being. Seeing him dressed as a cop with his little flaming horns peeking out of his hair did me in. I pointed at him, howled my laughter, and beat the shit out of my leg, unable to help myself. I ended up doubled over, gasping for air at the utter insanity of him trying to play at being a cop.

Perky snickered, and he patted my back. "Please forgive Detective McMarin, Lucy. She might one day handle you showing up with the same stoic grace the rest of us have mastered through extended exposure."

"I would be offended, except I kept the horns and flames hoping to get a reaction out of her. Hysterical laughter wasn't the expected reaction, but it'll do. How are you doing, Alec?"

"I'm good. We got a lot of good information out of the financials, so I'm feeling accomplished. Josefina, on the other hand, begged for a patrol this morning. She even got on her knees. She picked her target well, as Bailey does not seem capable of handling Josefina when she's displaying any form of distress. She really, really wanted to do some work she was familiar with. Samuel tried to convince her that detectives didn't go on patrol, but not even he could handle the begging."

After catching my breath, I straightened, although I failed at hiding my grin. "I have spent the majority of my career walking around outside on patrols or in a cruiser, patrolling, patrolling, patrolling. I'm sorry, Lucy. I shouldn't have laughed that hard at you."

"Oh, my darling told me you'd be laughing at me. I'm clearly too marvelous to pull off being a cop."

"You're too mischievous," I corrected. "You are also a king at avoiding punishment for the various felonies you've committed."

"It's only a little felony," the Devil complained. "What is the problem with a little felony?"

I shook my head at Lucifer. "Considering your felonies are usually murder, quite a lot, actually."

"Nobody likes the people I murder, and everyone is better off when I send them straight to my hells in a hurry anyway. I don't see the problem."

"If you're going to pretend you're a cop, at least manifest a proper kit." To teach Alec, I launched into a critique of the Devil's attire from head to toe, busting him on so many counts of inappropriate dress that Perky and Nilman lost their cool and doubled over laughing.

As though sensing I'd torment him until he represented the force properly, he snapped his fingers and manifested the appropriate gear. "Is that better?"

I eyed his firearm, but I decided I didn't want to know if it was properly registered. "It'll do. Your job is to make certain nothing negative happens to my cadet. Do not ask what will happen to you if he gets even a scratch."

Lucifer crossed his arms over his chest. "You are not supposed to be flirting with *me*, Detective McMarin."

While he snickered, Alec refrained from making any comments, a wise move in my opinion.

As there was no way in hell that I would let any of my co-workers catch me flirting with Alec, which I would do with wild abandon in the comfort of the apartment rapidly becoming *our* apartment, I scowled at him. "If my cadet gets a scratch, you *won't* be getting any scratches from your wife, as I will make certain she knows why you'll be on the couch for a few months. And you'll feed her without indulging yourself as needed."

Perky whistled. "Your threats do not need any work, McMarin."

I smiled at my fellow cop. "Why thank you, Perky."

"He'll be fine," Lucifer promised. "Your cadet will emerge from the patrol in better condition than he started it, brimming with knowledge and confidence. But, perhaps, you should request that *you're* not scratched?"

"That would take a miracle, Lucifer, and I'm not bargaining for a miracle today." At least once a week, I found some way to inflict an injury upon myself, which usually amounted to a broken, bleeding nail or some scratches. "I'm accepting benevolent gifting of nobody in our group dying from unforeseen circumstances."

"I will in exchange for a spa date with my wife, to happen on your next regular day off. I will go take your cadet off to a car show or something."

As my cadet had a secret love affair with cars with big engines and the math that made them work, I would break his heart if I refused the offer. "Only if you go test drive some new cars for Malcolm while you're at it."

"Sold." Lucifer grinned at Alec. "Wear a suit. I'll get some pictures of you with the vehicles as keepsakes, and you'll get special treatment at the dealerships when we go on the test drives."

If a day out with the Devil didn't drive Alec off, nothing would. As I enjoyed my spa days with Darlene, I would consider myself the ultimate victor of our bargain. I lived, and I got a day out with one of my favorite people.

"You disgust me," Lucifer muttered.

I grinned, rubbed my hands together, and admired the park with its plethora of possibilities for a lively patrol. "Patrols make me feel like a cop rather than a paper pusher, Lucy."

"You're going to have regrets," he warned me.

With Lucifer in the picture, when *didn't* I have some form of regret? Rather than worry about it, I went to work, delighting in a brief return to familiar duties and responsibilities.

THE NEXT TIME Lucifer warned me about something, I would remind myself that the Lord of Lies favored the truth as his preferred weapon. The patrol went well enough until I'd stumbled upon, rather literally, a trap set up by a criminal. Like most, their delusions regarding their own intelligence would cost them.

Dropping the corpse of a victim onto a cop's head was a damned good way of riling up every member of the force. I thanked my status as stubborn and hardheaded as the reason for my general survival. Getting clobbered with a corpse made a mess out of my day, especially as the impact knocked my lights out, but it could have been worse.

I could have died, been paralyzed, or otherwise injured beyond ready repair.

Fortunately for me, I regained consciousness within a minute or two of my close encounter with a falling corpse.

Once I could focus enough to recognize that Lucifer smirked, I accepted my status as wrong, somewhat stupid, and regretful. "It seems you are right as usual."

My tongue fought me, but I got the words out semi-intelligibly.

My cadet heaved a sigh from his spot kneeled at my side. "Should I bother asking how many fingers I'm holding up?"

"I'm going to need at least ten more minutes for that, Alec." The corpse, old enough to be stiff but fresh enough to be intact, lay nearby, twisted in a rather grimace-worthy position. "Yoga gone horribly wrong?"

Perky snorted, and he crouched beside me. "In bad news, I had to call it in right away. In worse news, both cindercorns are coming. I doubt it was yoga but rather rigor mortis from where he had been stuffed into the tree with the trap rigged up so the body would fall on the first unfortunate person to enter the area. You were right along the edge of the path, and it looks like you tripped over the side of the trap. The body clipped you on the way down. Lucifer deflected it somewhat."

"Well, she had bargained to stay alive, but she hadn't bargained against receiving a concussion," the Devil stated. "I maintained my side of the bargain."

I lifted my arm, determined everything still functioned, and flipped my middle finger at Lucifer. "Remind me next time to barter for full benevolence."

"Where's the fun in that?" Lucifer replied.

Rather than call him an asshole, I began the tedious process of checking my fingers and toes for signs of damage. Once I concluded I'd emerge with a sore neck and a concussion, I eased myself upright. "Can you at least call in that

I'm not unconscious? Spare me *some* embarrassment, Perky."

While he laughed at me, Perky got on the radio and called in I was still among the living, able to communicate sensibly, and had certain regrets about wanting to go on a patrol. That didn't stop the pair of cindercorns from showing up and fussing, and both steamed and blew flame.

Bailey bucked more than anyone appreciated, and she performed short charges at anyone who dared to encroach on her territory, snorting warnings.

It took Lucifer to calm her down, promising he wouldn't let any permanent harm come to me when present. While waiting for the ambulance, I opted to teach Alec the finer points of dealing with a fresh corpse.

Once I had everyone's attention, I said, "It's always wise to do your best to prevent any unexpected parties from dropping in on you."

Alec snickered, as he loved and appreciated puns more than was wise.

The Devil made strangling motions my way, and the chiefs, both of whom remained cindercorns, regarded me with white-rimmed eyes.

Perky bowed his head and said, "The corpse knocked the sense right out of her, Nilman."

"That is why we're sending her off to the hospital, but I feel she wants us to be punished for her latest trip to the body shop. We just have one problem. Which one of us is going to notify the commissioner that a murderer set a trap, McMarin wandered into it, and that she's headed off for treatment and observation due to taking a corpse to the head?"

"We could sacrifice Lucifer," I suggested. "I'm sure he can handle the commissioner."

"I think not," the Devil replied.

"Oh, I see. You're not man enough to handle the commissioner's wrath?" I replied, clucking my tongue as shaking my head would not end well for me. "I guess I'll have to recruit a real man to handle this. Alec?"

"Sure. If Lucifer can't handle it, I can take care of calling it in."

Lucifer gasped, and he clutched his chest. "Low blow, you two!"

Smiling my sweetest smile, I replied, "You could be the one required to notify my family of my close encounter with a corpse."

The Devil growled something, stomped a foot, and grabbed his phone. "I will find a way to make you pay for this, Josefina."

I blamed the ever-increasing headache for my inclination to hold my ground. Maintaining my smile, I said, "You'll try, but remember... your wife wants me. Not you. Me. And she who controls your wife's happiness controls *your* happiness."

After snarling some curses, he stepped away to make the calls. "Before I'm sent to the body shop, are there any other problems I need to solve?"

Alec grinned at me. "Would you like me to accompany you?"

"And deprive you of an eventful patrol with a body? Never."

"He could help fend off those cops destined to come storming in to check on you," Nilman said, raising a brow at me.

"I've changed my mind, Alec. Would you please accompany me? I want to survive the day, and the cops scare me a lot more than any corpse."

"Why do these cops scare you?"

"They're my brothers."

"Oh."

Oh, indeed.

THE ENTERTAINMENT of witnessing a cadet face off against my entire pack of brothers would amuse me for years to come. As my headache had grown teeth and devoured my brain, Alec swore if my brothers made too much noise and worsened my concussion or headache, he would ride Bastard and have the mean old horse step on them a few times.

Bastard had taken to Alec right away, making him the third person the horse would tolerate on his back. "He really will," I stated in one of the quiet moments where Alec scowled and dared my family to go against his wishes. "Bastard actually likes Alec. I'm not sure how, but Bastard is teaching Alec how to ride a horse, and Alec hasn't been sent to the body shop yet. Hell, he hasn't even taken a fall yet."

"Sugar cubes," Alec replied with pride in his voice. "I made certain to bribe your horse with sugar cubes. And then I groomed him, figured out what he likes the best, and gave him all the attention that he could handle."

That would do it. Bastard loved being groomed, and most everyone was terrified of the big horse. "Just keep your voices down because a corpse to the head hurts like hell. I really wanted Alec's first patrol case to be, well, normal, but there's nothing normal about this one."

"No kidding," Mrs. Chief Quinn said before shoving the whole group hovering in the doorway into the room. "You're crowding the hall and getting in the way. How are you doing, McMarin?"

"I've got a headache you wouldn't believe, but I'm hanging in there, unlike our corpse."

She snickered. "I see your sense of humor has survived. Lucy did take care of the commissioner, by the way. You will be pleased to learn it will be a quick solve. The culprit decided to leave a phone recording to see who would get clobbered with a corpse. Then he posted it to the internet. That made it quite simple to go knock on his door and arrest him. I'm afraid I had to bump the case over to somebody else, though. You'll get to testify about how you got beaned in the head with a corpse and did not consent to being recorded, as the owner of the phone was not present to utilize any loopholes regarding recording people."

"It always amused me that it's fine to record someone if you're present without their consent as long as you, the recording individual, engaged with the target of the recording—and that using security cameras on personal property is legal without requiring consent. Record somebody at a distance in a public place? Hello, lawsuit." I waved at my brothers. "I found a new way to get a few days off work and get paid for it. Tell Mom and Dad I'm stealing a cadet and we're coming over for dinner. No driving for me for at least three days." I grinned, as my overprotective younger brothers would tie themselves into knots over me experiencing the same exact level of risk they did while on duty. "Also, this is one of my bosses, so please don't get me into more trouble than I can get out of today."

Bailey snickered. "Nice to meet you. Do you go by your badge numbers or do you all respond when someone says your last name?"

I giggled. "We point at the McMarin we wish to address or just talk to everybody at once."

"McMarin, once you're released from the body shop, I am expecting you to go spend the rest of the day with your parents. Take your cadet with you," my boss ordered. To make it clear she wasn't joking about her edict, she placed her hands on her hips.

My other boss picked that moment to poke his head into the room. "It's paid time off per the commissioner's order, as he already reached out to the other forces involved with the unique situation in this hospital to make certain everyone could have the same day off together. I just spoke with the doctors and nurses, and if you pass a check in an hour, you can leave. It doesn't look like the concussion is as bad as we thought, although you're still barred from work for a minimum of three days. You'll have a doctor's appointment to confirm you're clear to return to duty. Alec, I've gotten you cleared and insured to drive your partner's SUV, so try not to let the glory rush to your head."

Alec laughed. "This explains why the driving courses were crammed at the start of my schooling rather than at the end."

"Just don't run the sirens or lights unless McMarin tells you to. McMarin, don't run the sirens or lights unless you witness a hit and run or some other form of murder or attempted murder."

I snorted, as the last time I'd run my sirens and lights, I'd done so to notify a would-be criminal there was nothing wise about trying to steal a police horse. That the police horse had been Bastard meant the would-be criminal had escaped with his life to go along with a warning.

Mrs. Chief Quinn, in her cindercorn form, had done the equine equivalent of tiptoe behind the idiot, ready to put an end to the theft with her horn if necessary.

I'd turned on the sirens and lights to prevent more chaos than New York City needed in one afternoon.

"You should have let me bite him," Bailey complained.

I grinned at the memory. "You can't bite people without just cause. If you don't bite anybody, I'll do my best to behave. We'll have an escort, anyway. How much trouble could we possibly get into?"

"More than I care to think about," Samuel informed me in a solemn tone. "All of you healthy McMarins, don't let her escape. She's slippery, and she likes trying to ditch out of the hospital before the paperwork is finished."

"Just how many times have you busted out of the body shop?" Henry asked,shooting a glare my way.

I began counting on my fingers. "Once, twice… honestly, I stopped counting after twice."

While my brothers would make me pay somehow, I looked forward to taking Alec home to my family.

THE CONCUSSION SCREWED around with my sense of balance, which meant instead of the expected three days, the doctors were willing to send me home but refused to authorize a return to work for at least five days. After five days, they might authorize my return to duty, assuming I could pass their basic exams.

As I couldn't walk a straight line even if I tried, I expected to be out of action for two weeks.

I waited until I was in the SUV to huff and puff.

Alec raised a brow at me. "Which part has gotten to you? The ban from using computers, the ban from active duty, or the strong suggestion that you should forgo any engagements with sexual partners for a week?"

"All of it! Bailey had a temper tantrum, Samuel looked like he was going to choke to death trying not to laugh at me, and my brothers were all horrified at the idea that their pristine sister *might* have some man in the wings. And your face betrayed you, sir. You pouted. You pouted at the first sign of abstinence."

"Of course. Why wouldn't I pout? We're both being punished. We could have done thorough testing of myths regarding activities that might lessen the severity of a woman's headache. I did remember I wasn't supposed to be pouting before your brothers caught me, at least."

"That's something." I put my seatbelt on, and I went through the prescriptions we needed to pick up on the way to my parents' house. "If I take these as prescribed, I won't be feeling any pain, that's for sure. They must be afraid of the cindercorns freaking out if I complain that something hurts."

"That I can believe. How long do you think it's going to take Bailey to figure out we've used her thoughtful present?"

"I give it six months. Samuel's doing a pretty good job of masking his reactions, and the various demons and devils in our lives are perfectly comfortable with lying."

Alec snickered. "Lucifer's utter looks of disappointment

in my prowess trip our chief's trigger, which means he's going to keep doing it for the fun of it. Riling her up is one of his favorite hobbies."

I returned my prescriptions to their envelope. "I'm paying for general servitude in platonic cuddling and minimal levels of whining. I'm hoping I'm also paying in my momma's tacos, but I suspect I'm going to be eating soup instead of carnitas tonight. My mother's carnitas are worth killing over. I suspect my father will be the one cooking, as my mother's second love in her life is spice. Concussions and spices probably don't mix."

"Should I be concerned?"

"Only if nobody gives you a lemon wedge or four," I replied. "Go suck a lemon is not an insult in my family. It's salvation when my mother has decided to imbue our food with the fires of hell. If I am telling you to go suck a lemon, I'm trying to spare you from a great deal of pain and suffering."

My phone rang, and the screen informed me that my brothers had nominated Ricardo to be their spokesman. Smiling, I swiped my finger across the screen. "Didn't I leave you like thirty seconds ago?"

My brother laughed, and I appreciated that he kept his voice soft. "We wanted to give your cadet an opportunity to escape. I volunteered to drive you everywhere if he doesn't want to deal with Mom and Dad."

"Hold on." I put the phone on speaker. "It's on speaker now. Alec, my brothers are offering to let you head back to your home and keep an eye on me if you want to escape."

"We could swing by the apartment and pick up some of the family board games," my cadet replied, and he raised a brow at me.

Crap. *The* apartment was not the same as *your* apartment, and Ricardo was not a fool. "We could. It'll surely take at least twenty minutes for the pharmacy to fill these prescriptions, and there's one nearby."

As expected, my brother asked, "The apartment?"

Alec smirked and blew a kiss my way.

I read between the lines. He wanted to meet my family, and he didn't want to be stuffed into the closet. "You know those fraternization policies we ignore in New York City? My precinct throws eligible bachelors and bachelorettes at each other until they're no longer bachelors or bachelorettes. Alec was nominated to deal with me. Technically, he has an apartment in the same building, but we mostly use it to store excess board games, off-season clothes, and stuff like that. Mr. Chief Quinn is aware. Mrs. Chief Quinn is not aware, and the various demons and devils in our lives are getting a little overenthusiastic about yanking on her chain because she's hilarious when matchmaking."

"That was a lot of words to say you're dating your cadet," my brother stated, and then he laughed at me. "So, you're hiding it from your one boss because she's funny?"

"Yes, that's right."

With a rather evil snicker, he said, "We can help with that if you'd like. We can start begging for salvation, as we're concerned for our beloved sister, too old and beautiful to be single."

"Can you wait until my head isn't killing me?"

"Of course. Anyway, we'll act like we aren't aware that you're a couple. You're not going to be up for a board game, though. Sorry to burst your bubble, Alec. She's going to sleep it off because the other option is cry, and my sister hates crying."

"Unless it is from laughter, which happens fairly frequently nowadays," Alec stated, and while his tone indicated he muttered, he controlled his volume to make certain my brother could hear him.

Apparently, I enjoyed sleeping with the enemy, but I would find some way to make him suffer for his cruel betrayals. As I generally failed at making him suffer, I expected we'd walk away from my attempt to discipline him with a severe case of mutual satisfaction.

Well, that would happen once the concussion symptoms eased enough I could engage in the behaviors my doctor explicitly recommended against.

"Is it true, Josefina?"

"I generally wait until my bosses leave before I lock myself in my office, fling myself onto the couch, and laugh until I'm crying," I confirmed. "Is this punishment for failing to notice the trap while on patrol?"

"Yes," my cadet replied. "I'm debating how I'm going to punish myself for not noticing the trap. I've already figured out how our partners will suffer."

Oh, this would be good. "What are you going to do to Perky and Nilman?"

"I'm going to take away their access to our chief's coffee."

There was mean, and then there was downright vicious and evil. I regarded Alec with wide eyes. "Ricardo, I don't know if I want you to relay that to our parents or not."

"As punishment for getting a concussion while on duty, I will be notifying them that your new cadet is even more ruthless than you are and is willing to withhold coffee," my brother informed me.

Well, that would result in my marriage within the next

one to two years, depending on how extravagant my mother wished to be. Having barely survived my quinceañera, I worried.

My mother had been willing to sacrifice most of her traditions, but the quinceañera was the one she had mandated, as she wanted me to have my day of being a proper princess. If we stuck to true Mexica traditions, I wouldn't have endured such a thing; the quinceañera was European in origin. If my mother had her way, I would be properly tying the knot rather than making use of modern rituals.

I could only hope my future partner would not object to the invasion of my family's traditions—or dealing with multiple weddings to appease all sides of our family.

"I might not make it. Remember my quinceañera?" I heaved a sigh.

Alec would understand the American version of the tradition, where the word represented the celebration itself rather than the star of the show, in this case, me. As my mother lacked a single scrap of European blood in her, she'd gleefully appropriated the ceremony, adding it into our traditions.

"As a matter of fact, I do remember your quinceañera. All the pictures are at our parents' place, and should you fail to show up in a timely fashion, your secrets will be made known," my brother warned. "Alec, I'll swing by a store for a few games if that's your jam. We aren't gamers, but if you like family games, we'll give it a try."

Alec shot me a questioning look, and I shrugged.

"Thanks, Ricardo," Alec replied. "I'll make sure that I bring her over in one piece, after we pick up her prescriptions and I make sure she's taken everything on schedule."

"Sounds good. I'll see you soon, Josefina."

WE ARRIVED forty minutes after my brothers, and a clear path in the driveway remained open for our use. I suspected the SUV would be blocked in the instant we parked.

My family would not let me leave until confident I'd recovered properly, which meant Alec would be a hostage for a few days. "I'm going to apologize now."

"Why are you apologizing?"

I pointed at the open spot. "That is a trap. Once you park, we will be staying, and they will use every vehicle here to block us in. They will not move their vehicles until satisfied I'm not going to fall over dead. That could be anywhere between twelve hours to a week. Your status as a hostage is determined by how quickly you charm my mother. You have no hope with my father. I am his little girl, I will forever be his little girl, and you are an interloping male. As I have six brothers, several of which are married, he understands full well how interloping males operate."

"And your mother is Mexican, and your father is Irish?"

"Yes."

"I play rugby. I can take him."

I almost accused him of making bad jokes, except he disappeared several times a week to indulge in his secret hobby. My eyes widened. "Your secret hobby is *rugby*?"

"It is."

"Don't tell my family you're a rugby player. I cannot miss this opportunity to fuck with them." I unbuckled my seatbelt, grabbed my bag of prescriptions, and took my time getting out of the car. "I'd say let me fall on my ass for being stubborn but please don't."

He killed the engine, got out of the vehicle, and came to my side, keeping a close eye on me while I battled to get my feet doing what I wanted. Once somewhat confident I wouldn't fall on my ass, I picked my way to the door, making use of the rails in the appropriate places.

My brothers beat Alec to opening the door, and they shot my cadet glares.

"Did you really think she'd let me carry her up the walkway?"

Had he offered, I might have considered it. "Piggyback rides are fun." As my brothers all had me by at least four inches, I cocked my head and glanced up at the lot of them. "The process of being carried would likely result in vomit. I don't want vomit in my life right now, nor do you."

"Valid point," Henry stated, and he shooed the rest of my brothers out of the way so I could come in.

I beelined right for the couch, eased down, grabbed the blanket on the back, armed myself with every pillow I could get my hands on, and made a nest. Had I been a little wiser, I would have taken off my work gear first, including the bulletproof vest I'd insisted on putting back on at the hospital because the last thing I needed was a serious case of shot.

"Shouldn't you take your vest off first?" Alec asked.

"Should I? Yes. Am I up for removing it? No."

My cadet snorted, came over, and wrestled the blanket out of my hold before tackling the clips and buckles of my apparel, freeing me from my bulletproof vest. I had to sit up for part of the process, but I did so with minimal protests. He claimed my firearm, checked that the chamber was clear, and ejected the magazine before asking, "Is there a gun safe here?"

The sound of happy sighs made me giggle. I pointed in the general direction of the safe we'd all pitched in on so we could visit our parents safely after work before returning to my nest, burrowing in the couch's soft embrace.

"Mom and Dad are in the kitchen working on dinner, so you're stuck with us, Alec. If Josefina is feeling bad enough she's already hiding on the couch, then we're going to have to use our indoor voices and keep things quiet. Are we missing any pertinent facts?" As the quietest of my brothers, Liam tended to dominate conversations when he did participate, as he partnered his quiet nature with a ridiculous amount of determination to be heard when he did bother to speak.

"Do you want the truth, an answer that makes you generally feel better about the situation, or what I would tell my bosses if asked that question?" Alec replied.

Uh oh. "Don't ask him for the truth, Liam. He'll tell you, and then I'll be doomed." Having learned about Alec's wicked side since teaming up with me, I understood he was about to exact partial punishment for taking a corpse to the head. The weeks had gone by in a blink of an eye, and I'd learned there was nothing truly meek about Alec.

Beneath his calm demeanor was a man willing to get his hands dirty for a good cause. He just liked peace in his life, and he had adopted docile behaviors to cultivate that environment.

Thus far, it worked well on the force, as he tended to help deescalate situations rather than worsen them.

"Doom my sister, cadet," Liam ordered.

"She's sleeping with a rugby player."

Before I could stop it, a snorted laugh escaped. I smooshed a pillow over my head. Thanks to the drugs, I could tolerate the discomfort. I blamed the same drugs for my inability to stop giggling over the situation. With six words, my cadet had surely lit a fire, one that would consume my brothers the entire night. By the time the dust settled, I would be the true winner of Alec's comment, especially if I got a demonstration of him taking out one of my brothers.

Henry gasped, and I peeked out from under the cushions in time to watch him fling his arm against his brow and fake swoon into Ricardo. "A *rugby* player?"

Tomas clucked his tongue. "I'm fine with a rugby player. A rugby player might be able to survive her if she decides she's taking him out."

I hoped Tomas survived the night, as the rest of my brothers turned on him with a variety of protests.

"She should be taking him on a *date*, not sending him to the hospital," Ricardo announced. "Wrong type of take out, Tomas. How are you ever going to survive the world of women if you don't learn the basics?"

"Stop picking on Tomas. It's not his fault he's gay," my mother called out from the kitchen.

I would die, not from a corpse to the head, but from laughing over my mother's belief my brother was gay due to his notorious lack of girlfriends. As Tomas would never forgive any of us if we didn't set the record straight, I sat up, cupped my hands around my mouth, and hollered, "Tomas just prefers paying the prostitutes a fair rate for their time, Mom. My evidence indicates, thus far, his prostitutes are women."

Tomas bowed his head. "I am not paying for prostitutes, Josefina."

"Well, that's rude. They deserve to be paid, Tomas." I considered the other options. "Wait, are you an incubus or something? That's the only reason I can think of that a prostitute might pass on a paycheck."

My mother came into the living room armed with a spatula, and she regarded us through narrowed eyes. "Which is it, Tomas? Your closet full of handsome men you'll bring home to your momma or prostitutes you should have paid fairly?"

The rest of my brothers laughed, and Alec came over, sat on the arm of the couch beside me, and pressed the back of his hand to my forehead. "I am token checking your temperature so the cindercorns don't get upset with me."

Aware the man loved affection, I went along with his ploy. "Be vigilant, else you might get bitten by our bosses. How am I doing?"

"Clearly, you are too ill to do anything other than sit on the couch and stay warm. If they do not have tea here, I will go get you tea. If they've blocked me in, they will either go on my behalf, or I'll have to call in backup. My backup has four hooves and is prone to having temper tantrums."

I laughed, snuggled into the blanket, and made myself comfortable on the couch, situating the cushions and pillows to maximize my comfort levels. "Tomas isn't gay, Mom. He just understands what hell his girlfriends would face should she enter the door. Look at Henry's wife. She *ran* the first time she came over."

"Well, I hadn't known we were having a guest, and Henry had made a comment about your work again. He deserved a shoe to the face."

Kelly came out of the kitchen, and like my mother, she was armed, although she had a ladle. "When doesn't he deserve a shoe to the face? Also, what's this I heard about a rugby player?"

"They seem a lot tougher than the American bred handegg players," I replied, grinning at the woman. "Did Henry call you with a sob story?"

"He told me you took a corpse to the head."

I nodded, and I pointed at where I'd taken the brunt of the victim's weight. "It was supposed to be a calm patrol in Central Park, getting my cadet used to the beat before exposing him to a tougher run. He got a few minutes of the beat before dealing with the hospital for the rest of the day. He's technically on duty, as his job is to make sure I make it back to duty."

"That's a dream assignment! What's your name, sweetheart?"

"Alec. You?"

"I'm Kelly. Just relax. The McMarins seem a little crazy, but they're all pretty good people. You know you're in with their mother if she starts throwing her slippers at you. You'll never be in with their father, because he is Irish and nobody will ever be good enough for his little princess."

"It's true," my father shouted from the kitchen. "But you can tell me more about this rugby player. That's already a step up from most of the American offerings."

As only some horribly lewd joke would do, I said, "Maybe I wanted a rugby player because he has to be good in the sack."

My brothers groaned and fled, save for Tomas, who raised a brow at me.

My mother threw her head back and laughed. "You

can't be feeling much pain yet if you're ripping that kind of line when your brothers can hear you. Your father handled your soup, and I made the crunchy bits of meat you seem to like whenever you come over. You can thank Ricardo, as he gave us plenty of warning to get the spit fired up along with the grill. I even fire-charred it for extra crunch."

"Thanks, Mom."

"Alec, be a dear and keep an eye on her. She has little tolerance for headaches, and she'll go from all right to sobbing in two seconds flat, which makes the headache worse. She'll cry herself sick, rather literally, so protect her hair. It's all over if we have to try to clean her hair while she's in that state. I'll get back in the kitchen and put her brothers to work so we can eat. I hope you didn't have any plans for going home tonight."

"As I'm not going to subject her to another long drive tonight, my backup plan had been to catch a nap on the nearest accessible surface."

"Good boy. Are you going to be a brave boy and suck some lemons for us?"

Alec let out a startled laugh before saying, "Sure."

Tomas sighed and shook his head. "Well, I'll go get the shovel, because it looks like we're going to have to bury a body tonight."

ALEC HELD SPICY SECRETS, and he devoured my mother's hottest foods with grace, delight, and an iron stomach. As cry-worthy peppers and concussions did not mix, my mother gave me extra lime crema, told me to suffer through the best grilled onions she could make for me, and to wait a week for a proper offering.

Rather than fell my cadet, my mother won his affection for life.

My father also fell prey to my cadet's charms, as little pleased him more than someone besting my mother at the spicy food game.

"So, about this rugby player," my father prompted.

As I could throw Alec under the bus just as well as he could toss me under, I gestured to him with my taco. Thanks to the painkillers, my brain swam around in cotton balls without a hint of the agony I'd endured before dinner and my next dose had been served.

I had thrown up, Alec had managed to preserve my hair, and he'd called my bosses to let them know I'd progressed to pain-induced vomiting, the precise time I'd been given my previous medications, and how I would be held hostage at my parents' place until recovery.

After twenty minutes of calling around, we'd identified when I could safely have my next dose, and my brothers had brawled for the right to pick up my two new prescriptions, which were the reason I enjoyed dinner rather than suffered.

Alec set aside the grilled peppers of death, which consisted of every type of hot pepper my mother could get her hands on in her quest to defeat him. He grabbed a lemon, sucking on it while he made use of a wet wipe to get any stray capsaicin off his hands. Digging into his wallet, he pulled out a card, which he handed over to me.

Before becoming a marketer and then an accountant, Alec had done a stint as a Major League Rugby player, and I held his rookie card. Laughing, I passed it to my mother.

She blinked. "I see you have found yourself a clever one, Josefina."

"I didn't even know he was a rugby player until today."

"Clever, charming, and perhaps excessively manly yet somehow trapped in a scrawny body." Shaking her head, my mother sent the card down the line. "When did you quit rugby?"

Tomas eyed the card with interest. "More importantly, why?"

"I liked tackling numbers more than tackling people," Alec admitted. "I also went in, did what I set out to do, and decided to go tackle those numbers while I was ahead of the game. I also didn't want to end up with more concussions. I had suffered through a few, and I'd gotten a warning from the doctor I would be courting long-term problems if I got many more of them. So, I quit. I used the money I'd earned to fund my education. I viewed rugby as a fun game, but I didn't want to dedicate my life to it. I still play for fun, but the teams are for those who, like me, can't afford to get more concussions. We have some younger players who just like the game but have jobs where they can't afford a break. We're an unofficial league, but we share the pitch with the serious teams. So, I play rugby to pretend I'm keeping in shape, and I help coach some kids who want to try for MLR but can't afford the professional trainers."

Well, that cinched that. I had a new hobby of watching men tackle each other while fighting over a ball. "But will you all play a match in suits for me?"

Alec laughed at me. "Why do you want us playing in suits?"

"I'd like it a lot."

He snorted. "I bet you would. I'll ask the boys if they're

game for wrecking a suit. If we do a light run as more of a demonstration, we can probably manage it. If we wear the vests under our jackets and shirts, all we'll need to do is sacrifice the look for the helmets. We do not play without helmets, ever."

The card made its way to my father, who huffed, puffed, grabbed the serving pot of my mother's *chilate de pollo*, and passed it on over to Alec. "Had I paid better attention to US rugby, I wouldn't have gotten blindsided with this. But aren't your physicals a mess right now?" My father eyed me. "You had mentioned something about that, right?"

Busted. "Sorry, Alec."

"Don't be sorry. I'm not. We play for the fun of it, a little exercise, and well, we break more than a few rules because we're tired men who just like to get on the pitch and play. Your brother mentioned your quinceañera. I want to see the pictures."

"You better show him, Mom. The drugs will surely ease my pain."

ALEC LOVED everything about the pictures of my fifteenth birthday. I'd picked a sky blue dress, and as I'd wanted to be accepted by all of my mother's family, I'd asked for all the older women to add something to the hem and sleeves. The result had been a masterpiece, taking nine months to complete.

As pictures couldn't do the dress justice, my father brought it out of the closet and held it while my mother explained every symbol on the skirts and sleeves. There were even references written in Nahuatl along with several other languages I didn't recognize. My mother had, though, and she'd cried when she'd found them among the embroidery.

She'd promised they'd stitched their love for me into the fabric.

Perhaps I'd faced some exclusions for being half-Irish and a girl, but the dress had gone a long way towards making me believe I had a family, even when we sometimes didn't see eye to eye.

Most had come to the celebration, making the trip from Mexico to welcome me into the adult world. I hadn't seen most of them since, as I'd learned more than a few bitter lessons regarding culture and acceptance. If I were ever invited to a ceremony of any sort, I'd go out of familial obligation, but I'd be waiting for a damned long time for the invitation—if one ever came.

The dress no longer fit, but one day, I'd take it home with me as a memento of the time my mother's side of the family had treated me like family.

Alec eyed me and then eyed the dress. "Judging from the size of this dress, you were of diminutive size at fifteen."

That was one way to put it. "I was a very tiny little princess, who upon turning seventeen, grew half a foot." As Alec's favorite type of math involved any equation involving my bra, he had a very intimate awareness of my breast size, which had grown substantially since my teen years. "I was a late bloomer."

He snickered, and he offered to help my parents put the dress back to somewhere safe where it wouldn't be damaged. Once out of the room, I crossed my eyes.

"Are you trying to encourage or discourage him?" Henry asked.

"I'm banned from everything fun and good in life for a week, Henry." I flopped onto the couch and subjected my brother to sad sighs and pouting.

"Mom, Josefina's whining," he complained.

"She took a corpse to the head. Give her what she wants and deal with it. Then go home. You are no longer a wanted child. You can come back tomorrow, after work, to check on your sister."

"The doctor told her she can't have who she wants, Mom," my brother replied.

I thought about murdering him for his failure to use his indoor voice, but I opted against it. I'd miss him eventually, and could I really blame him? My father's family defined what it meant to be loud, and my mother's family took their noise, especially at celebrations, to extremes.

We'd come out of the womb loud.

Alec returned, and he smiled at me. "You're done for the day, is it?"

I shoved a pillow over my head. "The drugs are going to wear off sooner than later."

My father pointed down the hall in the direction of the bedrooms. "Hers is the one with the pink leopard-print cat poster on the door. I'll put some tea out on the counter so it's easy to find. If she proves to be more than you can handle, knock on our door. There's some soup in the fridge, so if she starts trying to bite you, you can redirect her that way."

Alec laughed. "I'll keep that in mind. All right, Josefina. It's to bed with you. If we're lucky, your mom will make us spicy soup tomorrow. And if we're not, we'll sacrifice your brothers and whine until we get our way."

My mother came in and laughed at my cadet. "You

learned that one quick. Which one are you going to sacrifice first?"

"The quiet one. Everyone pays attention when he says something, and he's the only one you haven't tossed a slipper at tonight."

My mother graced Alec with an approving nod. "Excellent choice. I shall notify the younger children that they are being sacrificed. But will you be telling them to suck on lemons come dinner time?"

"If Josefina is unhappy for any reason, they don't get any lemons," he replied in his most serious tone. "And unless they can beat me at the pepper game, I am keeping their sister."

My mother turned to my father and said, "Tomorrow, we're going to the market. We've peppers to buy. Mark my words, those boys of ours will be weeping for mercy by the end of the day."

"Do you love or hate my brothers, Mom?" I asked.

"That's for me to know and you to find out."

EIGHTEEN

The Stolen Mugs

SOMEONE HAD STOLEN MY MUGS. All of them. I narrowed my eyes, scoured my cabinets, and peeked into every spot one of my precious travel mugs might fit.

I found nothing.

Someone would pay for invading my turf and stealing my mugs. I had earned them through pain and suffering, mostly in the form of having to ride Mrs. Chief Bailey Quinn whenever she was called out to handle explosives. Someone had also screwed around with my cindercorn plushy, moving it from my mug cabinet to my keyboard.

I checked over the cindercorn to make certain a soon-to-be-deceased co-worker hadn't damaged it. When all proved to be well, I set it safely back into the cabinet where my mugs should have resided.

Sitting at my computer, I unlocked it to discover the culprit had accessed my computer and changed my wallpaper to be a picture of a certain cadet, shirtless and rather sweaty while working out at the gym.

The former rugby player turned forensic accountant turned cop struggled with the force's base physical requirements, and he spent three days a week with Amanda and the other instructors getting him fit enough to keep up with me. I'd thrown him to the wolves, making a fuss over the physical elements as I couldn't fault him anywhere else.

I could see Alec being responsible for the wallpaper along with the disappearance of my mugs.

Giving him to Amanda three times a week counted as cruel and unusual punishment, but I gave it a month before he could handle a three mile run without claiming he might die. Yesterday, I'd enjoyed motivating him in the form of running a mile in seven minutes before slowing to an eight minute pace for another four miles.

I'd then headed back to work, leaving him to the not-so-tender mercy of the precinct's trainers.

Rather than watch me pursue cold cases, he'd opted for an extra day of torture in the gym.

I got up, headed for Mr. Chief Samuel Quinn's office, and tapped on the door, waiting for him to gesture for me to come in. Without a word, I went to his cabinet, opened it, and took one of his mugs. "There will be no need to investigate the string of murders that might happen in this station should I not have coffee this morning."

He snickered. "Like your new wallpaper?"

"Actually, yes. It's a good shot. Did an incubus take it?"

"Succubus, as Lucy thought you'd prefer a woman's eye getting a good shot. He doesn't even need to be thanked. He's trying to offer you some encouragement. You know, a preview of the wares."

Samuel, the sex demons, and Lucifer all understood I enjoyed my evenings with my cadet, but we continued to deceive the station to see how long it took Bailey to figure out we were playing her. "I'll admit, it's a mighty fine preview, especially now that he's eating better and getting into good shape. What's his current estimate for the physical fitness exam?"

After learning my cadet played rugby and still had physical health issues, I'd begun to worry—and I'd asked Amanda to ramp up his training to get to the bottom of it.

"Amanda has cleared him for patrols and some light work, but he still has a way to go on his endurance. She got two miles out of him on Monday, but she had an inhaler on hand."

That tracked. Alec handled short bursts of exercise well enough, but he struggled with his endurance. I jumped to the first bad conclusion I could think of. "Asthma?"

"She's not sure, so I'll have Lucy check to be certain."

As was often the case, the Devil popped into my chief's office, and he closed the door. In one hand, he held out one of his wife's iced coffees, which I'd found to my liking. As only a fool refused one of her drinks, I accepted it and got to work getting my much needed hit of coffee bliss. "You're the best, Lucy."

"I'll pass on your thanks to my wife, who is making me do nice things again. One day, I'll tell her no." He winced. "When I want a hungry kitty a month afterwards, because that's roughly how long she puts me on the couch before relenting."

I snickered, as Darlene liked putting the Devil back in his place, which involved neither of them feeding for a month as they tried to out-stubborn each other. Once one of them cracked, the pair disappeared for a few days. The last time that had happened, I'd ended up with an apartment crammed with succubi and incubi who wished to avoid being caught up in the insanity that was Lucifer let off his leash.

I'd liked the gaming, but the whining had almost done me in. Alec had found the situation to be hilarious, and he'd jumped on the chance to have more people to play games with him.

"So, Alec," my chief prompted.

"He does, in actuality, have asthma. It is currently minor, but it was induced from the levels of emotional distress he's suffered over the past few years. The stress he's suffered has caused a few unfortunate health consequences. Before you panic, Josefina, they're all resolvable. Considering these health complications, he's progressing well, although Amanda is becoming worried, as he is not improving at the rate she expects. She would be bringing it up to you next week, Sam."

I'd been around the precinct long enough to understand the Devil wanted to strike a deal with me. For the most part, we both walked away happy with the various bargains we'd struck. "At what price?"

"I have a few new fish species I can't take to my conservatory and require a home for."

For fuck's sake. I had an entire bedroom of my apartment dedicated to fish that Lucifer couldn't keep, and at the rate I was going, I'd end up with a second apartment for the newest residents of my home. "How many?"

"There are only two, but they might breed if given a better environment. I'll manipulate their children to establish diversity before working out if they can be reintroduced to the wild. They're just intolerant to devilish energy. They're the last of their kind, and at the very least, I want them to have a quiet, calm home until the end of their days."

All of my fish were intolerant to demonic and devilish energy, and I'd coerced archangels into shielding the room so Lucy could visit the beloved pets he couldn't keep. I'd transformed the space into a quiet reading den, which meant I could read a book, listen to the water, and generally enjoy myself with my finned roommates. "I think we can fit one more tank in there before we're going to have to take over another apartment or find somewhere larger."

"The apartment next to yours has four rooms, and it's empty right now. My little cupcake is fine with knocking out a wall in your fish room and expanding your territory. We could move most of the fish into the connecting apartment so you can keep your reading den. I can adjust the tanks so it's clear-fronted ponds with waterfalls."

As he described my personal version of heaven, I replied, "Sold. I can take up temporary residence in Alec's apartment until the base work is done." I took another sip of my coffee and held up my chief's mug, raising a brow at Lucifer.

"The cops in the cubicle farm miss you," he explained.

Seriously? My office had been robbed because I'd been neck deep in solving a few cold cases? I'd only been in hiding for a week. "And how many bargains did you make to help with the theft?"

"A few."

What a bastard. "Know this, Lucifer. I am coming for you, and I will train Marigold to serve as the only horse I need to start and finish the apocalypse."

While the youngest horse in the cop stables, my little flaxen liver chestnut showed a high tolerance for the absurd, adored the Devil when she wasn't trying to kill him, and would make an excellent police horse.

She tolerated leaves and plastic bags with grace. The gunfire and car horn tests irritated her more than anything else, and her response to devils, demons, and other oddities was to investigate, determine if she wanted to be friends with them, and beat the shit out of the ones she liked.

I needed to teach her not to pick fights with the non-human entities she liked.

Then again, when she found one she didn't like, she made her opinions clear, warning the unwanted individual away with snorts, stomps of her hooves, and short charges. If the fool ignored her, the yearling did her best to forever remove the scourge from the face of the Earth.

Fortunately for my sanity, Marigold adored the cindercorns, their foals, and their gorgon children, and when they went to the stables, she followed them around like a puppy in dire need of attention.

"She really means it, Lucy," my chief warned.

"I know, which is why it's so delightful. That filly of hers is something else. Josefina, does your brother know he bred the horse equivalent of a demon?"

I eyed my chief's phone, and with a laugh, he picked it up, cradled it between his ear and shoulder, and worked on his computer, likely pulling up my brother's work number. A moment later, he dialed. "Good morning, Sergeant McMarin. I had a question for you regarding Marigold. Are her parents anywhere near as demonic as she is, and if so, are they for sale?"

I giggled at the question, bowed my head, and wondered how it had turned into my boss trying to acquire a few more horses for our herd.

"Marigold is working out wonderfully. She's going to be steady and solid by the time she can be ridden, and she's taking to the ground training like a duck to water. That bastard you sent over for your sister is going to be a strong asset, too. Of course, he's a bastard to everyone except your sister and her cadet, but I appreciate my detective having a bodyguard shaped like a horse when she isn't riding us. I now have to pay her daily overtime to run to the stables to care for him, as he's a jackass on top of being a bastard and won't let the stable hands into his stall. I consider myself grateful that he will tolerate a lead line and a trip to the pastures or into the trailer as needed without attempting murder."

I loved my bastard of a horse, who had earned the name of Bastard from being his charming self. Bastard was an angel for me and only me. Thus far, only two other entities on Earth, in the heavens, or in the hells other than me could handle him.

Bastard loved the Devil and Alec, although he toyed with them both for the fun of it.

"Call the stable with the horses you think we can integrate into our herd, find out how long it will take to train them, and get the totals for the animals and the work. Our precinct is going to end up with a record number of mounted officers, so if you can get me animals of the same quality as Bastard but perhaps a little more inclined to play nicely with others, that'd be ideal." Samuel snickered. "Also, if you could speak to your parents and concoct a family dinner tonight to lure your sister and her cadet away from the area, that would be useful. I fear I might have a staffing shortage, as some of my officers decided the best way to get your sister's attention was to steal her mugs and touch her cindercorn. I'll even send them off early, shortly after she solves the mystery of her missing mugs."

I drooled at the thought of enjoying my mother's tacos. "But my cases, Samuel, sir?"

"You have done twelve hours of overtime in four days. Solve your mug mystery and get out of my station," he replied with a grin. "Sorry about that, Henry. If your parents call, I have learned your sister will answer, as she doesn't want to be targeted with the slipper. Thanks. Call me when you have a time, and I'll make sure she's on the way." Making eye contact with me, my chief stated, "You will go home, see your family, and have a good time. Tomorrow, you will stay at home with your cadet, as he will inevitably feel like he was steamrolled when Lucifer is finished with him. Your job will be nursing him back to health. Your cold cases can wait."

"It's true," Lucifer said, and he winced. "I can do the work, but let's just say I lack the finesse my brothers have with holy fire. He'll survive, but he won't like me for a few days."

Ouch. Having gotten sucker punched by an archangel, I understood the pain of holy fire. "Understood. How long do I have to solve my mug mystery, Samuel, sir?"

"Call it two hours. Your brother yelled in my ear, swore he would gather everyone, and promised you'd get your tacos, as your love of your mother's cooking is now legendary. Is that enough time to do your dirty deeds, Lucy?"

"It's plenty of time, and if you happen to stay over at your mother's place, I can be done with the apartment adjustments by morning."

"Sleepover party it is," I stated, and I retrieved my

phone to text my mother that I would be bringing my cadet over and we'd be spending the night. Her reply promised I'd be getting a round with the slipper, as she inquired if I would be sharing my room with my cadet again. I accepted my punishment with a grin, confirmed I would be sharing with my cadet, and warned my mother that he wouldn't be feeling well and could use some of her curative soup. "She is aware we won't be leaving after dinner."

"Do you want the SUV or the convertible?"

I laughed, as Lucifer had donated a convertible to the station for cops who deserved a reward. "I'll take the SUV, as it's not guaranteed my cadet will make it all the way to my parents' place without throwing up."

"Good call," Lucy informed me.

ARMED with the iced coffee gifted from my favorite woman in the heavens and the hells, I entered the cubicle farm, determined to ferret out who had stolen my mugs.

The mugs had bred, and I found a mug on every last one of my co-workers' desks. Each one rode a cindercorn, nightmare, or standard unicorn plushy.

The sight reduced me to a helpless fit of laughter. "You're all guilty! Guilty, guilty, guilty," I declared, and I waggled my finger at them. "You have successfully summoned me. I might be a demon or devil at this point, as I can't help but notice *somebody* touched my cindercorn. Death is too good of a fate for the guilty party."

Behind me, Samuel laughed, and he strode up to join the festivities. "She came into my office, and she stole one of my mugs. Fortunately for everyone, the Devil saved us all, giving her an iced coffee. Dare I ask what's going on?"

My co-workers shook their heads.

Still laughing, our boss left.

"Where's the gas guzzler, anyway?" I asked, narrowing my eyes.

"She's checking in with your cadet," Nilman informed me, and he gestured to the cubicle farm. "Your mugs are somewhere in this room. You must guess which one of us stole your mugs. Every incorrect guess is punished with a plushy, which you must take to your office and put on display."

The last time I'd been pranked, I'd been punished with a new, larger, and better couch, which made for an excellent place to read over paperwork with my cadet, who had likewise been punished with an office next to mine. I could play the game one of two ways: I could play to win or play to lose.

Losing could earn me an entire herd of plushies, which would make my couch especially comfortable when reading through pesky documentation. "And are the mugs with the actual culprits behind the theft, Nilman?"

"The masterminds of the theft are in possession of your mugs," he confirmed.

Well, well, well. I rubbed my hands together. "And how many culprits have more than one mug?"

"I'm afraid to report that your mugs have engaged in illegal breeding, and you now have ten of them, as you have not lost or damaged a single one. No one has two of your mugs."

Had it been over a year since I'd been promoted? Had my cadet somehow survived through numerous months of daily exposure to me? However, understanding that I'd reached my one-year anniversary in the station, all became clear. The chiefs always planned *something* for any fool determined enough to remain in the station on the eighth floor for an entire year. I turned, and as my chief had left his door opened, I yelled, "Samuel, sir?"

He snickered, came back out, and asked, "What's wrong, McMarin?"

As my chief would have a meltdown if I didn't have fun with his prank, I decided I'd play along and do the equivalent of let my hair down. "When is my cadet no longer going to be a cadet? Have I really been here a *year*? Is my yearling no longer a yearling? What is time? Where has it gone?"

He relaxed, and after a moment, he laughed at me. "He'll graduate with the next batch. Yes, you have been here for over a year. Yes, your yearling is two years old, but we figured we'd let her have her youth a little longer because she's a bit on the small side. She's still growing, and she's over our minimum hands requirement to work, so you have nothing to worry about. And yes, your SUV is no longer new, as it's over a year old now."

Damn. I pointed at Nilman and said, "Hand over the unicorn plushy."

Snickering, he obeyed, flinging the standard unicorn my way. I caught it with my free hand and shoved it against my face to buy myself some time to work through the passage of time.

"How did you guess I wasn't one of the culprits?" he asked.

"You can't lie worth a shit, and you would've had someone else be the spokesperson had you held responsibility, as you wouldn't be able to look me in the eyes had you been the one behind the attempt to delay me from my morning coffee."

"Busted," he replied with a grin. "That's one plushy for your office."

Lowering the stuffed animal from my face, I cradled it against my elbow. "My mug, Samuel."

My chief snapped his fingers. "Why are you busting me?"

As if anyone else would mastermind theft from a detective's office, especially one who locked her door when leaving. "You wouldn't allow anyone else to put such wallpaper on my computer; you are one of four people in this station with a key to my office, and I bet nobody in here is actually aware you switched out my wallpaper. I'm one of the key holders, and the other two key holders are not here right now. You would have been the primary mastermind, as you prefer when people think outside of the box. You always have a cindercorn plushy in your office, in case any of your children visit our floor. As such, you wouldn't participate in the plushy game in case your children invaded unexpectedly, but you would make me claim all the plushies in here because you think it's funny when I have my stuffed animal out. You all can escort my new plushies and mugs to my office, and one of my mugs better have hot coffee in it."

Perky laughed, and he held up a mug, showing it off to prove he held one of mine. "I'll handle the coffee. You could have played with us a little longer, McMarin!"

"When my cadet is promoted, we can welcome him properly," I suggested. "But instead of unicorns, we'll use stress balls, puzzle cubes, and empty notebooks. We need to make him think we actually like him, after all."

"That's too nice," Perky informed me.

"We'll make him guess how many stress balls are in his office, use the number as the code to unlock whatever thing we use to bar entry into his office, and refuse to give him any clues beyond how many notebooks and puzzle cubes are also in his office along with the precise measurements of his office furniture. We'll be nice and give him a piece of paper and a pencil for his mathematical equations to determine the correct number of stress balls filling the space."

Everyone stared at me, and after a long time, Perky asked, "Do you like or hate him, McMarin?"

"I love him, but don't you be telling anybody that, especially him," I replied.

Pilot: Star-nosed... what?

Author's Note:

This short story is a pilot of a world concept where everybody is a shifter of some sort without exception. This unfortunate character, Meredith, has a rather unique secondary form, and something has caught her attention...

When I'm conceptualizing something, the pilot (or first crack of a character) often doesn't make it to the final version of the world they helped to create. If I were to turn Meredith's story into a novel, it would likely begin the first time she picked up on that delicious scent she wants to hunt down and include some form of office drama or mystery to it. Then, after nicely settling into the character's life, the event(s) from the pilot might be used, albeit in a different fashion. There'd very likely be some general exploration and perhaps some additional drama.

Yes, this pilot isn't "up to snuff" for general publication. That's why it's a pilot. But I hope you have enjoyed this exploration of a potential character and the world she lives in.

If you enjoy this short story and would like to see a full-length novel about this character or the world she lives in, swing by my blog (thesneakykittycritic.com) or Facebook, find the release post for 101 Ways to Die, and let me know in the comments! (Comments regarding the pilot will be considered between June and July of 2023.)

Please view this as a sneak peek into the creative process. (And if you dislike typos, plot foopahs, general silliness, and exploration of elements without absolute conclusions, you may wish to pass on reading any pilots. These are generally written for the sheer joy of writing, and it's an extra I'm choosing to share as part of the creation process.)

Pilot: Star-nosed... what?

Magic worked in mysterious ways, but why had it decided I should shapeshift into a star-nosed mole? If it hadn't been for someone else telling me what I became, I wouldn't have had a clue in hell.

Star-nosed moles lacked a functional sense of sight.

Worse, shapeshifting did not imbue me, the victim, with a convenient instruction manual on how to cope with a whole new set of senses. The basics of taste, touch, and sound came with relative ease, but having to use a blend of these to replace sight?

My life had gone down a shit creek without the benefit of a paddle, and my boat had holes.

As I tried not to wallow over my circumstances, I attempted to find the silver lining. With ample motivation in the form of avoiding shapeshifting, I'd mastered the art of controlling when I shifted. The magic gathered over time, and I'd determined I could go three weeks without having to transform. At the three-week mark, I needed to embrace my smaller side, bleed off the excess energies, and spend a few hours snuffling about and doing star-nosed mole things.

So far, I'd determined star-nosed moles enjoyed sniffing things more than I appreciated. In air, on land, or under water, if it had a scent, I could find it. As I abhorred sitting around and doing nothing for several hours while I bled off the magic I didn't want, I put my oversensitive nose to work.

Someone wore a gentle perfume or cologne I loved at work, and I wanted to know who, so I could ask for the brand. The whole lack of vision part would challenge me on my quest, but I figured all I needed to do was identify where the person parked while a star-nosed mole and then check it out while human.

Sometimes, a woman needed to go to extreme measures to get what she wanted, and I wanted to spray everything I owned in the scent. As human or star-nosed mole, I loved it.

Going to work after hours, in the dead of night, to snuffle around, counted as one of the crazier things I'd done. As long as I acted like an animal, kept moving, and put my nose to work, nobody in the real estate investment firm would know my dirty little secret.

My co-workers all had sensible animals, most of them predatory. As I had no desire to be uncovered as one of the odder critters North America had to offer, I needed to shuffle around the building's exterior, get a fix on the scent, and track down who wore it.

Once I identified the who, all I needed to do was figure out how to approach the scent's owner and inquire where I might get a bottle for myself.

Pilot: Star-nosed... what?

Under no circumstances would I betray how badly I wanted to spray my bed with the essence of joy and roll around until satisfied.

While shapeshifting into a star-nosed mole battered my pride, I still retained some of my dignity. But only some. By the time the night ended, I would have a better idea of who drove me insane with the perfume or cologne—and have a lead on where to get it. Once I appeased my sense of smell, life could go on as normal.

I would shapeshift strictly in the comfort of my home, make use of the pond I'd installed in my yard for my enjoyment, and life would be good.

Sight would have made my job a lot easier. To maximize my chances of pulling off the trick without getting caught, I parked my car several blocks away, in a straight walk along the sidewalk to my destination. To help me locate the appropriate place, I'd spritzed one of my favorite citrus body sprays onto the bush outside the front door when leaving. Thanks to my supersensitive nose, I'd be able to locate the bush and do my investigation from memory and scent.

The issue would be my inability to transform back to human easily.

For some reason, people frowned upon naked women just showing up in the middle of the street, even at night. Thanks to my mother's obsession with beauty pageants, I'd become accustomed to people staring at me in almost nude states, as I'd begun wearing barely there bikinis as early as age seven. As an adult, I'd worked hard to become something other than eye candy, choosing jobs in the background rather than using my looks to get ahead in life.

I wore my makeup to mask my feathers, pulling tricks to make me appear a little less attractive. I wore loose clothes, fake glasses with gaudy lenses that didn't match my face all too well, and spent more time turning my hair into a rumpled mess that met the minimum requirements for my job.

I suspected my tendency to hide the beauty my mother had loved more than me had resulted in my shapeshifting magic turning me into a star-nosed mole.

Nobody, and I mean nobody, swooned spotting a star-nosed mole. Most screamed and ran away—or burst into fits of uncontrollable laughter.

Rather than complain over the nature of life and its twisted eccentricities, I stripped, triple-checked for any nearby observers, got out of my car, closed the door, faced the direction of my work, and shapeshifted. Due to bottling magic up for weeks, I transformed faster than I could blink, a trick that helped to bleed off excess energy faster. While it hurt a little, I shook off the discomfort, and went about my business, scurrying off in the direction of my work. Over time, I'd grown accustomed to the bombardment of scents and feelings. Rather than rely on sight, I felt my way around. From blades of grass rustling nearby to the distant rumble of cars, vibration and sounds hammered at me. While I couldn't precisely see, my nose directed me. I stayed away from the sidewalk's edge, using the grass as my guide. I didn't have to go far to pick up the trail of my body spray, but the scent I appreciated the most taunted my nose.

As I needed the bush with my body spray to serve as a landmark to find my way back, I went to it, discovering numerous trails of my quarry. Puzzled, I followed, to discover the scent went around the building as well as into it. While there were paths around the building, few used them.

They led to restricted sections, the company's dumpsters, and a storage shed we used for signs and large items.

While unexpected, the discovery helped me to eliminate numerous co-workers. We had a few staff janitors, but most of them only came in a few times a week, with employees expected to handle minor cleaning tasks in between their shifts. With fresh doses of the scent daily, the owner needed to be someone who came into work daily. The real estate agents refused to go to the back of the building, as it was beneath them, thus eliminating the entire lot as possibilities. The janitors never came in frequently enough.

Traces of the scent, old and new, clung to everything around the back of the building.

Whomever went into the back tended to avoid the front of the dumpster, although I caught hints of the smell towards the sides and back.

Only two types of employees fit the pattern: security and maintenance.

As the company was run by older men, everyone in security and maintenance were men. I did a little mole dance by the dumpster, as the smell driving me insane belonged to a man. To my delight, I couldn't think of a single unkind man in the entirety of the security and maintenance crew.

While I used some math daily as part of the team making sure the real estate investors could make money and build their empires, I rarely enjoyed the equations.

For a change, the formula I worked with thrilled me.

Nice men plus good scent equaled an interesting time at work.

Satisfied with my discovery, I left the company's backyard and explored to determine where else the subject of

Pilot: Star-nosed... what?

my interest went. I returned to the bush I'd marked, making use of my nose and other senses to get a better feel of how far afield my quarry went. One trail, used numerous times and with varying degrees of strength to the scent, led to the employee parking lot. As vehicles and star-nosed moles formed unsatisfactory relationships, I opted for caution, abandoning identifying which spot my target used.

Tomorrow, I could hunt in a more traditional fashion, with my weaker human nose.

In the meantime, I would put some serious thought into a plan on identifying the cologne and its wearer. Satisfied, I returned to my car and hid beneath it until I burned off enough magic to buy myself a few more weeks of peace and humanity.

* * *

As I refused to dress up to draw the attention of some man, I went with the plan least likely to draw attention to myself. I went to work as normal, herded real estate agents, paper pushers, and property sellers and managers on my quest to become the perfect office gopher. I envied the actual gophers. While the company I worked for didn't have any on staff, one of our contracting management firms did.

Without fail, they got cherry picked for the best tasks.

When in doubt, always pick the tried and true office gopher.

"Meredith, I need a set of signs from the shed."

Thanks to my star-nosed mole secret, my sense of hearing had improved, and I'd gotten a lot better at picking up on the tonal notes of comments. The real estate agent in question, Robert Deneries, was about twenty seconds shy of

Pilot: Star-nosed... what?

having a meltdown, although he struggled to hide his anxiety.

It came out as the faintest of wavers in his voice, along with a higher pitch than normal for him. There was also an almost bitter or sour undertone to his scent, which made me want to sneeze.

Robert disliked the general formalities of the office, and once I checked we were alone in my office, little more than a closet offering me some privacy for sensitive phone calls, I asked, "Which signs, Rob?"

He relaxed, and something about his scent changed.

I doubted I would ever get used to people having distinct scents while a human, but the magic did what it wanted, and in my case, my nose betrayed me daily, subjecting me to an endless flood of information about people, often including certain states of mind I wished I could avoid.

I had zero interest in knowing when men found me to be sexually appealing to them. Alas, my nose informed me each and every time.

Fortunately for my sanity, Robert preferred chubbier women with ample curves, which spared me from excess discomfort. Unfortunately for my sanity, I worked with a few women he found to be attractive, and his favorite also happened to be his wife.

His wife, on the other hand, found everybody to be attractive, especially her husband. Overall, the situation worked well for everybody—except for me and my wretchedly sensitive nose.

I worried for the man, as he needed more than a minute or two to collect himself, after which he said, "I need three for sale signs, I need a reinvestment sign, and I need any warning signs we have about a dangerous property." He

Pilot: Star-nosed... what?

gulped. "And I need someone to put the warning signs up at the place in question."

Ah. I understood. Robert's anxiety was linked to certain terrain types due to an accident in his childhood, and one of the firm's new properties must have had some form of hazard he couldn't handle. I could read between the lines: he wanted someone to go handle the signage for him.

"I can ask the boss for approval to go put up the signs for you," I replied, forcing as much happiness as I could into my tone.

"I'll make sure you get the approval. May I text your personal phone with the address?"

As I wasn't customer-facing most of the time, I didn't have a work phone, and company policy required employees acquire permission to text other employees on personal devices. "You can, and I'll go email HR that you have my permission to text me on my personal device with the address, so I can install the signs. That's not a problem at all. Can you also email and text me with the list of hazards, so I can make certain the signage is correct?"

"I'll send you the documents. There's definitely a soured oil tank on the property, and the warning list is about twenty pages long."

Well, that would color my day, burn my nose, and create an interesting time for me. "I'll make sure all the signage is correct," I promised. "I'll need a hard hat."

"Maintenance can give you one, and if you can't find someone in maintenance, ask security. They know where the equipment is at. They also keep steel-toed boots in most sizes, so see if they have a pair you can wear. If not, I'll have you comped for buying a personal pair for the job on the way."

Pilot: Star-nosed... what?

Whatever had Robert rattled had him rattled enough he was willing to deal with HR, and as such, I'd do my best to help him. "I'll go to my boss's office and let him know I'm helping you, in case he has anything critical on the wire I have to shuffle in, and then I'll get the equipment and grab the signage after I have a chance to go over the document." To help put him at ease, I hurried off, heading for my boss's office, one of the investors who had a tolerance for dealing with management.

I tapped on his door three times, paused, and tapped two more times, our general signal we had a matter of some importance we needed to discuss with him.

Mr. Westin answered, "Come in."

One day, someone would give everyone doors capable of buffering sound better—or I'd wear ear plugs to mitigate my heightened sense of hearing. I let myself into my boss's office, fixed my gaze onto his desk, and said, "Mr. Deneries has a signage issue he asked for help with, sir. Is there anything critical on the wire I need to attend to prior to helping him?"

"As I'm the jackass who sent that nightmare his way, go help him, please."

"I was going to get the gear and install the signage," I added, careful to keep my tone tentative.

Mr. Westin made a grunty noise, which I'd learned meant I behaved as he expected. "Take your time, make sure you wear all your safety gear, and if your vehicle is damaged, file a claim with your insurance and give accounting the bill. I'll make sure everyone knows you will be busy for the rest of the day."

Well, my day had taken an interesting turn. What sort of

hell hole was the firm trying to sell? I wasn't sure I wanted to know, but I would find out sooner than later.

I wished myself luck, bobbed my head like a good office gopher, and headed off to handle everything needed, already regretting my decision to be helpful. I consoled myself with one simple fact. They were paying me to be helpful, although I feared nobody was paid enough to handle the chore I'd foolishly volunteered to take over.

* * *

Dressed in more safety gear than I cared to think about, including a yellow safety vest meant to make me visible, goggles so I'd preserve my vision, a hard hat, safety shoes, thick gloves, and special cleats over the boots to aid with my footing, I loaded the trunk of my car with the plethora of varying signage to install at the site an hour's drive away from my work.

Once upon a time, the place had been an asbestos and chromium mine; it also featured a ridiculous assortment of other stones and minerals and had served as a dumping ground of all things toxic over the years following the mine shutting down.

The sign declaring the mine to be for sale meant little. According to the documents I'd read before heading over to face potential doom, the investors meant to scrap and profit from all the metal they could, check to see if the mine could be revitalized, and transform it into something productive rather than an eyesore.

My job was to remind potential trespassers of the dangers, take photographs of as much of the site as I could, and try not to die.

Pilot: Star-nosed... what?

Upon arrival, I'd taken care of the first set of caution signs where the mine's road began. Fortunately, the storage shed had a collection of all the signs needed, and I'd cleared the entire thing out.

Everything had barely fit in my poor car.

I regretted my decision to be an ethical star-nosed mole, choosing to rein in my desire to locate the delicious scent taunting me at work through any means necessary. Jail seemed much safer than the hell I ventured into. Rather than complain, I checked the first set of signs, decided they'd stay put, and ventured deeper into the property. I parked my car at the locked gate, took the keys to the padlock, unlocked it, and unwound the chains. I wrestled the steel monstrosity open, moved my car inside, and restored the chains.

Locking myself in seemed less than wise, but I did it anyway.

"If you want to try out for a horror movie, go to Hollywood next time. Put on some makeup. Wear formfitting clothes. Show a little skin. Make use of those pageant wins, woman. Strut the catwalk like you mean it. Practice screaming... and not in an abandoned mine," I muttered. According to the directions, I needed to put a collection of the hazard signs both inside the property and outside of it.

According to the map, I needed to drive for over a mile to reach the mine buildings where the majority of the signage would be installed. Great.

The map indicated that mine shafts riddled the entire place, and it was entirely possible one might collapse should I drive over it. I counted possible shafts, determining I had ten total chances to fall into a shaft, which ranged from five to twenty-five feet underground.

As though warning me of my fate to come, some bird circled overhead and let out a loud and long call.

I flipped my middle finger at the avian harbinger. "Screw you and your wings, buddy!"

The bird let out another cry, rather harrowing in nature.

I put in some serious thought about transforming and living out the rest of my life around the mine, which had all of the nice things star-nosed moles enjoyed, including a lack of people determined to make a mess of my day.

* * *

In good news for me, I survived the five foot drop into the mine shaft. In bad news, my car would never be the same. Thanks to the shallow depth, the fashion in which the shaft collapsed, and the presence of supporting beams meant to keep the whole thing from tumbling down on the miners, I escaped with a collection of bumps and bruises. As designed, my windshield exploded in a shower of pretty glass beads, which irritated the hell out of me but did little else. My back would dislike me for a little while, but I called it a win.

In a final bit of good news, the trunk of my poor car had popped open during the crash, making it trivial to access the signs I needed to install before I called my boss to inform him that the mine had attempted—but failed—to kill me.

As the mine shaft jammed my doors closed, I made use of the shattered windshield to escape my car, shaking my head at the destruction.

It could have been worse. It could have been the mine shaft twenty-five feet deep. Five feet would give me enough problems, especially as I'd almost made it to the main buildings.

As the signage wouldn't install itself, I began the tedious process of emptying my car of everything.

I began with hammering a caution sign ten feet beyond the tail end of my trashed vehicle to warn people of the hole. Then, as nobody would be making it through the thick foliage around the road, I went ahead and installed the plethora of other signs warning people of various hazards. As there was no way in hell I was hiking to the mine itself, I encircled the ruins of my car with a fence of various real estate signs as a haphazard cordon.

For at least twenty minutes, I stared at the installation and the wreck of my vehicle, debating what to do.

As my phone had one bar of reception, I took a picture of the scene, composed an email to my boss, and requested that someone come pick me up at the gate, as I would not be able to return to the office without an intervention, a crane, and a tow truck.

Then, as I hadn't been wise enough to request permission to text anyone before leaving, I ditched the heavy safety equipment, retrieved my shoes from the trunk of my car, and made the hike to the road to wait. Every now and then, I checked my email.

Nothing.

I gave it an hour, and then I set off in the direction of home and walked.

* * *

Thanks to a helpful motorist who took pity on me, I made it home six and a half hours after leaving the mine.

Pilot: Star-nosed... what?

For five hours of the hike, I'd stewed over the situation. The instant I got home, I checked my savings account, confirmed I'd squirreled enough money away to last six months if I failed to find a new job, and did what I should have done upon reading about my assignment: I quit.

I even managed to use professional language in my resignation letter, although I quit all the same.

As I wasn't going to let the jackasses get away with ruining my car over some damned signs I shouldn't have been sent out to install anyway, I sent the pictures of the wreckage to HR, forwarded the resignation I'd sent to my boss, and informed them I had hitchhiked home due to a lack of functioning transportation.

Then, expecting the company to go on the cheap, I reached out to my insurance company, informed them of my work's decision to send me to a mine, showed them pictures of the wreckage, and forwarded them a copy of the email from my boss promising that they'd pay back any damages to my vehicle. I requested that they deal with my employer, as they were the reason I no longer had a functioning vehicle.

Frustrated with the circumstances, aware the crash would give me a pain check sooner than later, and sick and tired of humanity, I tidied my home, washed and dried my laundry, and made sure my little mole hole was open before shapeshifting and going to make use of my pond.

When the going got tough, the tough dug holes, worked on her burrow, and indulged in a good sulk.

* * *

I spent two days in my burrow nursing my bumps and

bruises before making use of my mole hole, changing back into a human, and taking a long, hot shower. During those two days, I'd done good work on expanding my home away from home. As I was a spoiled star-nosed mole, my next step would be leaving some creature comforts I appreciated at the burrow's entry, where I'd drag it into place and transform it into a little paradise for rest and relaxation.

After getting properly clean, dressed, and fed, I checked my email to determine my former place of employment had some regrets over their assignment and begged for my return.

It turned out when a good office gopher left without warning, things fell apart.

I declined their invitation to return to work, especially as the invitation offered me nothing beyond an apology for failing to provide appropriate transportation home. My insurance company, aware I'd be unavailable for a few days, had emailed me with an update. Initially, my former employer had refused to accept responsibility for the vehicle. After indicating they had a copy of my resignation and photographs of the vehicle, a copy of the map indicating where the car had been damaged, and a copy of the email indicating responsibility, they'd decided to play ball.

The insurance company had threatened to involve some worker-safety group, claiming the accident could have been lethal, they would have to get someone to access the mine and evaluate it to see if my car could be recovered, and if it couldn't be recovered, that the company was responsible for any environmental hazards resulting from my car's demise.

Any other day, the drama would have amused me. Rather than amusement, I regarded the whole mess with weariness. As I'd burned my employment bridges, I got online and began looking up new opportunities. I filed some applications, and near the end of the day, the owner of my former place of employment emailed me. I'd never met the man in person, but I'd heard rumor of him.

Hot. Single. Driven to Succeed. The hot and single were what tripped most triggers. The sole picture I'd seen of him, dressed in a suit, with brown hair, piercing blue eyes, and a somewhat stern demeanor supported the hot portion of the equation. The single part meant little to me.

I didn't date within my place of employment.

The evidence he'd been driven to succeed existed in his company, which ran well until someone made a mess of an office gopher's day.

Curiosity got the better of me, and Mr. Brandons opened his email with an apology for the gross mistreatment of my person and my vehicle, and the news that he personally had acquired a replacement, which he wished to deliver as soon as was convenient for me. Furthermore, he noted that the replacement was not being done through my insurance company, and that I could enjoy taking his company for all my little car was worth.

That made me laugh, and I replied he could come over at any time, but I was not changing my opinion regarding my resignation.

Twenty minutes later, someone knocked at my door.

I peeked out the window to discover Mr. Brandons meant it when he said he'd be over at my convenience, as he'd come calling, and two sporty cars waited in my driveway. That left me with a problem: the owner of my ex-company had brought me a car approximately twenty steps up from my old vehicle.

Pilot: Star-nosed... what?

I opened the door, wondering what he'd think of me when dressed down and ready to go to town.

To my horror, the alluring scent of the cologne I liked wafted off the man. The star-nosed mole in me fainted from joy and delight.

I considered fainting from sheer horror.

How could I ask a real estate investment genius where he'd gotten his cologne?

When in doubt, I could rely on my long years of office gopher professionalism to get me through any situation. "Mr. Brandons," I greeted.

He grinned at me and offered his hand. Rather bemused he wanted to shake with me, I accepted the offer. While he had a firm grip, he didn't issue a challenge. "First, I'd like to apologize for the mess. Had I been in the office that day, none of that would have happened—at least not in that fashion. I would have been accompanying you, as I always go to the more interesting sites on the docket. I certainly wouldn't have let anyone go to a hazardous mine alone."

"I'd say it's all right, but the fact I resigned clearly states I wasn't all right with the situation." I shrugged. "I do appreciate it, and I accept your apology, though. It wasn't your fault."

"Ah, but they're under my management, and they knew better. So, I have a great deal to thank you for, as this incident allowed me to do an audit of company policies and how the executives currently running the firm were handling certain affairs. Unacceptably, as I've determined since being notified of the situation. Accounting was given strict instructions to work with the insurance company, and I filed the incident with the worker safety board myself."

Pilot: Star-nosed... what?

"You threw your own firm under a bus?" I blurted, my eyes widening.

"Some people in the firm forgot the only reason a business is successful is due to those working within it. So, while I am genuinely sorry for how this worked out, I'm grateful it worked out as it did—and that you quitting is the absolute correct response." Mr. Brandons gestured to the car parked closest to my house. "This is the vehicle I've picked for you. I will have the title and registration transferred to you as soon as I can get your signature for the transfer. I've also taken the liberty of handling your insurance." He pulled out a sheet of paper and handed it over.

Sure enough, it was a copy of the insurance policy for the vehicle, and it had both our names on it. "This is a little more than I was expecting, Mr. Brandons." I eyed the car, which fit into the wishful thinking territory. "My car was not quite as nice as this one."

"Your car, before it met its unfortunate end in a mine shaft, was a modern marvel of mechanical brilliance. Part of the reason I wanted to come over personally was to ask who was doing the maintenance work on it. By all rights, that shouldn't have still been running, especially with its mileage."

I laughed, as my car's mileage was a thing of wonder. "When I bought it, it already had three hundred thousand on it. I've had it for a long time."

He eyed me for a moment, his expression thoughtful. "To put on that much extra mileage, you must enjoy road trips. There was over a half a million miles on it."

"Did you get it out of the shaft?"

With a low chuckle, he nodded. "Before seeing the car, my plan had been to do anything necessary to repair it, but

Pilot: Star-nosed... what?

then I saw it, and I decided only something new would do. There are twelve miles on the vehicle, and ten of them were from driving from the dealership to here."

"Well, I really appreciate it, Mr. Brandons." Careful to keep my expression neutral, I asked, "Would it be all right if I asked a strange question?"

"Sure. What do you want to know?"

"Who makes your cologne?" I blurted. My face warmed, and I stared at him with wide eyes.

He cleared his throat, and the corners of his mouth twitched. "I was going to ask you the same question, actually."

Well, since I was no longer working for him and my species wouldn't make a whit of difference, I opened the door further and gestured for him to come inside. "I'll show you, if you'd like. Mostly, I wear the stuff to cover up the scent of my shifted species."

"You're a star-nosed mole," he announced.

I staggered a step, blinked, and stared at him, my eyes widening even further. "Clearly, I was not covering up the scent enough."

"It just explains what I've been smelling." He came in, taking a look around my living room and chuckling at the rustic decor. "We have similar tastes. Pond in the back, a nice place to burrow?"

"Want to see the perfumes and body sprays first or the back?"

"The back."

I led him through my house, opened the back door, and showed him my star-nosed mole paradise. "I've been working on this for years." Then it clicked. He knew my

Pilot: Star-nosed... what?

species from scent? How did he know with such certainty? The possibilities were... "Wait. You're a star-nosed mole?"

"As a matter of fact, yes."

We stared at each other for a long time and took a few tentative sniffs. "You are wearing cologne, right?"

"I am, although I suspect it's likely the scent of a male star-nosed mole that's catching your attention rather than my cologne. I was aware that there was another star-nosed mole nearby, but I failed to realize my fellow mole was a woman. My brothers tend to enjoy security and maintenance work, so I was sniffing around where those staff members go. And they go all over the building, much like you do, so I couldn't pinpoint where the scent was coming from."

"I hadn't clued in there was another of our kind nearby at all," I admitted. "I just wanted to ask you where you were buying your cologne."

So I could spritz it all throughout my burrow and roll in it for the rest of eternity.

"It happens. Most members of my family are moles, although our species varies. Two of my brothers are also star-nosed moles, and our scents are drastically different enough, I didn't realize you weren't just another male, probably a distant relative." He laughed. "This explains a lot. Frankly, I'm now relieved you didn't just decide to shift and go exploring the mine shafts. I would have! Let's try this again. My name is Les. Technically, it's Lester, but I'd rather choke on an egg than go around introducing myself as Lester."

"Judging from the insurance information, you already know my name, but I'm Meredith."

"If you're willing to drop me off at home later, I can

Pilot: Star-nosed... what?

send off my brother, who would surely attempt to act as an unwanted chaperone. I definitely do not want to share your perfume secrets with him. He's a ground squirrel, and just between us, star-nosed moles are far superior to mere ground squirrels."

Well, maybe I didn't have a job, but I could have something better: the company of someone stuck in the same exact predicament as me. "I don't know if I want some ground squirrel messing up my burrow," I confessed.

"I shall go vanquish my brother and inform him you are not interested in murdering me at this time. And once we finish exploring your burrow, I would be pleased to show you mine."

"I think I'd like that."

About R.J. Blain

RJ Blain suffers from a Moleskine journal obsession, a pen fixation, and a terrible tendency to pun without warning.

When she isn't playing pretend, she likes to think she's a cartographer and a sumi-e painter.

In her spare time, she daydreams about being a spy. Should that fail, her contingency plan involves tying her best of enemies to spinning wheels and quoting James Bond villains until she is satisfied.

RJ also writes as Susan Copperfield and Bernadette Franklin. Visit RJ and her pets (the Management) at thesneakykittycritic.com.

Follow RJ & her alter egos on Bookbub:
RJ Blain
Susan Copperfield
Bernadette Franklin

Printed in Great Britain
by Amazon